WHAT IS IT ALL WORTH?

Mr Stephen James Bamford

Copyright © 2014 Mr Stephen James Bamford
All rights reserved.

ISBN: 1500684724
ISBN 13: 9781500684723

AUTHOR'S NOTE

The story that you are about to read is entirely fictional, but I have framed the book around actual characters, institutions, and events. The story includes criminal activities, and there is no suggestion that these happened in reality…but they may well have done! I mention real stockbroking firms and banks and have created fictional ones as well, because many events that have happened in the last sixty years appear too far-fetched to be credible but really did take place. The title of the book is drawn from the ideas of the Beatles song "Can't Buy Me Love" and the ABBA song "Money, Money, Money." I want to pose a simple question to the reader: what's it all worth, and what values are we all willing to sacrifice to get what we want? I have suggested courses of action, but all of you will, I hope, think differently. That for me is the glory of life and the fun of writing a book!

Front Cover – The Bank of England makes the rules but not everyone chooses to obey them!

PART I

CHAPTER ONE

Julian Barker was born in 1941. His first recollections as a child were of chickens running around and his mother collecting the eggs and exchanging them in the local butcher's for meat. This was post war Britain, and austerity and rationing still existed in the late 1940s and early 1950s. His parents had a very ordinary, beige Singer car that had been allocated to them. There was no consumer choice back then; you got what you were given. Julian's mother so disliked this car that as he grew older, she stated quite bluntly that it was "fart colour."

Their family was upper-middle-class, and Julian's father was a partner of an old stockbroking firm and had served in the army in the war. He had been in the Allied D-Day landings and had a range of stories that fascinated Julian. The expectation was that he and his sister, Jane, would go to private school and join all the right clubs. Despite the prevailing economic climate, the children had been born with silver spoons in their mouths, and the likelihood was that their lives would turn out well.

Since Julian's father had to work in the city of London and that was never going to change, the family had settled into the classic commuter-belt town of Walton-on-Thames in Surrey. The train service to Waterloo was just thirty minutes, and the famous one-stop train from Waterloo to the city, nicknamed the "Drain," finished off the journey to the office in a total of about an hour. In Julian's young days, he always remembered his father, who of course had a moustache, leaving the house in his dark suit, white shirt with a stiff, detachable collar, and bowler hat, with his very smart, black, rolled umbrella. Casual dress had certainly not arrived in that era.

After attending a local junior school in Walton, he started at a private preparatory school in Sussex where he was to become a boarder. The first night he cuddled up under the sheets and cried. The idea that he would only see his parents on three Sundays in a three-month term sounded horrific. Fact, however, is stranger than fiction, and as he settled in, he made a lot of friends whom he could play with all the time. At this point Julian realised that boarding school could be great, and although he missed his parents and sister a little, there was too much fun to be had to get stressed about it. And his attitude to going away to school never changed until he left public school at the age of eighteen. He loved school and enjoyed the sport enormously, and it was only the work and passing exams that ever worried him.

Julian was always attentive and interested in his classes, but when it came to exam time, he never really got it right and was always nearer the bottom than the top. Up until he was twelve, the masters never really pressured him because he always appeared to be trying. His reports were consistently polite but with a clear message that exam results were important and that at thirteen, a major test called Common Entrance awaited him, and that would determine whether he could go on to a school of his choice or not.

Twelve years old was a watershed for Julian. Life was becoming important. He was good at rugby but probably not strong enough to get into the first fifteen a year early. Nevertheless, he was going to train really hard and see whether he could make it. Events were not kind to him. This batch of thirteen year olds were excellent, and played well together, and their team produced good results. Therefore, second-fifteen rugby was all that was on offer to him, but he lapped it up. He realised quickly that the place kicker of his year was pretty indifferent, so Julian decided to learn how to do it and put in many hours of training to become good. By the end of the winter term, he had replaced the kicker of the second fifteen and felt totally confident that in his final year, he would be a key player in the top side and not just a forward. This place kicking skill, he reasoned, would make him much harder to "drop" if he had a poor game, and events proved him to be totally correct. He played in every game of his final season, was a highly effective place kicker, and was awarded his school colours.

Sadly, sport is only a part of what school is all about, and Julian's academic achievements were not improving. Much as he enjoyed classes, he found it difficult to put his answers down on paper in the way that the examiner wanted, and it became clear that this Common Entrance Exam was going to be a problem.

Julian had been put down for a famous public school in Berkshire where his father had gone. The sport was extraordinary, and there was no doubt that Julian would really enjoy it…but it was a very popular school, and the marks required to get in would be high. On current predictions, passing was going to be difficult.

During the holidays his father had the first serious conversation he had ever had with his son. What made it worse was that Jane, his elder sister, was very bright and had just passed her exams to get into the best local girls' school. Jane was also developing into a very attractive young lady, which Julian found a little irksome, although he loved her dearly. The good news from his point of view was that she was useless at sport!

His father was very direct. "The way things are going," he said to Julian, "I think it is becoming increasingly unlikely that you are going to pass Common Entrance to the school of your choice. Is that a fair observation or not?" Julian sat in silence. Although he had been disciplined by his father before on minor matters, this was the first time that he had sensed anger in his tone, and it really hurt him. He began to cry and through his tears said that he was trying as hard as he could, but he could not seem to do well in exams. The conversation went on for quite some time as Julian tried to explain that he did well in class and that his reports always said that he was keen to learn.

"The fact is," his father said, "that in life it doesn't matter how much you cry and get emotional; you have to convince the examiner that you are worthy of a place at your next school, and if you can't, you will have to think again." He then dropped a bombshell. "How badly do you want to go to my old school? There are many other good schools, and they would be easier to get into. You seem to enjoy school, so you do not have to go for the top tier just because I went there. The truth is that in my day, if you knew one of the governors, your son was accepted because he was a friend of a friend, and I was certainly no brighter than you."

He finished by telling Julian that after the summer and by Christmas at the latest, they would have to make a final decision, and the period ahead was vital. He said that he would be in regular touch with the headmaster. He was aware that Julian's reports never suggested any laziness, but things had to get better.

Julian went back to school absolutely determined to do two things. The first was to work really hard and get better and better marks in the exams, and the second was to get into the school's cricket team a year early. Much as he enjoyed all sports, particularly beating his elder sister, father, and mother at tennis, cricket was his main love. He bowled, batted, and loved throwing the cricket ball in from the boundary to the amazement of the teachers. It didn't matter how much practice was required; Julian was always ready to do more, and the many hours spent in the nets paid dividends. By May, Julian found out that he had been picked to play for the cricket first eleven. He was so proud that he got permission to ring home.

Back in 1953 the telephone was an expensive novelty. To make a call, one lifted the receiver and waited for the operator to speak. Julian was asked what number he wanted, and he very carefully said, "Walton-on-Thames 3491." There was a lengthy pause, and then the operator said, "I am putting you through." Ringing began, and Julian's mother answered. The moment she heard his voice, panic overwhelmed her: "Are you all right, dear? Has there been an accident? Are you ill?" Julian said that he had been picked for the first eleven cricket team, and wasn't it the most amazing news? "Is that all?" said his mother, still a little flustered. "Well done, but you should only ring home if there is something really important to tell us." Julian ended the call feeling utterly deflated and mystified that his mother had not grasped the enormity of him getting a place in the top cricket team at twelve years old. It was wonderful, amazing, and incredible...perhaps his father would be more excited.

CHAPTER TWO

Sport and passing exams were the major focus of Julian's life when he was twelve, but something of a very personal nature started to emerge as an issue for him as well. On an increasingly regular basis, he would wake up in the morning and realise that the foreskin of his cock had retracted (he never used to use the word "penis," since it sounded so medical). He found this odd, but it simply returned to normal and he went about his day.

However, something occurred a little later that shocked him. When he woke up one morning, not only had the same thing happened again, but there was a small, wet patch in the bed. He knew that he had not wet his bed like the little boys did occasionally, but this was odd. For the first time in his life, he realised that he loved to do research and really understand things, and he needed to get to the bottom of this!

His first stop was his best school friend, Robert Moore. In graphic detail, he explained what had happened and asked if it had happened to him. Robert said no, but he had heard two older boys talking about "wet dreams" and how to stop them. Julian was completely intrigued. Apparently you had to do a thing they called "wanking," and the wet dreams would stop. He continued by saying that the official word for it was "master something."

Julian had enough to be going on with and went to the library. He got out the school's dictionary and turned to "master." The words after master were "masterful," "masterly," "mastery," "mastic," "masticate," "mastiff," "mastodon," "mastoid," and "masturbate." After that came "mat."

The explanations were as follows for the possible words:

Mastic—gum or resin extruded from certain trees
Masticate—chew
Mastiff—large, strong kind of dog
Mastodon—extinct animal resembling an elephant
Mastoid—1. shaped like a woman's breast; 2. conical prominence on temporal bone
Masturbate—produce sexual arousal by manual stimulation of the genitals

Julian now looked up "genital." The dictionary said "1. of animal reproduction or reproductive organs; 2. external genital organs."

He therefore worked out that "the genitals" was a polite name for a boy's cock, and manual stimulation of it was to masturbate. He now decided to look at the boys in the showers, which he had done every day with no particular interest. But now he was curious. After his casual review, he decided that there were five types of cock—three uncircumcised and two circumcised. The circumcised boys had either been done well or poorly; the second type looked rather unfortunate. The uncircumcised boys fell into three groups. Some had an excess of foreskin and a tassel on the end, which looked somewhat comical. Most others had the correct amount of foreskin and looked normal. But a few had too little, and the foreskin did not completely cover the knob; they looked distinctly odd.

Julian realised to his great distress that he was in this final category. One night, however, he was lying in bed and thinking about the findings of his research when he suddenly found that he was becoming aroused. As he reached his first full erection, the foreskin of his cock retracted without him touching it. He now understood what had been happening in his sleep and why each morning he woke up effectively circumcised. At this point he touched his erect cock, and amazing sensations began to flow through his body. The feelings were so good that he was slightly frightened and kept stopping because he felt that he was going to pee. The sensations got bigger and bigger after each pause until suddenly, even though he stopped, the feelings reached a crescendo, and a liquid shot out. At this point he knew what masturbation was.

The next morning Julian decided that he would not close his foreskin and see what would happen. Nothing did happen, but that left him with the dilemma of going into the showers in a different form than the day before. As showers approached after sport, he wondered whether he would be ridiculed and laughed at, or worse, whether someone would tell him to behave himself. What happened next taught him a life lesson. As he walked nervously into the showers with fear in every footstep, he awaited the first comment. What would it be? But there were none—he sensed a few glances in his direction, but no one said a thing. What Julian learned from this was that in general, men do not readily talk about personal matters; they are really very private. Ladies like to talk things over, but men prefer to converse about sport or business and would not dream of asking close friends about the intricacies of their love lives and definitely not about their bodies.

CHAPTER THREE

Julian was aware that his Christmas meeting with his father was going to be very important. Julian loved him a great deal, but he also knew that with his father, things were very black and white. He might have learned this in the army, but Julian sensed that his decisiveness was part of his character.

The question on the table was quite simple: was he going to pass Common Entrance? That autumn term, he had worked really hard, and his math, geography, and science had improved. The essay subjects, however, were still very weak. His spelling was something near tragic, and his teachers were annoyed about it.

He did have a piece of good luck. His Latin teacher wrote with an italic fountain pen called an Osmiroid 65. You could change the nibs, and if you mastered the art of italic writing, the work looked really impressive and attractive on the page. One day Julian asked Mr Latimer whether he would show him how to do it, and he agreed. This Latin master was a keen writer of short stories which were very good but all shared a common trait. They were all handwritten in italic, and quite frankly, the words on the page looked beautiful.

Mr Latimer gave him a book which showed every letter of the alphabet perfectly formed, and then he gave Julian one of his stories. He said in his kind way, "Really learn how to form every letter until you never have to think about it, and then I want you to write out my story as an exact copy. I will then compare them, and we can see how you are getting along. The fact is, Barker, [no Christian names in the 1950s] that I see you on the rugby field kicking away for hours on end, and you have become very good. It is the same with this kind of writing. Practise, practise, practise; there is no substitute for it."

Mr Latimer really made a difference to his life at school, and Julian worked really hard at his italic writing and became outstandingly good. His teacher once laughed at him and said that his work was so elegantly scripted that he could forgive the atrocious spelling, and that he believed that many examiners who were ploughing through scruffy, poorly written papers might be kinder to Julian in his forthcoming Common Entrance than they really should be. Julian sincerely hoped so.

As his father sat down, Julian felt like he had been called into the headmaster's study on a disciplinary matter, of which there had been a number. Although not a bad boy, he was very talkative, and that got him into trouble in the classroom and after lights out in the dormitory. He got whacked on a number of occasions but learned that if you broke the rules, you got punished, and he didn't think that there was anything unfair in that.

Julian's father began sternly, "I have had a number of conversations with your headmaster, and these are my notes. Do not speak until I have finished." Julian wouldn't have dared—he was in the presence of a military officer in full flow! His father continued, "He says that you are working very hard and that I should be proud of you, which of course I am, *but*—and there is a but—as of today it is very touch-and-go whether you will pass the Common Entrance Exam to the school of your choice. He says that you have become a wonderful italic writer, and a Mr Latimer says that you have done huge amounts of work outside schooling hours, and no one can fault you for lack of effort. Your headmaster has suggested to me a plan B, which we have discussed at length, and it has merit. Apparently there is a newish public school in Kent that is building up its numbers each year and is gaining a good reputation. Your headmaster knows their headmaster very well and has spoken about you. The gist of the conversation is that your sporting profile and your work ethic have impressed the two headmasters, and as long as you continue to work hard, you will get it in. You and I need to talk about this now, and although we will not make any decisions today, we will conclude this matter by the end of this week." Julian was in no doubt that the presentation was over.

Julian's father now tapped his pipe in the ashtray and added a little tobacco. He lit it, and a cloud of smoke rose gently to the ceiling. Julian knew that particular aroma so well that whenever he smelt it, he knew that he would think of his father. And it happened many years later—when he was visiting a mine in Western Australia, the mine manager took him into his office and lit his pipe. He clearly smoked the same brand of tobacco as Julian's father had, and the aroma instantly brought thoughts of his father flooding back, although he had long since passed away. The power of smell is very real indeed.

As the conversation began, Julian saw a new side to his father, and he warmed to it immediately. The army man with the moustache had gone, and here was a man who wanted to support his son. He gently told him that whatever route he chose to go, he would support his decision wholeheartedly. He stressed that plan A was high-risk, and plan B was low-risk. During the conversation Julian expressed that he really wanted to follow plan A and go to his father's old school, and a few of his best friends were going there too. After a few days, it was decided that Julian would take the high-risk route.

When Julian went back to school, his father got to work. Julian had been put down for his father's old school when he was born. That was what upper- and middle-class parents did in those days. Some parents even stipulated the house that their son would go to. This was in fact rather stupid, since the housemaster is a very important figure in a child's life at public school and would be different from father to son.

Julian's father had a great friend from his schooldays who had gone into the teaching profession, and after gaining considerable experience at other schools, this friend had returned to his old institution and was now a housemaster there. He was academically brilliant, having gone to Cambridge where he got a first-class honours degree and was a low-single-figure golfer who had got a blue. Quite frankly, Julian's father reasoned, that made him an ideal housemaster for his own son. He set up a meeting.

As the old school pals met, the years just rolled back, and their friendship seemed just the same as when they had left school at eighteen years old. A little extra weight, a touch of grey hair, and even some hair missing, but nothing had fundamentally changed.

Julian's father trusted his friend completely and so told him the full story. "My son, Julian, is not good at exams, and although he gets great reports from school for effort, I have been told it is touch-and-go whether he will get in here, and I have worked on an alternative. He is a great sportsman and will definitely pull his weight in that department here. Julian has set his heart on coming here, and if all goes well,

I would really like you to be his housemaster. I must admit that I am really worried that if he failed to pass, it would crush his enthusiasm that is such a great part of his personality." His friend replied, "In this school, it is a known fact that those that struggle throughout their time here and work really hard often become the 'Kings of Industry' and provide employment for those that passed all their exams and got their degrees!" The two friends laughed out loud. He continued, "The most important thing to me and the headmaster is Julian's headmaster's report. We take these incredibly seriously, since children develop at different speeds, and the slow developers should not lose out. We also realise that there is much more to a rounded individual than merely passing exams. If Julian gets a report that suggests a variety of positives, despite some academic weakness, this will be taken into account, and we can be flexible. You didn't hear that from me, and so you know that our Common Entrance pass mark is fifty-five per cent. Having said that, I would be delighted to have Julian join us here and join my house."

As Julian's father drove home, he got the feeling that things were perhaps going in the right direction. Later that day he rang up the headmaster of Julian's school and asked, "Please, can you tell me about the headmaster's report that you will be writing about Julian later this year?" The headmaster gave a long-winded reply suggesting that some very academic schools only took exam papers and didn't really care about them unless they were dreadful. Some used them as a rubber stamp to confirm the exams, but some considered them almost more important than the Common Entrance Exam itself. Julian's father now asked him to explain what he would say about Julian. At once he knew that he had gone too far and retracted his question immediately, apologising for appearing to be a "pushy parent." "Mr Barker, I accept your apology, but I can tell you that you are definitely not a pushy parent and do not come even close. Dealing with them is the nightmare of my life!" The call ended in a very friendly way.

The final year for Julian at his prep school was fantastic. He had been made a prefect, and as summer arrived, he was told that he was to be the captain of the first eleven cricket team. Matches came and went, and he starred with both bat and ball. It appeared that he had no problems, but of course he did. He kept getting told off for misunderstanding the questions that he was asked in "mock examinations," and he got increasingly frustrated. When one teacher stated that he could offer Julian no marks because he had given an excellent answer but not to the question asked, he finally exploded and shouted at the teacher loudly and abusively. He was sent straight to the headmaster in disgrace and was whacked for insolence to the teacher. He accepted the punishment in good grace, but this difficulty with understanding exam questions was driving him mad.

Suddenly, time had run out, and Julian's Common Entrance Exam was upon him. His first paper was Latin, which went well, and then geography, which he liked, but the day ended with English literature, which he sensed went badly. The second day incorporated English language, his nightmare subject, but his mathematics was really good, and he felt it went well. French and others followed, and by the end of it, he was feeling that all might be well. On the final afternoon of the exams, there was a first eleven match, and Julian scored sixty-five runs, which virtually single-handedly won them the match. He went to bed comforted by the fact that he was good at something.

The next week was terrible for Julian as the tension of awaiting the results built. He began to dread the letter of failure that would ruin his plans. Facing his mother and father as a failure was more than he could bear, and what would Jane, his sister, say, who was doing really well at her school? He knew that it would be close, and it terrified him. Many of his friends were barely bothered. They knew that they would pass with flying colours and just enjoyed the end of their final term before they left for "adventures aplenty" at their new schools.

What is it all worth?

He kept waking up in the night before the results were due, as he had dreams about opening the envelope and seeing the word "fail." He had that dream three times that night and was near to tears. It was truly the longest night that he had ever known; the hours seemed to refuse to pass quickly, and he longed for the wake-up bell that he usually disliked. Finally, it went, and all the boys washed and dressed and went down to breakfast. Towards the end of the meal, the headmaster rang the bell, and there was immediate silence. "Would the boys who are awaiting their Common Entrance results please come here, and I will give you your envelope. You are free to take it to a private place to look at the contents. When you are ready, come to my study, and you can ring your respective homes."

The ten students walked forward and collected the envelopes, and by now there was an air of drama over the whole school as they took them. It was June, and clutching his envelope, Julian walked slowly to the sports field. He felt safe there. The letter was on the letterhead of the school, addressed to him, and the words were simple: "Congratulations, you have passed your Common Entrance Exam, and I will be writing to your parents very shortly to confirm the arrangements for your first term starting in September." It was signed off by the headmaster. Julian began to shake and then to sob noisily, and it took him a full few minutes to gather himself together. Suddenly, the tears and tension were gone, and he was running at full pelt to find his friends to celebrate.

This phone call home was very well received. Julian's mother was delighted and praised him for all the work that he had done, and she said that she would immediately ring Julian's father at his office to tell him the wonderful news. Two of the ten boys had failed, and they were devastated. They spent all of the morning in the headmaster's study, and he spoke to his contacts to see if other schools would take them. One was placed, but one was not. Julian felt empathy for them both, since he knew that this could so easily have been him. The boy who could not find a school was much disliked by most of Julian's year, and the headmaster constantly had to punish him. As a result, not many people stayed sorry for him for all that long.

CHAPTER FOUR

Julian's father looked at the letter from his old school, and the one thing that struck him was the mark that Julian had scored. It was 55 per cent, which he had been told was the exact pass mark for the school. He said nothing at all to Julian, who was dancing around the house in a joyous mood that he had hardly ever seen before. This clearly meant everything to him, and he was happy. He had a burning desire to ring his old friend the housemaster, but after thinking about it, he knew that it would be the wrong thing to do.

With his new uniform from specialist outfitters in Guildford, Julian was ready for his new school. As they drove through the ornate gates, he looked with joy at the most beautiful cricket ground that he had ever seen and longed for the day when he could play there. They then approached the vast, impressive building that was the core of the school. There were all sorts of smaller buildings around it, and to one of these they went. On the door was the name "Hopkirk House," and that was to be Julian's home for the next five years. Everything was taken inside, and Julian's mother unpacked everything neatly in drawers and hung things in cupboards.

There was a tea-taking place in the main atrium, and the housemaster and his wife were wandering around introducing themselves to anyone who didn't know them. After tea, all the new boys from all the houses were to meet in a large hall, and the headmaster was to address them all. It was then that Julian understood the sheer size of the school. Julian's prep school had been just under one hundred boys, but here there were ten houses of sixty boys each.

The headmaster started by asking a question: "How many of you boys played in a top team at your last school?" Julian raised his hand, along with 80 to 90 per cent of the one hundred other boys in the room. "You must understand that only eleven or fifteen can do that here," he continued, "and hence we pride ourselves in beating everyone at five levels in rugby and four levels in cricket, hockey, and the rest. We take huge pride in a fifth team having an unbeaten season." Julian lost interest after that, as the speech went on to talk about academics and teenage problems, and that bored Julian. After the meeting he noticed that his father was having a private chat with his housemaster.

The day was ended, and the parents went home. Public school had begun. As Julian's father drove home with his wife, he thought about what his old friend had just told him. "I am delighted that you have not asked me about Julian, so I will tell you as a friend. To be blunt, Julian failed the CE Exam, but the headmaster's report from his prep school was so outstanding and full of praise for his work ethic that the headmaster and I decided to use our flexibility. I am sure you realise that this is strictly between you and me." Julian's father further thought that whatever his son's problem was, he had knuckled down and worked hard. He had learned that nothing in this world comes easily, and this would be a valuable life lesson for him. This secret would never be shared with anyone, not his wife, not Julian, not anyone.

CHAPTER FIVE

The parents had all gone, and it was 7:30 p.m. in the evening on Julian's first day at public school. He was informed by older boys that he must look at the notice board in Hopkirk House every day to see if anything was required of him. He accepted that this was not unreasonable and went to see the board. Most of the notes had little relevance to him, but he saw one with his name on it entitled "Fagging & Domestic Duties."

In his last year at prep school, he had heard stories about "fagging," and they sounded spooky. He had been told that in his first year at public school, he would become a fag, and the person that he worked for could do anything to him that he wanted. A boy Julian knew well, who was at a day school in Weybridge, informed him that a fag was expected to wank his fagmaster at least twice a week! Julian was appalled by this and saw that his fagmaster was to be an Anthony Beckett, who was a prefect in his house. He noticed also that many others of his year had "domestic duties."

The note finished by instructing him to report to his fagmaster at 8:30 a.m. the next morning, which he duly did. Anthony Beckett turned out to be captain of the college cricket team. To Julian, he appeared friendly, and he found out that his fagmaster was the school's most outstanding batsman and a good all-round player. He was, however, worried about what fagging entailed.

Beckett, as Julian was expected to call him, told him to sit down, and he then began to explain. "The fagging system and domestic duties were originally set up to engender respect," he said. "That is, respect for property and respect for the individual. If you, Barker, sweep out a dormitory and tidy a room up, and then some boy comes in and throws his clothes all over the floor and spills a glass of water, you are going to be angry, and so you should be, because that slovenly behaviour has ruined your work, and by doing this, he has disrespected you, and that is likely to make you annoyed. Furthermore, all the major rooms in the school are cleaned by first-year boys and inspected by prefects every day. What these domestic duties instil into the first-year boys is that we are all inter-reliant, because it is our school, and we keep it clean and tidy. In my own first year, I cleaned a classroom and bashed up a boy who left sweet packets and papers everywhere and refused to put them into the wastepaper basket. He did not do it again! Barker, be aware that if you drop papers in any room in this school, you are in danger, since someone will be angry with you. Fagging is different and is intended to make first-year boys understand that they have a role to play in working to help others. I will expect you to do simple jobs, like polish my shoes, sweep my room, oil my cricket bat, and tidy my desk as necessary."

"Anything else, Julian asked nervously. Beckett laughed and said, "I expect that your day school friends have told you terrible tales about fagging; what have you heard?" Julian was not quite sure how to phrase this but suggested that things of a more personal nature might be required. Beckett burst out laughing and said, "Ah yes, the twice-a-week wanking thing! Barker, one thing that you have to understand is that people love to start rumours. Some boys hate school and make things up to discredit it, but most of it is rubbish. Now let me tell you the truth. At the end of last term, the headmaster called us prefects into his study and gave us a lecture, and it went like this: 'In your last year at the college, I am asking you to become a "fagmaster" to teach you how to manage an individual. In later life you will potentially have to do this and will find that it is not as easy as you think. The school expects high standards of its prefects, and scruffy shoes, dusty rooms, and untidy desks in your rooms will not be tolerated. We therefore offer you the perk of a fag, which is akin to a batman in the military services. If you are overly aggressive, this will harbour resentment, and trouble will surely follow. If you are too casual, standards will drop, and you will be in trouble yourself. What you will find, and this will follow you through life, is that respect is earned and not demanded. The first-year boys will tell all their friends that so-and-so is a tough but fair fagmaster and is a good guy and is therefore to be respected, and that will spread around the school. If, however, you are a poor fagmaster, the first-year boy will tell his friends that so-and-so is a waste of space. This will also spread around the school, and that person will not be held in high regard.' The headmaster finished by saying that this was our first management role, and we should learn from it. If, however, he heard of any abusive behaviour taking place towards fags, expulsion would become a real threat."

Julian was hugely relieved and realised that fagging for the captain of the college cricket team might be fun, since he loved the game so much himself. As the weeks went by, he did his best to keep standards high, but every now and then, he would do tasks in a slapdash fashion, and Beckett was onto it in a flash. He would then give Julian a difficult job like cleaning his rugby boots and then applying dubbin to them to keep the leather soft. Julian learned that if he did his tasks well, then fagging was quite easy, and Beckett was good company. As the year went on, he told all his friends that Anthony Beckett was tough but fair, and Beckett became highly regarded in Hopkirk House. The headmaster had clearly got it right. To add to this, a friend of Julian's told him that his fagmaster was an "A1 shit" and blamed Julian's friend for everything that went wrong, even though it was not his fault…no one in the first year respected that prefect at all.

Julian had heard a lot of stories about homosexuality at boarding schools, and he wondered how it would manifest itself to him—but it didn't. He was aware that boys in the dormitory were wanking most nights, because he heard the odd squeak from the springs of the beds, and he heard that some boys went down to the woods and wanked each other for fun, but he was not aware of anything worse than this. He did, however, once get asked by a fellow first-year boy what wanking was and how to do it. Julian explained, and the next day the boy came racing up to him and said, "I did it last night for the first time, and it was amazing; thanks, Julian, you are a pal!" Was that full-blown homosexuality? Certainly not!

The facilities of the school were amazing, and everyone found something to do. The art section was full, music concerts were on most weeks, and plays were acted out and were impressive to Julian's eyes even though he never wanted to be in one. His was the sporty world. At prep school he had played the major sports like rugby, football, cricket, and athletics, but at this school he could play hockey, badminton, squash, rackets, real tennis, golf, and even archery, and he always had a friend to play them with—for Julian, this was totally brilliant.

The dreaded subject of work continued to plague him. He kept failing exams, and when the O-level results came out, they were poor but just sufficient to get him into the sixth form and complete his final two years. His essay work was still very weak, so he chose A-level subjects that required a minimum of writing, like maths, geography, and biology. His housemaster told his father that he was an outstanding member of Hopkirk House and that Julian had treated his fag firmly but fairly and was highly regarded all around the school, but he followed these comments up with a simple statement: "I do not think university is for you, Julian."

So as Julian finished his glittering school days that he had so enjoyed, he had to think about what he was going to do with the rest of his life.

CHAPTER SIX

Julian's father called him into his study and sat down, and the implication was for Julian to sit down too. Julian saw in his father's face the same look that he had seen at the time of his Common Entrance. He knew that the full military presentation was about to begin, but what was the subject to be?

His father began, "I want to talk to you in detail about sex, and this is going to be acutely embarrassing for me and in all likelihood excruciating for you, but it has to be done. Would I be right to assume that you have yet to have sex with a woman?" Julian nodded. "Good," his father said. "I now want to explain some things that I have experienced myself and information that I gleaned from an Italian friend, who thought himself to be an outstanding lover. That may have been the truth, but he explained a lot of things to me which I didn't know, and hence I will pass his advice on to you."

Apparently this Italian had told Julian's father that the English were brilliant at running the world, generating great soldiers, and creating civil services to administer colonies throughout the world, but in the area of sex, they were useless. His view of Italy was utterly dismissive, since he said their governments were changing all the time, their administration was a shambles, and their army was cowardly. In the area of sex, however, they were unequalled, and the great Italian siesta gave them plenty of time to experiment in the afternoons. The key to lovemaking is to remember that ladies love to be touched and caressed and cuddled, and the longer a man does it, the better she likes it. Englishmen believe that sexual intercourse is the main component of sex, and that is where they get it wrong at the outset. He followed this up by saying that an Italian man would never even consider entering a woman until after he had made her climax by some other means. The reason for this is that for a woman to stay interested in sex throughout her life, she must have many climaxes, and hopefully more than one on special occasions. If this is the case, then she will always feel not only loved but excited too. Englishmen start intercourse too quickly and climax in a hurry, and their wives are left unsatisfied and as a result go off sex in their middle years. This, our Italian explained, was because their English lovers did not make them truly excited, and the ladies got bored with the whole process and gave up on sex altogether.

Julian's father was now going a little red and said, "The fact is, Julian, most English men of my generation were inclined to the 'wham, bam, thank you, ma'am' type of sex, and many of my friends complain furiously that their wives have cut off sex completely. Is it any surprise? This is very embarrassing for me to say, but you must follow my Italian friend's rules and learn. To woo a lady, give her lots of cuddles, lots of kisses, you know, all over, and do not start intercourse until you have made things happen for her. You may be surprised to know that I have followed my friend's advice myself, and it has been very successful. Your mother and I are very happy together. I don't think that there is anything more to be said on this matter, but do not forget what my Italian said, because it is important for your future happiness."

Julian's father now opened a desk drawer, took out two small cardboard sachets, and put them on the table in front of him. The name on the packets was Durex, and apparently each of these packets had three items within them. "Julian," his father said, "when you have sex with a woman, you must put one of these on yourself, and it will protect you from VD and stop you making the girl pregnant. I cannot stress enough that you must always, and I mean always, carry a packet of these in your wallet, because sex seldom happens when you expect it, and you do not want to be caught out. You may wonder why I have given you two packets, but that is simple: if you undertake any task in life, you must first practise. These blighters," he said, "are very fiddly to get on, and you do not want to be struggling with them when you are with a girl. I always buy them at the barber's, since the day when I was ordering them at the chemist's, and a good friend of your mother's came up and talked to me and saw what I was buying. It was a very embarrassing moment. Buy at the barber's; it is safer."

Julian was mightily relieved when this presentation was over. He and his father went into the living room, and two White Shield Worthington beers were served. Both of them needed a drink!

That night, Julian, full of curiosity, tried to put one of the Durex products on and got into a terrible tangle. So bad was his clumsiness that he climaxed before it was fully on. He sincerely hoped that the next time he would get the hang of it more easily, and thankfully, he did.

CHAPTER SEVEN

Julian and his father had long conversations about jobs, and in 1959 there were plenty to choose from. University, although a major focus of public and the top grammar schools, was not a major deal for employers. Ten per cent or less of students got a degree, and graduate entry was seen as a fast track for those that spent the three to four years achieving it. For those that used the same time learning the nuts and bolts of their business, it was fairly equal between the two groups, and the non graduates did not lose out by much as long as they were hungry to learn. There was little doubt that Julian would be recognised as one of those.

The two of them created a short list, and Julian's father was adamant that Julian was to make this decision himself with no pressure from him. "Your career, young man, will last the better part of fifty years, so make sure that you enjoy it. If you pick badly now, you are going to get very bored and will have to change careers midstream, and that tends to look bad to future employers."

The short list was as follows:

His father told him that Marks & Spencer took in management trainees, and if the candidate completed three years with them, they could walk into any retailing business in a good position. This was the power of the M&S brand name.

He could article as an accountant. Julian knew that he was excellent with numbers, and his father said that partners in accountancy practices tended to be well off.

Locally, there were good specialist engineering companies, and he could apply for management trainee schemes there and follow the route of business.

Lloyd's of London was the pre-eminent insurance organisation in the world and was one hour from home. Julian's father suggested that insurance broking and underwriting was global, and this may be an avenue for him.

And finally, there was stockbroking, the career of his father.

Decisions, decisions! Julian worried, but once he began to go to interviews, some light began to shine on the matter, and he inched towards his goal.

His first interview was at Marks & Spencer, and it was going really well. He had done a lot of research on the company and had found out something fascinating—at least, he found it fascinating! The shares of Marks & Spencer had doubled during the Great Depression, whilst the general market had fallen 70 per cent over the same period. The person who interviewed him was very impressed by Julian's story and then informed him that if he was chosen, he would work five days a week, but Saturday would always be one of them because this was their most important trading day. The interview ended, and he was told that he would receive a letter within a week informing him of their decision. That evening over dinner, his parents asked him how it had all gone. He told them emphatically that Marks & Spencer was a great company and the interview had gone well, but he had decided that even if he was offered a place on the management trainee course, he would not take it up. His mother was shocked and said that she could not believe that he would turn down a job before he had even been offered it, and she suggested that Julian was being a little arrogant. Julian's father was more measured and with the full look of a military commander asked for an explanation to help him understand.

"Well," Julian began, "Father told me that whatever I choose as a career, I must be happy to do it for ages, and I agree. As I came back from the interview with Marks & Spencer, I realised that sport is going to be a very important part of my life. As you know, I play cricket, which is Saturday and Sunday; rugby, which is definitely on Saturday; and tennis and golf, which are mainly played on Saturdays and Sundays too. If I joined Marks & Spencer, it would be like cutting my leg off. I am afraid that my decision is no."

Julian's mother reacted the same way as she had done when he had telephoned home from prep school to impart the vital and exciting news that he had been picked for the first eleven cricket team. "Cricket," she wailed. "You are turning down Marks & Spencer for cricket. I cannot believe what I am hearing." The tirade went on, but Julian's father said nothing. Julian adored his mother, but she clearly had a blank spot for sport.

After dinner when he was alone with his father, he asked, "What do you think, Dad?"

"Julian," he replied, "I told you that this choice of career is a very important one and that I would not try and influence you in any way—and I will not. Your love of sport is obvious to me, and I think your decision is both logical and sensible. Continue searching, and learn from each interview." Julian's love for his father knew no bounds. Despite his strict outward appearance to those that did not know him well, this man was very special indeed, and he worshipped him.

He had three interviews at local companies, none of which appealed to him, and one at a major record label. He decided very quickly that this place and the world of arts and music were not for him. In 1959 homosexuality was still illegal, and although he was only guessing, he reckoned he saw more of it in that building than he had ever seen at his public school!

He had a friend in articles at an accountancy practice, who told him that he had to count five thousand eggs as part of a "stock take" in an audit and sounded genuinely excited by the process...so Julian was now down to two options: insurance at Lloyd's of London or stockbroking.

As always, and ahead of his interview, he went down to the local library and began to learn about the history of Lloyd's of London, and he was fascinated. Apparently, in the seventeenth century, London had become more and more important as a trading centre, and there was a rapid rise in the need for ship and cargo insurance. In 1688, an Edward Lloyd allowed customers to use his coffee house as a place to gather, and it soon became the centre of the London insurance market. Julian also learned that what makes a great reputation is how you behave when things are bad. In 1906 San Francisco was struck by an earthquake of massive proportions, and it effectively wiped out the city. The claims at that time were $55,000,000, and in today's money, that figure would be billions. Cuthbert Heath, who was seen as a pioneering insurance figure at the time, instructed that all the claims at Lloyd's of London must be paid in full, without argument and at once. This was the defining moment, and the insurance buyers of the world flocked to London. Julian also read that the loss of the *Titanic* had cost Lloyd's £1,000,000 as a single event claim.

Armed with his research, he travelled on the train to the city and arrived at Lloyd's of London, where he saw the Lutine Bell, which was salvaged from HMS *Lutine* and was recognised as the market's most famous maritime loss. He was genuinely excited and felt that this might be the career that he wanted.

Oh, what a let-down, Julian thought as he left the building utterly deflated. He had been met by a Mr Jenkins and taken into an office for the interview. "Risk," Mr Jenkins started. "Risk is what we do—it doesn't matter whether it is a hurricane, a ship, an oil rig, or an aeroplane; it is all about risk. Now, Barker, this business is about numbers. We charge a customer a small sum of money, called a premium, to protect him from loss. The key to this business is to get the customer to pay you many, many premiums before he ever claims." He droned on and on about claims frequency, loss adjusters, and whatever... Julian was bored rigid. He was not sure whether he did not like Mr Jenkins or that the business sounded like a huge and ongoing maths class. Maybe he was being grossly unfair, but this was definitely not the job for him.

All of this left him with stockbroking, the career of his father. Truth be told, Julian had no clue what his father did at his office. He knew that his father loved his work, and his mother noticed that he often returned from work a little the worse for wear. He brushed it off in his normal army terms. "Meeting with clients, went on a bit, few too many gin and tonics, had to be done!" Whether Julian's mother believed him or not was not really important, since he was often amusing on those evenings and promptly fell asleep after dinner in front of the TV. He seemed to wake up just in time to go up to bed.

Julian again went down to the library to start his research into the London Stock Exchange. This exchange was one of the oldest in the world, being some three hundred years old, and had seen its fair share of disasters. Julian read about the Tulip Mania in Holland, the South Sea Bubble, and of course the 1929 Wall Street Crash, which bankrupted so many and ruined many famous families, and then the Great Depression that followed, which made things hugely worse.

Ten years after Edward Lloyd opened his coffee house to insurers, a John Castaing began to issue a list of stock and commodity prices, and he stated that these came from his office in Jonathan's Coffee House. This list could be seen as the beginnings of a London trading floor where buyers and sellers gathered around to trade. Julian's research also unearthed the way that specialties developed. A man with money might hear that a rubber estate was on offer after the death of the owner and that he might secure it at a favourable price. This person had no interest in dealing with lots of people, so he would make sure that the business was being run well and had adequate finances, and then he would mark the price up for his work and offer it to a stockbroker, whose job it was to find a whole raft of buyers. These financiers became known as merchant bankers. The most famous that Julian had heard of were the Rothschilds. After the shares had been placed, people would buy and sell, but not always at the same time. Some bright financial people worked out that they could pay a sensible price for these parcels of shares as they became available, but later when the buyers were hungry for shares, they could pass them on at a marked-up price. These specialists became known as jobbers, and the difference between what they bought and sold at became known as "the jobber's turn."

Finally, there were the investors who wanted to earn money from their savings, and these brave people talked to the stockbrokers, who helped them find the right investments for their money and worked out what fitted their needs. Sometimes a group of investors in a wealthy area got together, and in 1887 the Scottish Investment Trust was launched. Rich Victorian Scots, who had made vast fortunes exporting their amazing ships and engineering products throughout the world, could now plough their own fortunes, together with others, into extraordinary frontier projects like the great railways of America. The key to this was to have a small part of a big deal, and it definitely worked.

Julian was hooked. His father had told him bluntly that although he would support him completely, there was no way that Julian could work for his father's firm, Charles Stanforth. As he put it, "It just wouldn't be right, and anyway you must make your own successes and mistakes and do well." What he did do was get Julian an interview with the firm of Taylor, Dudley & Everett, and he was to be seen by the head of research, a Mr Ambrose Dudley.

CHAPTER EIGHT

The day of the interview arrived, and by this time, Julian knew exactly what his father did as a stockbroker. He had always worked in the selling side of the business. Initially, it had been with the rich, private clients, where he talked about what the investor was trying to achieve and what level of risk was acceptable. "Most of our clients," Julian's father said, "want to take huge risks but do not want lose any money. That is like a cricket captain telling his star batsmen to play all his flamboyant shots but under no circumstances to get out." This cricketing analogy was perfect for Julian, and he realised how true it must be. Latterly, his father had been selling to the big household investment institutions like the Prudential, the Scottish Investment Trust, and the newly formed unit trust industry.

As Julian walked into the offices of Taylor, Dudley & Everett, he got a sinking feeling, and it frightened him that this was his last choice on the short list. What if it turned out to be the same as his interview at Lloyd's of London? What made it more nerve-racking was that he had received an offer from the Marks & Spencer management trainee course, and his mother was still grumbling that cricket should not come ahead of work. He had sent a very polite note of rejection with suitable excuses—he was wondering whether he had been stupid.

A very friendly lady in her thirties came to reception and stated that her name was Rebecca and that she was Mr Dudley's girl Friday and sort of organised him and pretty much everything in the research department. Julian liked her immediately. She took him into the boardroom and sat him down.

A man walked in, who Julian felt was a little smaller than him and carried a little bit of extra weight but had a big smile on his face. He began, "My name is Ambrose Dudley, and I am the partner in charge of research at this firm. You will call me 'sir' for about six months, and when I tell you and not a day sooner, you will call me Mr Dudley, and when I think that you are invaluable, I will tell you to call me Ambrose. Rebecca is the only person in our research team that calls me Ambrose, so if you upset her, you are in deep trouble." There was something so delightful in the way that "sir" delivered this lecture that Julian knew that he had met someone of real quality whom he would have no problem in respecting at all.

Julian was asked to tell Ambrose Dudley about himself and his reasons for not going to university, and although he was extremely nervous, he admitted that he found written work very difficult, and this had held him back at school. He was then asked about his sporting interests. Julian felt much happier about this area and modestly related a number of his successes. Ambrose explained that the firm played in an annual golf match at Sunningdale Golf Club versus the Prudential and M&G, and they almost always came last. He said, "I know that you are not meant to thrash your clients, but to beat them occasionally would be an excellent idea. Julian, I hope that when you say that you are quite good at golf, you mean it. What is your handicap?" When Julian said that it was eleven, Ambrose was delighted and declared him to be a star. He told him that he had a handicap of eighteen but seldom played to it, although he loved the game enormously.

He then became serious and began, "I like to take on A-level students and teach them over three years as much as I and the back office team can about our real business. I find that a history graduate, for example, who is an authority on King John and the Magna Carta or the Napoleonic Wars is all well and good, but the relevance to our firm is lost on me. What I want from you is an ability to think, to imagine, and to dream of what might be relevant in the future. What we do here is to find shares that are cheap or simply good value and explain to our clients why they should own them. If we do not do the legwork and find these interesting stocks, this firm has no future and will wither and die. Do you understand that?" Before waiting for an answer, Ambrose went on, "We also have a special area of interest, and that is natural resources. In truth we research mining shares in South Africa, Canada, and to a lesser extent Australia. We do look at oil shares as well." Ambrose went on talking about bull markets, when markets rise, and bear markets, when markets fall, and how the firm made its money earning commissions for their advice. Typically, Julian was told that 1.65 per cent was added to the contract total, but this figure fell as the bargains got larger. Julian began to think how fascinating this whole world was, and the idea of researching to find new stories and looking at the world outside England was exciting to him.

Suddenly Ambrose had finished and looked at Julian intently. "Well, what do you think? The first three years, when you might have been at university, will not be exciting. I want you to learn everything that makes this company work. A simple list would include how we settle with the jobbers, how we settle with the clients, the collection of dividends on unregistered shares, bank reconciliations, how we deal overseas, how the partners fund the business, and how we could go bust. Then, and only then, will you be ready to become a real investment analyst. It is daunting, and I promise you that it will not be easy, but at the end of those three years, you will be knowledgeable and ready to start what I believe to be the most exciting career in the world."

Julian was sold on the idea; he had struggled through school and was frustrated by his problems just to pass exams. Ambrose said this was going to be tough for three years, and then there would be the chance to join a fascinating world. How could he possibly refuse? Julian spoke tentatively. "If you are willing to take a risk on me, I would be honoured to join your firm, sir."

Excellent, I think that we can make something of you. I am afraid that the pay is poor at the start, but in our business in good years, the pay can be very good. If you knuckle down and work hard in the back office, your salary should start to rise nicely. I have to go to another meeting now, but you can tell your father that I like the way that you present yourself, and I am impressed that you admitted to me that you struggled with written work—not many would. You will get a letter soon. Sorry, got to go, good-bye." He shook Julian firmly by the hand and was gone.

Julian sat there not knowing what to do until Rebecca appeared at the door and said, "He can be a bit of a whirlwind at times; his brain works so fast that us mere mortals find it hard to keep up. As he passed me, he said that he had offered you the job and to get on to the staff department and fix things. Well done. Let me show you out, and I look forward to seeing you again soon."

Julian shook Rebecca's hand at the door and walked towards Bank Underground Station, and suddenly it hit him—his decision was made, he had a job, and he was ecstatic about it. When he got home, he told every minute detail of the day to his parents, passed on Ambrose's comments to his father, and informed them both that he had been offered the job. Julian's mother was cautious. "I think we should wait for the letter before we open the champagne." Julian's father then said with his most delightfully pompous tone, "*Dictum Meum Pactum*", and it means 'my word is my bond,' and it is the statement on the coat of arms of the London Stock Exchange. If a partner of a stockbroker in London makes a verbal deal—it is done. Julian, dear boy, you have a job; you deserve it, and I am absolutely delighted for you." He got up, marched to the kitchen, and returned with a bottle of Moet & Chandon. He popped the cork out, and they drank it happily. Marks & Spencer and cricket was never mentioned again!

Three days later a letter arrived from Taylor, Dudley & Everett from a Mr Gordon, the staff partner. The gist of it was as follows:

Julian Barker was to join the firm in the role of assistant research analyst.

He would report to Mr Ambrose Dudley, the research partner.

He would serve a six-month probationary period before being taken on to the permanent staff.

His annual salary would be £208.

He would be eligible for a partner-agreed bonus in good years.

He would receive a luncheon voucher each day to help with the cost of lunch.

Suits must be worn, and they could be dark blue or grey.
Shirts must be white and have a stiff, detachable collar.
Moustaches were acceptable, but not beards.
Shoes must be black and properly polished.
Suit jackets may only be taken off in working office areas and never in front of a client.

Annual holiday would be two weeks.
The office hours were 9:30 a.m. to 5:30 p.m.

And finally, please confirm the acceptance of this position in your own handwriting, using a fountain pen.

Julian thought that this was brilliant. The clothes arrangements were little different from school, where he had worn stiff collars and actually quite liked them. The rest looked fine.

He got out his Osmiroid 65 italic pen, wrote his letter of acceptance, and asked his father to check it. He found two spelling mistakes but passed Julian's rewrite as good. Julian walked down to the post office box and dropped the letter in. He was still eighteen, and his working life was about to begin.

CHAPTER NINE

Julian was bought two suits and smart black shoes for his new job, and he was ready to go. He had agreed to start on the first of November 1959. Thankfully, his first commuter train was on schedule, and he arrived at the offices of Taylor, Dudley & Everett a few minutes before the 9:30 a.m. start time.

On his first day Rebecca greeted him, "Welcome Mr Barker, you will be working for a Mr Tom Smith who is the Manager in charge of the back office business.". She handed him an envelope, "These are a month's worth of luncheon vouchers and I have recommended a few restaurants that are basic but good. Ambrose is visiting a company in Southampton today but will be in touch on his return. if there anything else that you need just ask me."

Tom Smith was about forty, and to Julian, he seemed old. Unlike Ambrose, who appeared young at heart, he seemed dull and lacked any spark of humour. It turned out that he was from Bow in East London and had a short commute along the Central line, and he had a strong cockney accent. His first words to Julian were a little on the aggressive side. "In the back office, we are fifteen in number, out of a total staff at the firm of forty-seven. We work to exacting standards, and I will not tolerate sloppy or inaccurate work. The fact that you have come into the company to eventually work for Mr Dudley does not matter to me at all. While you learn in my office, you had better not show any public school arrogance, or I will make your life hell. If you work hard and produce accurate results, there is a chance that we will get along."

Mr Smith, as he was to be called, took Julian into a large office with books, papers, and telephones everywhere. He was introduced to all the staff, and he felt extremely uncomfortable. For the first year in his new employment, he was going to be subject to inverted snobbery. Everyone knows what snobbery is, but few know the reverse. The fact was that all fifteen of the employees disliked Julian for no other reason than because he was a research assistant, he was "posh," he was from public school, he did not speak like them, and, what they hated most, they were in this section for life, whilst he was only learning the ropes and would eventually move on to research and leave them behind. The fact was that they resented him.

As the weeks and months passed by, he became very lonely. All day he was ignored, he was never asked to join anyone for lunch, and every time that he made a mistake, he was given a severe ticking off and referred to as a public school idiot.

Julian learned how to do contracts, bank reconciliations, stock settlements, foreign exchange transactions, collecting dividends, the writing up of stock ledgers, and finally the preparation of cash-flow models for the partners. He actually liked the work, if not the people, and realised that the team was very professional, but he was acutely aware that the work was very hard. One day quite early on, Mr Smith asked him how he would calculate the cost of buying 7,657 shares at one pound, thirteen shillings, and sixpence. Julian wondered if this was a trick question but answered, "To work that out, you would need to use log tables, wouldn't you?"

"Yes, indeed you would, so how are you at using them, Barker?" Julian had always liked maths at school and reckoned that he was pretty good at calculations, so he replied positively. Mr Smith appeared pleased, telling him that he would be moved to contracts on the next Monday.

Almost a year went by, and he only saw Ambrose about half a dozen times, but he did lots of his own investigations and read every research note that had been produced by the company. Very soon, he knew each story in detail and why the company was recommending the shares. He realised that a thirty-minute train journey there and back from the office gave him plenty of time to study…and he did.

One morning Mr Smith called Julian over and told him that his time in the back office was coming to an end. He was to tidy up his personal things and go and see Rebecca, who was organising the next stage of his training. "Before you go, Barker, I would like to say something to you, and I hope that you will believe that it is genuine. I am well aware that my back office has been very unfriendly to you over the last year, and so I am very impressed at the way that you have knuckled down and learned our trade without showing any resentment to the others; in fact, I think that you have been a great example to them all. To be honest, if anyone in the team had had to put up with what you have been through, there would have been tantrums and fireworks. I really wish you well in the future, and I hope that as time goes by, you will not see me as too much of an ogre. I have passed these thoughts on to Mr Dudley." Julian had very mixed emotions, since on the one hand, he blamed Mr Smith for his unhappy year, but on the other hand, he realised that he ran a first-rate department, had taught him an enormous amount, and had just passed him a very nice compliment. He clearly was not all bad.

CHAPTER TEN

Julian and Rebecca walked into Ambrose's office and sat down. The atmosphere was light and friendly, and Ambrose spoke first. "Julian, I have heard from Tom that you have shown great diligence in the last year, and despite being unpopular with your colleagues, you have learned a great deal. You now understand how we administer our business. The truth is that the administration team are envious of you, and harsh though it is, you have had to grow up to handle it. Well done.

"Your next role will be that of a floor trader's assistant. This role is very important, and it will get you in touch with the jobbers and also our major customers. We have institutional clients that deal throughout the day, but the only way that they can get the up-to-date prices and see the movements of the market is through you. Each day you will go around the market with your list, fill in the prices from the jobbers every couple of hours, and telephone them through to the office or directly to our clients' dealers. It can be tedious, but it is vital. If I have written a major report on, say, BP, everyone will want to know how the price is reacting so that we can effectively accumulate the shares at the best prices. I may need a new price every thirty minutes. If you are lazy, you can simply be a messenger, but if you want to really learn about the market, talk to our dealers and find out what they are feeling. After you have done this for a year, you will be well on the way to becoming 'valuable.' Stanley Church is our head dealer and has an outstanding brain—learn from him, because there is little that he does not know about how the jobbers work. Before Rebecca takes you over to the Exchange, I will suggest one thing…in twelve months' time, you will be a great deal fitter than you are today, you will have to have your shoes resoled, and you will truly know every step of the way from our office to the market and back, come rain or shine. And by the way, you may now call me Mr Dudley."

He realised that his unhappiness over the last year had been part of the test and part of the learning process, and he told Mr Dudley that it had not been all that bad. That was a lie, but he felt that he should not admit to being unhappy, since he did not want to appear weak.

Stanley Church was clearly an important figure on the stock exchange floor, and although he was called Stan by everyone and told Julian to do the same, he was respected by all the jobbers. They laughed and joked with him after the trades had been booked and passed to Julian, who then either rang them through to the offices or took them there by hand. Stan's assistant was called Brian, and it became clear that Julian and he would be working very closely. Brian was about ten years older than Julian and was making his way up the firm's ladder and doing well. The message that he passed to Julian was a simple one—accuracy, accuracy, accuracy. If you gave clients bad information, they would deal on that incorrect price, and that would be a disaster. The fact was that everyone made mistakes, but you had to make damn sure that you did not do it too often.

Collecting prices and reporting them to various people had sounded boring when Ambrose had told him about it, but when Julian realised that a share price was a "living thing" and moved up all day or down all day or sometimes a bit of both, he became fascinated by it all. He rushed around to the jobbers' junior members and asked why so-and-so share was rising today, and when he got the answers, it excited him more and more. One day Stan got into a conversation with Julian and started to tell him what to look for in a quote. "If a share is hard to buy and the jobber is only offering small parcels of shares, take a note of it and report it. There is an old expression here that suggests when it's hard to buy, it is right to buy. The same is true in reverse—if there is lots of stock on offer, tell your client's dealer, since he may well want to drop his price and get the shares a few pennies cheaper. Frankly, Julian, it is like dealing in apples and oranges—if I have two oranges and eight apples, and you offer me more apples, I will have to offer you less because I have already got a lot of apples, but if you come and ask to buy oranges, I will ask for a higher price because I will have none left if I sell them to you. Whatever the complications of the stock exchange, the rules remain the same—too many buyers and the price goes up; too many sellers and the price goes down. If you only learn one thing from me, my boy, that should be it!"

The year passed by in a flash, and Julian was captivated by the task. He made friends with the dealers at the big institutions and tried to get as much extra information to them as he could. Their reaction was simple: they placed more and more orders with Taylor, Dudley & Everett. He was proud of his work, and in the background, his bosses were noticing. He found that there was a very social side to the business and much drinking done. The dealers invited him to join them in the pub, and as a result, he met their bosses. He sensed that this was a good thing. Brian and he often lunched together, and Julian asked him to teach him about the firm's speciality of mining and resource shares. He soon got to realise that his firm was very strong in South African gold shares and Canadian mining shares. The firm did a reasonable amount of business in Australia, but Brian told him that Aubyn St John Peters was a bit of a waste of space, and although a partner of the firm, he was seen by the dealers as a bit of a public school plonker!

Julian absorbed everything and deliberately got to know all the mining jobbers as well as he could. He saw that Ambrose wrote all the big reports for South Africa and Canada, and they were first class, but even at his young age, he could see that the Australian reports were poor and not very convincing.

Suddenly, his year was up on the stock exchange trading floor, and Stan told him to come to the pub after work. When they got there, he said, "Ambrose wants me to give him an assessment of your year with us, and I felt that I should tell you my conclusions over a pint or two. To begin with, you talk too much and ask too many questions. Whilst this is admirable and everyone loves having you around, you have two ears and one mouth, and you should learn to use them in the correct proportion. If you ask one good question and then wait patiently for the answer, you will learn a great deal; just think about that a little. Your enthusiasm is infectious, and I think Brian is achieving much more since you have been on the floor. He is a little shy, but you have really brought him out, which is great, because I want to retire eventually, and Brian should be capable of taking over from me. A year ago I am not sure that I would have felt that—well done. Finally, you are very accurate, you report very clearly, and I hear that you are a big hit with the institutional dealers, because you give them so much more than just a price. In many ways, I wish you could stay with us, since you are a breath of fresh air in this stuffy old place. Good luck with Ambrose; I hope that he appreciates you as much as we do. Now to the serious business of the evening—mine's a pint, and you are buying!"

Julian went to the bar a very happy man, but it was tinged with sadness because he had really loved it with the dealers. He hoped that his next job would be anywhere near as good.

CHAPTER ELEVEN

Julian was established at work and happy with his club sports, but at twenty years old, he was seriously upset that he remained a virgin. The only girls that he met were very nice, middle-class girls, and they allowed a little bit of fumbling but no more, and full sex was out of the question. There were some rough girls around, who some of his friends had experimented with, but he was worried about VD and left them well alone. Someone at work who had travelled to West Africa laughingly told Julian that he had been informed by a local ex-pat manager that the sexual rules there were simple. Over a large pink gin, he declared, "Out here, old boy, you keep your cock where you can see it, and you'll be all right!" Julian was fed up and could see no end to his dilemma, but what he didn't know was that his luck was about to change, and very much for the better.

Each morning he arrived at Walton-on-Thames Station, and the fifty-odd people on the platform got on the train and were transported to Waterloo. He bought his *Financial Times*, which was paid for by his company, and walked to the exact same place every day. The same people were there every morning, and not a word was spoken by anyone—it was robotic. One day, however, a most attractive young lady walked to the spot where Julian was standing and followed him into the railway carriage. He looked at her when he thought that she was not aware of it, and he loved what he saw. He guessed that she was at least seven years older than him, but she was gorgeous. She was fairly tall and slender and had midsize breasts that he could not stop peeking at. This was no tarty lady; she was elegant and beautiful, and Julian was awestruck. At Waterloo, she wandered off towards the Underground and hence clearly did not work in the city. After a day or two, Julian noticed the train that she returned on and made an effort to sit near to her on the return leg of their commuter journey. Nothing was said, but one fine day, luck intervened.

Back in the early 1960s, each carriage was split into sections, one set of seats facing the front and one facing the back, and four people sat on either side. On this evening, Julian was sitting on the opposite side from her so he could look at her. As the time of departure came close and the train was about to leave, a man with a bunch of flowers burst into the carriage, threw the flowers onto the rack above, and flopped into his seat. About thirty seconds later, a small but heavy stream of water left the plastic wrapping around the flowers and fell all over an elderly lady sitting next to him. The scene that followed could have graced a West End theatre. The man was distraught, the lady was acting like a complete prima donna, and the remaining six passengers were trying desperately not to laugh, with varying degrees of success. As the lady star of the show saw the giggles, she shouted, "It's not funny; I am absolutely drenched, and all you can do is laugh." As the scene developed, everyone fell into uncontrollable giggles, and the more the lady protested and complained, the more everyone laughed. The train rolled in to Clapham Junction and came to a stop, and the lady fled, with the passenger and the flowers hot on her heels. Suddenly, an event occurred that never happens—everyone in the carriage was laughing and talking to complete strangers that they had never met before. The beautiful lady, looking straight at Julian, said, "That is truly one of the funniest things that I have ever witnessed." As Julian agreed with her, he knew that the ice had been broken, and he could now talk to her. He asked her what her name was, and she informed him that it was Christine. She asked him his and followed up by asking where he worked. He then asked her the same question, and it turned out that she worked in an advertising agency near Oxford Circus Tube Station.

As they arrived at the Walton-on-Thames station and got off the train, she suddenly said, "After such an amazing event, I think we should celebrate with a drink, unless you are in a hurry to get somewhere." Julian replied to her clearly that he was doing nothing that evening and would be delighted to join her. There was a pub directly by the front entrance to the station, and in they went. The evening that followed was a delight to Julian. Christine was vivacious and worldly, and her eyes twinkled as she spoke. They left after a couple of hours as friends, and Julian knew that they would now be able to talk together every day.

About a week later, after an enormous amount of chatting during those seven days, Christine looked very intently at Julian in the pub and said, "I am going to ask you a question now, and I really want you to be truthful with your answer." Julian had no idea what was coming, and he waited. "Are you a virgin?" she asked. Julian sat there in total shock and then sheepishly admitted that he was. "Good," she said, "would you like to come back to my flat, so we can discuss this further?" Julian could not believe what was happening and realised that he was getting an erection already. They walked the ten minutes to her flat arm in arm.

As they sat on the settee next to each other, she explained what she wanted to happen next. "My rules are simple: there will be no intercourse, but we will explore other avenues of sexual excitement. Before anything happens, both of us will go to the bathroom and wash our bodies properly, and I mean properly, and then we will meet in my bedroom." Although he was very excited, the thought of no intercourse sounded bad, and he felt that even after this encounter, he would still be a virgin.

They arrived together totally naked and stood in front of each other next to her large double bed. He looked at her body and thought that it was the most beautiful thing that he had ever seen. She suddenly asked him, "What are you thinking about right this minute?" He honestly replied that he thought that she was incredibly beautiful, but he was embarrassed to say it. Christine now said, "Ladies love to be complimented, and if you think a young woman is beautiful, tell her. She is never going to be upset with you—in fact, quite the contrary." She followed it up with a wonderful compliment to Julian: "For some weeks now and long before we spoke, I have admired how you hold yourself. You look at times almost regal, and now I see that you have a beautiful cock as well."

By now Julian was so aroused that he was ready to explode. Christine then explained to him that because he was a virgin, she thought that it would be better if she guided him through the events that would follow. He agreed without objection. She laid him down on the bed, nestled up to him, and very gently took hold of his cock and began to move it very slowly. Julian could not believe how amazing her touch was, and he ejaculated within a minute. As she took a Kleenex from the side of the bed and wiped him clean, she said, "No young man can hold back his first climax, so it is better to get it out of the way quickly." He was amazed but actually delighted that he had not done something terribly wrong. Clearly very aroused by the feel of Julian climaxing in her hand, she now said, "Let us enjoy kissing, and when I suggest it, please can you gently touch my breasts and then kiss them very softly? This arouses me a great deal." He needed no further encouragement, and they kissed passionately. Christine was now extremely aroused, and Julian's erection had returned. She slid down the bed a little and asked Julian to kneel above her and position his cock above her breasts. He obeyed…this was amazing! She took hold of his throbbing penis and began to massage her nipples very sensually. Her breaths and gasps were now becoming very short. Julian had no idea what would happen next, and he waited, loving every stroke of his knob against her erected nipples. He was now aware that she wanted him to move his cock towards her face, and then he felt her mouth close around him and experienced extraordinary pleasure as he felt her tongue discover him. Because he had already come, he had some sort of control, but Christine realised that it would not last long if she continued. She therefore let go of him and asked him to kiss her "down there," as she described it. In the next five minutes, Julian learned something very important. The pleasure that he got from kissing Christine in her most intimate parts gave him a truly exquisite feeling, and as she had an enormous orgasm, he was truly excited for her, and his own needs became totally irrelevant.

Christine now said, "I want you to finish with something that I hope that you will like. Lie on your back." She now knelt above him with her breasts above his cock. "Take hold of my breasts with each of your hands and put your cock between them. Now move yourself gently backwards and forwards, close your eyes, and think that you are inside me. There is no final whistle in this game, so enjoy it as long as you want to." As Julian moved very, very slowly, not only did he become immensely aroused, but he also realised that his cock resting against Christine's breasts was making her unbelievably excited, and they both climaxed at almost the same instant.

As Julian walked home, having left Christine with a powerful hug, he pondered a simple question. Was he still a virgin, since he had not had intercourse? By the time that he walked into the driveway of his parents' house, he virtually shouted out loud, "Who gives a monkey's?" because that sexual encounter was beyond his wildest dreams.

Christine had clearly been as excited by the events of that night as Julian, and for three months they had spectacular sex but never intercourse. The relationship was about to end, and when it did, it was sudden. Christine explained that for the last five years, she had been going out with an army officer who had been sent to Cyprus, but his tour of duty was about to end. She explained that she had decided that if Julian admitted to being a virgin, she would have a bit of fun on a one-off basis and then end it. The problem for her was that she had played out all her fantasies with Julian and simply could not believe what extraordinary sexual feelings he had awakened in her. She admitted that she had never come close to sex like they had had with any other man in her entire thirty years. Christine reasoned that her fiancé was a goodish lover and a very good man, and she would be crazy to toss it all away just because she had had an extraordinary sexual encounter with a gorgeous young man.

Julian was devastated for a while but was wise enough, even at his tender age, to realise that reality must return. He believed that what Christine had taught him in three months would help him become a genuinely sensitive lover for the lady who would eventually become his wife…and so it transpired.

CHAPTER TWELVE

Julian walked into Ambrose's office, having completed his time on the London Stock Exchange trading floor. He had loved every minute of it, and he genuinely believed that he had learned a huge amount and was ready for anything that Ambrose was going to give him as further training. As he walked in, Julian felt a little tense, but he liked his boss's manner and believed that he would be sensible in anything that he might suggest.

Ambrose began, "Julian, I took you on as an A-level student because I genuinely believed that after three years, you could become a really valuable member of my team. In the time that you would have been completing your university education, you have gained hands-on experience of our work practices. You now know how our business administers itself, and you know now how our business trades in the market, but there is still one vital ingredient missing, and that is, how do we put together a broker's research circular, and how do we present it to our clients? That, my friend, is your next task. I have heard a rumour that you read every document that our firm's research department produces. Is that true?"

Julian paused a little nervously but answered, "Yes, I love the work of the research department, and I really try and work out which of the shares I would buy if I had some money. I also read documents from other firms that I have found on the stock exchange trading floor and try and work out whether ours are more believable than theirs."

"Ouch," said Ambrose, "and what is your conclusion?" Julian was diplomatic and said that most of the firm's material was up with the best standards. Ambrose grasped the veiled criticism and suggested that this was going to be a core part of his learning process. "Initially, you will research data for me, and we will create a document that I will write myself. After a period of time, you will research a document yourself, and it will go out under your own name. This you should see as good and bad news. If the client makes money from your recommendation, you are a hero, but if the share proves to be a dud… only you are to blame; there is no one else. In our world there is no place to hide and no one else to criticise; you are the villain because it is your report. In the next two or three years, you can hide behind my name and learn the trade, and if we make mistakes, the villainy falls to me! Do not rush to expose yourself to the real world…it can be very cruel, and worse, it is often very unfair." Julian realised how true this was and settled down to work in the shadows and learn from Ambrose. He was truly looking forward to it.

Julian had read Ambrose's reports on the mining shares of South Africa and Canada, and it became clear that Ambrose enjoyed South Africa more than Canada. He always planned a trip to Cape Town and Johannesburg during January, which of course is their summer, and enjoyed the wines, cricket, and golf down there before writing outstanding reports on his return. Julian learned a simple lesson: you could work hard and have fun at the same time. This was an example that he wished to follow. Ambrose dealt with a Canadian called Phil

Campbell from a company called Beacon & Partners of Toronto. He came to London regularly and was full of facts and information, and Julian questioned him thoroughly. Phil liked Julian and said, "I am on expenses whilst I am here, so why don't you grill me with your many questions in a nice restaurant, and we can enjoy a meal together?" This was amazing for Julian, since Phil seemed to know everyone in Canada and was full of stories about the dodgy goings-on in Vancouver shares and the true enormity of the vast natural resources of Canada. At the end of Phil's trip, Julian wanted to write a major report for Ambrose because he was so excited at the opportunities that existed there.

He went to his friend Rebecca and asked her if she could help him with his written work for Ambrose, since he knew how bad he was at this. She laughed and said, "Have you ever heard of a Dictaphone?" Julian admitted that he had not, and then Rebecca showed him the machine and explained how it worked. Rebecca said, "I love this machine because you or Ambrose can tell me your stories, I can turn them into good English with good punctuation, and the final document is mine!" Julian could not believe it. He recorded the whole story of Canadian natural resources and put in all his thoughts as to why shares were potentially cheap or expensive and what clients might wish to do. He knew that all the facts had come from Phil, but he felt that his report added a lot of value. Rebecca took the Dictaphone tape away, and the most wonderful English document was returned to him, which he could never have written in a million years. He was so excited that he gave Rebecca a kiss and told her that she was amazing. Far from being offended, she appeared delighted and told Julian that she would take it to Ambrose. "Oh no, no, no," Julian said, "please send it to Phil at Beacon & Partners and ask him if I have got any facts wrong or if he doesn't like any of it." The document winged its way to Canada, and a day or two later, the phone rang—it was Phil Campbell. "Julian, if any of my clients paid as much attention to what

I said as you have done, I would be a very rich man. Your document is fantastic, and I am certain that Ambrose will be delighted with it. Please put me through to Rebecca, because I would like her to change a few minor points, but nothing of substance." Julian's firm and Phil's had an unwritten agreement that if they did Canadian business for their clients, they always placed it with his Toronto outfit and vice versa, and all the commissions were shared. It was, as the Americans like to say, a win-win deal.

Ambrose was delighted and said, "This is so good that I would like to put it out in your name, but it is too early. Some of these ideas might not work, and you should not be exposed to potential criticism quite yet. What I want you to do is keep up a regular contact with Phil Campbell and see if the two of you can build up our mutual business together." Julian was beyond happy—he had discovered the Dictaphone, and Rebecca got pleasure out of creating well-written documents. What could be better?

As 1963 began, Mr Dudley told Julian that the time had come to call him Ambrose, since he had now become a valuable member of the team, His research workload got bigger as he worked on UK companies with Ambrose and wrote a great deal on the Canadian natural resource sector. At home he played a great deal of sport, and in the summer he met a lovely girl called Alice. He was very attracted to her, but she was not interested in sex. He really missed Christine, but that's life.

Aubyn St John Peters was irritating Julian. He went to Australia every year to do so-called in-depth research on the potential for mining and natural resources there. Taylor, Dudley & Everett had a relationship in Perth with a firm called Porter and Partners, and Aubyn was meant to come back with insights and good recommendations, but all he seemed to do was go out to lunch with clients and charge it to the firm's account. Julian remembered that the dealers thought that he was a waste of space, and now, after first-hand experience, he agreed with them.

Ambrose called him in one day and dropped a bombshell on Julian. "I want you to work with Aubyn and help him with the Australian natural resource sector. What I need you to do is similar to what you have done for me in Canada. You must build a relationship with our Perth partners, create some strong stories for our clients, and get them written up. More and more of our clients are looking in that direction, and we have to improve our offering, or we will miss the boat. You should see this as a good opportunity to improve your knowledge, gain experience, and make you a better analyst." As Julian left the office, he thought to himself that this was a poisoned chalice and not a great opportunity, but Ambrose had spoken, and what he said always happened. He was stuck with it.

After a few days, Aubyn came back to the office after an excellent lunch full of good spirits and said to Julian with a smile, "You and I need to go on a course together." Julian wondered what on earth he was talking about and waited for the next statement. "A golf course, old boy, and I can tell you my plans and what I have in store for you. Meet me at my golf club at 8:30 a.m. tomorrow, and we can tee off at 9:00 a.m., and then of course we can have a spot of lunch. Bring a blazer and tie with you." He wrote down the club's name on a piece of paper. Julian was delighted, since he knew that it was a very prestigious place, and it was only about ten miles from his home. He told Rebecca about it, and she confirmed that it was OK.

Julian got there very early and was shown into the lounge of the golf club and offered a coffee. What struck him immediately was that the name A. St J. Peters was all over the honours boards. He seemed to have won everything at some time or other. He was clearly an outstanding player.

Aubyn was on time and asked what handicap Julian played off, and Julian informed him that it was eleven. (For those of you that do not know about golf in the 1960s, the highest handicap was twenty-four, and the lowest was zero, which is nicknamed "scratch." In simple terms, the higher the number the worse you are, and the lower you are the better.) Aubyn now stated that in singles, Julian would receive three-quarters of the difference in their handicaps, and that would be nine shots. Julian thought that even if Aubyn was scratch, he would only get eight shots, so he challenged him politely. "Don't worry, Julian; I play off plus one, which is better than scratch," said Aubyn. Julian was flabbergasted, since he had never heard of anyone being better than scratch. Aubyn must be amazing, and so he proved to be. Even with Julian's nine extra shots, he got nowhere near beating him.

As lunch began, Aubyn became serious. "Julian, what I am going to tell you today is in the strictest confidence, and you will tell no one. I know that you are very close to Ambrose and Rebecca, but I mean them especially. Let me tell you the history of the Peters family and Taylor, Dudley & Everett. Pre the Second World War, the Taylors and the Everetts were much in evidence in the partnership, but in the 1930s the economic catastrophe hurt them both very badly, and they could not pay their way. Lord Glenconner, who is now our senior partner, built up his percentage of the business as they faded away. It was all very amicable but recognised economic reality. His family are huge landowners in Scotland today, but their big money came from some large investments in the United States at the end of the last century.

"During the war I was a pilot, and although I had some very frightening moments, which I will not bore you with, I came out unscathed.

My father and I were both realists and knew that I was not very bright, and the idea of working was very low on my list of priorities. All I wanted to do was to play golf for my country and get a place in the Walker Cup team. As you know, this is not a professional event for money but a truly amateur event for gentlemen. This was always my dream, and I am very proud that I achieved it. One of the reasons that I brought you here today is that I wanted you to see my spiritual home, where I believe that I am a king, or at least a prince.

"Post the war, our partnership was looking for some fresh capital to grow the business, and my father, who was very rich, decided that he would buy into it. His terms were straightforward. I was to be employed for as long as our money was in the partnership, and that has meant that no one can ask me to leave until I wish to go. I was asked to look after Australian matters because I was not likely to do much harm, and I had once flown myself there in delivering a plane from England to Sydney in my youth. The joke was that this made me a real expert!

"Julian, what you must learn from this is that life is not fair, and however bad that is, it is a reality. The brutal facts of our world are tied up in an old expression, 'He who owns the gold makes the rules.' So my message to you, young man, is to become wealthy, because with money, you may not be happy, but you will always be comfortable."

Julian could not believe what he was hearing but clearly understood that golf was Aubyn's life, and he was rich enough to take it very seriously. For him to have played for his country against the United States in the Walker Cup team was an achievement of enormous proportions, and although he was rightly seen as a buffoon at the office, his golfing status had to earn Julian's respect.

Aubyn continued, "What I want to suggest to you now will probably sound offensive, but life is about compromises, and this one could work well for us both. Ambrose has worked with Phil Campbell in Canada and has done a good job, but since you have become involved, the quality of insights that you have brought and your close working relationship with Phil have added a great deal to Ambrose's reports, and I have actually made money buying your recommendations myself.

"Absolutely nobody knows this, but in one year's time, I am going to retire and leave, so what I want you to do is to make our Australian reports as good as the Canadian ones so that I can leave on a high. I will do almost none of the work but take most of the credit myself, but I will acknowledge that you have helped me along the way. My aim is to go when the company is happy with me and not when everyone thinks that I am an idiot, and I believe that you are capable of doing that for me. I know that this is a terrible cheek, but I believe that I can repay you for this favour in the future, if you are willing to help me now."

Julian was stunned and barely understood what had been said, but whatever it was, it was underhand. Julian was to do all the work, and Aubyn was to take all the credit…what a bloody nerve!

The year that followed proved to be really interesting, and he was introduced by telephone to a Michael Porter of Porter Partners. Aubyn thought that he was a really good man and an excellent golfer. As his conversations with Mr Porter grew friendlier, Julian found out that Aubyn and Michael were the undisputed golf champions of Western Australia. It was all strictly amateur, but they had won this big event six times in the last seven years. It was no wonder, Julian thought, that Aubyn's reports were so poor, since he was always playing golf and never visiting gold prospects. It also became clear that Michael had as much interest in golf as Aubyn, and his insights on the market there were useless.

One day, as he asked a complicated question about a mining venture, Michael gave up. "Frankly, Julian, I haven't got a clue what the answer is, but if you want to pursue it, we have a young geologist who would be likely to help you. He is very bright but very working class, but we value his judgement. Talk to him and learn from him, but beware; he will ask you as many questions as you ask him, and he expects good answers." Within days, Julian was speaking to a Rick Jones, and in no time, he realised that this man, who on the telephone sounded incredibly Australian, was better than bright—he was brilliant.

At the end of the year, with huge help from Julian and Rick, "Aubyn's" Australian reports were seen as excellent, and client business grew extremely well. Out of the blue, Ambrose called Julian into his office and said, "I have just had a great surprise. Aubyn has decided to retire. I know very well you have been writing Aubyn's reports for him, although no one else does, and when he has gone, we can discuss the future."

Aubyn had a wonderful leaving party with the partners at Claridge's, and an era in the firm had ended. On that last day, there was a note on Julian's desk, with an envelope beside it. The note read, "Golf tomorrow at my club—8:30 a.m. Come by taxi. See you there. Taxi fare in the envelope—Aubyn." Julian opened the envelope, and inside it was a twenty-pound note. He had never seen one before and examined it closely. Julian wondered how much a round trip of twenty miles could be from his home in Walton-on-Thames. At the taxi rank by the station, he asked for the price of a fare to take him there and said that he would ring when he wanted to be collected to bring him home. The price was two pounds, ten shillings.

During the year, Aubyn had played golf with Julian a number of times and never lost. Julian often played very well, but try as he might, Aubyn always seemed to have something extra, and it was no different on this final day. As they sat down to lunch, Aubyn began,

"I asked you to come by taxi because today I am celebrating, and I am very happy. We are going to drink the best wines that this club can provide and lots of it, and then I am going to introduce you to a great drink called Kümmel. Julian, the reason that I am so happy is because you have shown me the very best that a young man can offer, and that is integrity. You and I know that what I asked you to do here last year was not right. I asked you to make me look good and get little recognition yourself, and you have done it brilliantly well. I am not sure where you got all your facts from, but I know that Michael knows very little, and you definitely didn't get it from him! My reports, shall we call them, were so good that I have made a fair bit of money this year, and our clients are happy too. I will never forget what you have done for me, and I will find a moment when I can do something important for you in the future." Julian and Aubyn drank and drank, and then this Kümmel arrived from the freezer, and Julian loved it.

When he got home, his mother scolded him for being drunk and said that he was a disgrace, but his father smiled at him and said, "These things happen, and life's for living."

The next day, fighting a terrible hangover, Julian sat down at his desk and toyed with his coffee. Out of the blue, Ambrose appeared and said, "Would you be prepared to take on Australia for the firm?" His hangover disappeared instantly, and he said yes at once. Ambrose then said, "Aubyn had informed me that there is a good geologist in Perth that you have started working with, and he thinks that a trip to Perth to meet the man would make sense. I think that this is a good idea, and you deserve it for all that you have done. With Aubyn gone, the expenses on the Australian section will fall dramatically, so funding you for two weeks in Perth will not be that expensive!" Julian then rang Rick Jones and asked him to produce a trip for them both so that he could really get to understand Western Australia. Rebecca organised everything, and he was ready to go.

CHAPTER THIRTEEN

Alice Mary Jenkins was born around the end of the Second World War in April 1945. Her parents were Michael and Rebecca Jenkins, and lived in a really smart and expensive private estate in Weybridge, Surrey, called St George's Hill. Without knowing the facts or figures because discussing money in the house was regarded as tacky, she was certain that her father must be very wealthy, because the house was very large, and there was a garden that was nearly two acres. Her father worked at Vickers Armstrong, which was a factory just outside the estate in the area of the famous old racetrack called Brooklands. One of her first memories was hearing the siren sounding every morning to tell the workers that it was time for work. She was aware that he designed and built things for the aviation industry and was very proud of the fact that he had worked with the very famous Barnes Wallis on the Upkeep mine, which became known as the "bouncing bomb." In their living room at home, there was a photograph of her father shaking hands with Barnes Wallis and the bomb itself was in front of them. When guests would arrive at the house for the first time, everyone would say, "Oh my God, you worked with Barnes Wallis; that is amazing." Frankly, Alice was bored to sobs with all this until in later life, when she began to appreciate the enormity of what that small team had created from an idea in Barnes Wallis's mind in early 1942, as he watched stones skipping across the water, to the bombs hitting the dams in May 1943. It was hard for her to believe that it really happened, and if someone told her a story like that, she would probably dismiss it as impossible. Her father's work was considered so vital to the war effort that he never had to join the forces.

She went to a private school for girls in her home town and enjoyed it to a degree. The idea, she believed, was to create genteel ladies who would manage the household accounts, prepare first-class dinner parties, and of course bring up children. Going to work was not an option, and university was pretty much unheard of. She was bright enough but mischievous. She and her friends liked to play tricks on the other girls and never took anything too seriously. She loved outdoor activities; sports and tree climbing were fun. Was she a "tomboy"? Maybe just a little, but she loved clothes and trying to look as pretty as she could be, so there was no masculine side to her nature at all.

Sex is a huge deal for a young girl, and when her mother told her that a man with a hard penis would stick it inside her to make a baby, she wanted to be sick on the spot. It was bad enough that she had to bleed to death every month, but this as well…this was truly unimpressed, and nobody was going to try that on her until she was very much older!

When she was fourteen, something happened that slightly changed her view, but not much. She was climbing up the apple tree in their garden and sat with her legs astride a strong branch of the tree. As she sat there, a very nice and tingly feeling began to envelop her body. She stopped collecting apples and just sat there enjoying the buzz, which seemed to be growing stronger. After a while she decided that she had better stop and collect the apples, which of course was why she was up the tree in the first place. Seeing an excellent apple a little way in front of her she leant forward to get it. Wow! Her body seemed to explode in the most amazing way, and she very clearly experienced her first climax. It felt fantastic, and although she had no idea what it was, she always offered to get the apples from the tree after that. It was clearly a task that was enjoyed every autumn.

Back in the 1960s, nice girls definitely said no, and it drove the boys mad. One of the girls at her school who offered herself liberally got the cruel nickname "the Blackwell Tunnel." When she asked what it meant, her friend told her that "everyone has been there, but no one wanted to stay." Girls can be really cruel.

She definitely thought that my looks were better than average, and this was confirmed by the number of boys that asked her to dance at the junior ball at St George's Hill Tennis Club. Her parents were keen on tennis and had been members there for many years, and both played a great deal. The club was just a stone's throw away from their house, and it was inevitable that she would play tennis, because it was just so convenient. There was also a badminton court there that was set up in the main ballroom, and she enjoyed that too. Boys came and went, and she found out that she really liked kissing, but some boys were really terrible at it, and they didn't last long. She liked her breasts being stroked through her blouse or sweater, but absolutely would not allow anyone to touch beneath her clothes. She became aware of the lump in a boy's trousers and occasionally stroked the trousers, to their quite obvious pleasure. It seemed to her at the time that if you stroked a boy's trousers, he would become putty in your hands, so to speak, and he would do almost anything that she wanted.

This was a good life lesson for her, and if a woman knows how to satisfy a man well, he will do almost anything that she wants him to.

Her first serious relationship was with a boy called Paul. He was good-looking and fun, and they had a great relationship. She was twenty-one at the time and had been with Paul for a year. Initially, he was happy to kiss her and stroke her breasts, and she reciprocated by rubbing his trousers. Her mother, who she soon realised was way ahead of her time, sat her down one day and asked about Paul. Her questioning was gentle but direct, and it was clear that she wanted to know whether Paul and she had slept together. She told her that they had not, but Paul kept hoping that they would. Her mother then shocked Alice to the core. She said, "I think you should." She was flabbergasted and asked why. "Well," she said, "in my day, every girl from a good background was a virgin, and in the early part of their marriages, they found out that they were totally incompatible with their husbands sexually. But by then, it was too late, and it was a catastrophe, and I really do not want that for you. Go to bed with Paul and see how it works, and make sure he wears a French letter. Your father and I were lucky, but I want you to get some experience. But please do not tell your father about this conversation—he would have fifty fits!" Alice had heard of French letters at school, along with rubber johnnies and Durex, but had no idea what they looked like, but knew that it was imperative for the boy to use one.

The sex with Paul proved to be a disaster, and afterwards, their relationship withered quickly and finished one month later. On the day that she decided to lose her virginity, she invited Paul over to the house. He had been over many times, and much stroking, cuddling, and kissing had taken place in her bedroom. She knew that her parents were going to a function in London and would not be home until very late. When Paul arrived, they kissed, and she asked him if he had any protection with him. He opened his wallet and proudly showed her a little package. "I have been carrying this around for three months in the hope that you might want to have sex with me one day," he said. She replied with a downright lie, "I think that I have been a little harsh on you, and I think it is time we did." Once in the bedroom, he approached her enthusiastically. It wasn't aggressive or anything of that nature, but Paul was in a kind of aroused frenzy. He started unbuttoning her blouse and took it off with a flourish. She could see the lump in his trousers, and at that point it dawned on her that she had never actually seen a man's penis. Her father always locked the bathroom door, and Alice didn't have a brother, so as she took Paul's pants off, she wondered what it would look like. She found herself very confused. Even though she was aroused from the kissing and being undressed, there was an inner tension that was very strong. It was a summer evening and still light outside, so when she saw it, she could see every detail. It was fully erect, and to a virgin's eyes, it looked huge. The thought of that thing being pushed into her was terrifying. She looked at it more closely. It was like a pole with skin all over it. Her first reaction was that it looked rather silly, but Paul was looking at her breasts very intently; she guessed that they were the first ones he had ever seen. She decided to touch him and see what it would feel like. At this moment Alice was really enjoying herself-This was fun.

"Pull it open," he said. Alice had no idea what he was talking about but suggested that he show her what to do. He took her hand and placed it around the skin, and then, guiding her hand, he pulled down, and the skin at the top rolled back. Underneath there was a kind of hat, which he referred to as his knob. This knob was very pink and slimy. She touched it, and frankly, didn't like the feel of it at all. She began to wish that her mother had not suggested this. Paul now opened the package from his wallet and started to roll the Condom onto himself. When this was done, his penis looked really silly. The rubber thing had a tassel on the top—Alice found it hard not to laugh. He now tore off the bedclothes and laid her down. After a little bit of kissing, she felt a pushing sensation, and then there was pain. Alice begged him to stop, but he wouldn't; he pushed ferociously into her, and she burst into tears. Paul certainly came, and Alice certainly didn't, and afterwards she spoke very harshly to him. "Why didn't you stop thrusting when I asked you to stop?"

"I was coming, and if I had stopped, it would have ruined it," he replied. The fact that Alice was in pain didn't seem to bother him at all, and that day she saw a side to Paul that she really didn't like. His days were numbered, and she never wanted to have sex with him, or anyone else, ever again. As they got up, Alice realised that there was blood on the bottom sheet, but she knew that her mother would think it was something to do with her period, so Alice simply changed the bed and went downstairs. Paul was now looking rather sheepish, and she told him bluntly that the whole sex thing had been a disaster, and they would never do it again. He had clearly loved the experience himself and looked very upset at her statement.

After Paul there were a number of other boys but never any sex. Alice was now twenty-two. One afternoon, she was going to play tennis, and her friend suggested that they play a mixed doubles game with some boys. The boy who Alice ended up partnering was good-looking and tall, and she definitely liked what she saw. He was called Julian Barker and was an excellent tennis player. They won easily, and then the four of them retired to the bar for drinks. It was a glorious summer's evening, and they went outside and sat by the lake there. There were people swimming and sunning themselves on a raft that was anchored in the middle of the lake. Alice now set about learning more about Julian, whilst her girlfriend was clearly doing the same with her partner, Tom.

Julian lived at home with his parents in Walton-on-Thames, which is a town virtually next to Weybridge. He worked in the city of

London as an analyst. He had not been to university, which surprised Alice somewhat, since he seemed like someone who would have been. Sport was clearly his thing, and besides tennis, he played cricket locally and was a member of St George's Hill Golf Club, in the estate, and loved golf. What she liked about him was his easy charm: he had a kind of charisma about him, and she felt very delighted to have met him. The day finished on a low note, however, when he failed to either ask her for her phone number or suggest that they meet again. Alice was crestfallen and fed up as she walked the short distance to her family home.

The next day the phone rang in the house, and Alice's mother answered it. She said, "There is a Julian Barker on the line who would like to speak to you," and then with her hand over the mouthpiece, she added, "He has a lovely speaking voice and sounds rather nice." As Alice took the phone and started to speak to him, she agreed with her mother that he spoke really well, and the telephone seemed to highlight it. "Would you like to go out with me this Friday evening?" he asked. She said yes, but was curious to know how he had found her phone number. He laughed and suggested that being a researcher by training this was not the hardest task he had ever undertaken. Clearly making fun of me, he said that there was a member's handbook, and her name and address were in it, as were his own, if she cared to check. Part of Alice was upset as she obviously appeared completely stupid, but most of her was thrilled -she had a date!

The relationship between Julian and Alice blossomed, and she knew that this was going to be special, but she was really worried. It was this sex thing that hung over her like a cloud. Alice had liked Paul, but after sex it was over. She really liked Julian and wondered if the same thing might happen. It was a dilemma. Alice had very strong feelings for Julian, and he hugged and kissed her in a very affectionate way; she knew beyond any reasonable doubt that he wanted sex.

What is it all worth?

With great trepidation, Alice decided that she must do this. Again, she made sure that they would be alone when Julian arrived. She asked him about protection, and he said that he had got it. Alice wondered at the time if all men were optimists and carried these little packets around in their wallets just in case. "Yes", she concluded, they probably did. Once things began Alice felt totally different with Julian. He seemed to be very calm, and for some reason she told him that she had only had sex once, and it was dreadful. "Why on earth did I tell him that?" she asked herself. Perhaps it was trust, because she felt totally safe with Julian, whatever was going to happen. They kissed and cuddled, and clothes came off until Alice was completely naked, but he still had his pants on. He stopped and said to Alice, "You really have a most lovely body." This made Alice feel so good that as she took his pants down, she was ready to face anything. To her great surprise, Julian was completely different from Paul—the skin at the top of his penis was already pulled back, and his knob, as Paul had called it, was smooth and dry. Before she had time for any more thoughts, Julian eased her gently down onto the bed and lay down beside her. He started to kiss her and stroke her breasts, and their excitement grew. Alice was not at all sure what she was meant to do, but her curiosity about this penis got the better of her, and she began to stroke it. From Julian's reaction, there was little doubt that she was doing the right thing. Julian now began to kiss and caress her breasts whilst at the same time stroking her vagina and clitoris with his hand. Alice had no idea how long it took, but she suddenly had the most enormous orgasm. Her body shook, and she rolled all over the bed in a complete world of her own. By the time Alice had calmed down, Julian had put on the condom and climbed on top of her. Because of her huge orgasm, she was very wet indeed, and Julian slid into Alice with ease; there was no pain at all. He was so aroused that he came very quickly, but the intimacy and the feeling of really being connected overwhelmed them both gloriously.

After that wonderful first sexual encounter, Julian asked Alice to tell him what pleased her, and sex got better and better; it remained extraordinary for the rest of their lives. Alice knew that it may have sounded rather arrogant, but she knew Julian would invite her to be his wife from the very first time that she had that amazing orgasm. Alice was acutely aware that what had happened was very special; it was "making love" and not just sex. They really bonded at a deep level, and they just knew that we were made for each other and that it would be special forever, and it was until the day that Julian died.

As they learned about each other's bodies and loved the touch and feel of them, Alice and Julian become more and more adventurous. They created their own sex game which they called "No Climax Sex." It was always played on Friday nights, and it lasted around an hour, during which time neither of them was allowed to climax.

Alice would start things off by very gently stroking his erect penis. The aim of the exercise was to drive him closer and closer to climax but not let him get there. Initially, he would tell her when to stop, but as they played their game more and more, they got to know when to stop. At that point Julian would start to kiss and cuddle Alice in an incredibly sensual way. He would stroke her breasts, which were very responsive to his touch and kisses, and he followed this up by very gently stroking her vagina and clitoris. She found this foreplay exquisite. As Alice approached her climax, she gently held his hand, and he stopped. She now went down and licked his very erect cock and put the knob in her mouth. This was wonderful for them both, and when Julian almost reached the point of no return, he stroked her hair and Alice immediately stopped. Julian now began to kiss and lick her clitoris until Alice was climbing up the wall, but as her climax approached, they stopped. And there the game ended. Readers may well think that this is extremely odd, since most people are desperate to climax. For Julian and Alice, though, it was different. They knew that we could make each other climax at any time, but what this achieved for them was around a whole hour of the most intimate and glorious stimulation and the most intense and loving feelings towards each other. The next day there was a lovely, tingly feeling inside Alice's body, and Julian felt the same. Throughout the day they would touch each other in a playful way. Julian would slide his hand down her trousers and fondle her bottom, or he would come up behind her, wrap his arms around her, and gently stroke her breasts through her blouse. Alice in turn kept stroking Julian's trousers and making him become erect. By the time Saturday evening came, they were both so aroused from this intermittent foreplay that had gone on throughout the day that they fell onto the bed and exploded together in the most spectacular way. People joke about the earth moving, but the climaxes they had after effectively twenty-four hours of semi-foreplay were quite simply extraordinary. They played this game off and on for all their lives, and genuinely believed that their relationship become closer and closer as a result. Alice once told her best girlfriend what they did and she simply said, "How frustrating and boring that must be." So clearly it's not for everyone, but for Julian and Alice it was brilliant!

Within a month of their first making love, Julian proposed to Alice, and she accepted without a second's hesitation. Julian told her that he was paid fairly well, but there would not be much money around if they wanted a house. He was very aware that Alice had been born into a very wealthy lifestyle, which he could never compete with. Alice loved her childhood home, but was sensible enough to realise that they would have to start somewhere, and it would clearly not be in a private estate.

Alice's parents were ecstatic with the news. Her mother said that she was really pleased that she had not let Julian slip through her fingers, and her father, who checked on these things, proclaimed that

Taylor, Dudley & Everett was an excellent stockbroking business, and he felt that Julian had good prospects. Alice met Julian's parents long before they got engaged. They were quite old-fashioned, but were kind and welcoming, and they all got on well. Julian's father worked for a different stockbroker called Charles Stanforth, which was apparently one of the oldest in London. Alice asked him once why Julian hadn't joined him in his firm. In his military sort of way, he said, "Bad idea, my dear Alice; Julian must plough his own furrow, make his own mistakes, and hopefully learn enough to make it to the top, and I believe that he will." Alice knew that he was a wise old bird. Julian had a married sister called Jane who was nearly six years older than Alice. She was always kind, but the age gap in their twenties seemed large. As Alice got older, however, she and Jane became very close, and when her marriage hit the rocks, Alice felt very honoured that Jane came to her as an adviser and a shoulder to cry on.

The day of the wedding came in May 1967. The weather was dry, but there was a cold easterly wind that was difficult for the ladies. The men in their morning dress suits were well wrapped up and lucky for that. The service was held in the local church in Weybridge, and the reception held at the High Pine Club, which had a lovely garden and lake. The whole day was very special to them both and generated many very happy memories.

Julian travelled about three times a year, mainly to Australia and Canada but sometimes to South Africa. His firm specialised in mining, but Julian spent many a day trying to find the next winner in the UK market, and he often did. The fact was, he lived and breathed his work, and research for him was a fabulous hobby and not a job at all.

They bought their first house between Walton-on-Thames and Hersham. Property here was much cheaper than Weybridge, and one got much more house for your money. Hersham had an old

Hackbridge factory there, and each morning a siren went off. So Alice swapped the Vickers siren for the Hackbridge siren! She was delighted when they were phased out. The house was a three-bedroom, semi-detached Victorian house, and they had to pay £3,500 for it. At the building society, they were offered two and a half times Julian's salary, which was about £1,000 a year, as a loan. To make up for the shortfall and get them the deposit, Julian's parents gave the couple a wedding present of £1,500, and so the numbers worked, and the house could be furnished as well. They were on their way. Julian was clever and sporty, but DIY was beyond him; a friend once suggested that DIY stood for "Don't Involve Yourself," a sentiment that he wholeheartedly agreed with. Alice therefore had to become the odd-job man of the family and really got to like wallpapering and painting, but electrical issues and plumbing were way beyond her, and they called in the experts. The garden was done together, and they made it very pretty. Julian and Alice were really proud of their little house.

Children were discussed but it was decided that they would wait a bit since finances were tight. In the spring of 1970, however, Julian got a huge bonus, which he said was related to Australia, and from then on money was never an issue for them again.

Around that time, they stopped taking family planning precautions, and after a few months, Alice fell pregnant. The baby was due in the summer of 1971. She wanted a healthy boy, and Julian did too. Alice went to Walton Hospital, had all the check-ups, and learned about breathing and panting, natural birth, and gas and air. She assumed that nothing could go wrong, since ladies have been having babies since time began.

As the due date came near, everyone was offering advice. Julian's mother and sister, Alice's mother, and most of her girlfriends all offered their thoughts. When the first contractions came, they collected the pre-packed case, and off they went to the hospital. Alice did not think of herself as a wimp, but could not believe how painful the contractions were. Alice complained to Julian that no one had told her was how long childbirth goes on for. In her naivety, she had thought it would just be bad at the end, but actually her birth lasted for hours and hours.

In her later life, someone told Alice that 80 per cent of communication is nonverbal, and she could confirm that this was true. No one at the hospital said anything to either of them, but Julian and Alice knew something was wrong. As the hours went on and on, she became weaker and weaker, and when a surgeon arrived to update them, they knew it must was serious. "Your baby is in distress and is the wrong way round, and you are now bleeding internally quite badly," he said. For the first time ever, Alice saw Julian in a panic, and he asked, "Am I going to lose both of them?" The surgeon explained very calmly that he was going to operate and take the baby out and then deal with the bleeding. He felt that this was not life-threatening but very serious nonetheless. Alice was now taken down to the operating theatre, and Julian was sent out to the waiting room.

When Alice came around from the anaesthetic, she was woozy but awake enough to hear Julian telling her that they had a son, and he was completely OK. Even though he didn't say a world, Alice could see all over Julian's face that something was badly wrong. Alice was so exhausted that she didn't ask anything until the next morning when the surgeon came round and she was alone with him. Alice was direct, "I know there is a problem," she said, "so please tell me what it is?" The consultant was incredibly kind but explained that there was a small growth in Alice's womb that had ruptured during the labour. He explained that he had removed all the material and sent it off for analysis, but unfortunately, there would not be any more children. A week later, the hospital informed the couple that the growth was not cancerous, which was a huge relief to them both.

The baby boy was to be called Simon Anthony Barker, which Julian and Alice thought had a nice ring to it, and she bonded with their baby at once. She felt so proud of what she had achieved but got tearful with Julian because Alice knew that he wanted more than one child. She knew that he was a kind and lovely man and believed him when he said that it didn't matter. "Simon will be special to us, and that is all that matters."

PART II

CHAPTER FOURTEEN

Richard Edward Jones was born in Midland, Western Australia, in 1936 and spent the whole of his young life there. His parents had little or no money beyond what they needed to live on. In 1913, his grandfather had left the east of the country, where he felt underappreciated, and decided to take up a labouring job involved in the construction of the western end of Trans-Australian Railway. He figured that this massive opening up of Western Australia would bring him fame and fortune. Sadly, the reality was different, and it brought him neither. The devastating truth was that he spent the rest of his life working for those entrepreneurs who really were making their fame and fortunes. Unlike many who turned to the bottle or became lazy and resentful, he instilled a fiercely strong work ethic into his grandson and affectionately called him Rick and the name has stuck.

His father recognised very early on that if you were a working man, you had to operate in an area where there was nearly always work. In his early twenties, he begged his father to enrol him on a course that would teach him how to drive the biggest trucks, but initially, his own father resisted the idea because he had so little money. Although Gramps, as everyone called him, worked for the Western Rail Company in Midland and held a responsible position there, a course of this nature was very expensive. "Go and work for a company that will train you to drive and you will learn for free," he was told by his father. Eventually Rick's grandfather realised that jobs like that were like gold dust and would take years of waiting. He caved in telling his son that all he ever wanted from him in return for this specialist driving course was a promise that he would work hard and not waste the opportunity that he was being given.

In the late 1920s and '30s, having an independent diploma from a high-calibre driving school meant that Rick's father was always in work. Even in the Great Depression during the 1930s, although life was extremely tense and wage rates fell sharply, he always remained employed, and Rick's upbringing and family life were very happy time. A key part to his own happiness was the love he had for Gramps and his father, both of whom he respected greatly.

His mother was a simple, working-class girl who barely ever left Midland. She looked after everyone, and when Rick's grandmother boarded a train one day and returned to Sydney, never to come back, she took in Gramps, and everyone stayed together. His parents told him that they had wanted more children, but they had done the numbers and decided that they could not afford any more mouths to feed. Around their Western Australian home, the Aborigines lived in great poverty, so it would be wrong to exaggerate the extent of their deprivation, but they were very much at the lower end of the economic tables throughout the Depression. Later in the 1950s, growth picked up, and Rick's father's skills were in high demand, and the family lived much more comfortably in later life, which was thoroughly deserved.

What is it all worth?

The local school in Midland was better than average. The railway company had endowed it with considerable funds, since many of the directors sent their children there, and as a result, it wanted for nothing. This was exciting to Rick's parents, because they knew that if he could do well at a good school, he might escape from the lowly background that he had been born into. From the start he loved his classes and was excited to learn. Many of the boys like him rebelled and did no studying at all, and they were destined to follow a humdrum existence with little chance of escape. For Rick it was different—the history of Australia was wonderful, stories of the British Empire captivated him, and the geography of Western Australia and its mineral wealth, for some strange reason absorbed him.

Gramps taught him to swim in a nearby lake. They fished together for many long hours, and he told Rick amazing stories of the rituals and wonders of Aboriginal culture. In the eyes of a young boy, his grandfather was the font of all knowledge, and although he constantly told me that he did not know very much, it was quite enough. When I reached fourteen years old, Gramps told me that we were going to Perth for the day. As a long-time member of the railway company, he could use the trains for free, and since everyone knew him, the guard did not ask him to pay for me. My mother made us up a box of sandwiches, we took a towel and swimming trunks, and at six o'clock in the morning, we joined the main train that had come all across Australia for its last leg from Midland into Perth. He told me with a smile that we could do anything in our state capital as long as it was free. At Perth Station, I saw an advertisement for the Museum of Western Australia, and it stated quite clearly—Admission Free. We were both delighted and arrived there in an excited state. The museum was incredible, and there were so many exhibits to see that neither of us knew where to start, until we both saw an item at the very same moment—the Myths, Rituals, and Legends of the Aboriginal Tribes of Western Australia.

We both agreed at once that this was for us, and into this huge, high-ceilinged room we went. Gramps and I decided to play a game and see which of the exhibits was the most fascinating. There were so many to choose from. We learned about the terrible cruelty inflicted on the natives. In 1893, a bishop named Matthew Gibney used the word "inevitability," which the museum suggested was a convenient euphemism for "genocide," and he wrote:

> The Aboriginal races are inevitably doomed to disappear before the advances of the white man. Over how many bloody outrages, over what an amount of greed on the part of some, weakness on the part of government and apathy on the part of the public does this convenient euphemism throw a thin but decent disguise.

Gramps had always told me that the Aborigines had been very badly treated, but this quotation made me realise that "badly treated" was the understatement of the century. We moved on, looking for something more amusing, and we found it after a short search. The exhibit was on rituals relating to a young Aboriginal boy's coming of age. Because it said that this occurred between eleven and fourteen years old, and I was fourteen, we stopped.

Apparently, the Aborigines believe that all the evil spirits of a boy are held in the foreskin of his penis, and he cannot enter manhood until this evil is removed. A major service is held in front of the whole tribe, an expert from the tribe cuts the foreskin off with a sharp stone, and the "casting away of the foreskin" is then celebrated.

Underneath this, there was a note that stated simply that because Australia was a hot and dusty place, the Health Department insisted that all boys be circumcised at birth for health reasons, and that Australia, along with the Jewish people and Muslims, had the highest rates of circumcision in the world.

Rick said to his grandfather that he had thought that all boys were born that way, since everyone at school was the same. They left the museum laughing and joking and saying that the idea of a sharp stone brought a tear to the eye!

The next free stop was the beach and the beautiful ocean. Rick had never seen the sea before, and he put on his swimming trunks and rushed headlong into the water. It was truly wonderful, and as he sat on the beach eating the picnic, he reckoned that this was far and away the best day of his life. Gramps took him to Perth on the train many more times after that day, and Rick began to become fascinated by the geology of Western Australia and the history of the mines. His grandfather was not very interested in this but was happy to read a newspaper that had been left behind by someone while Rick explored the museum. He knew what pleasure that his grandson was getting from this and was delighted to let him get on with it. They always went to the beach after the museum, and from there Rick developed a love of the sea.

Midland was predominantly a working-class town, and there was nothing very sophisticated about Rick's growth into adulthood. The school was co-educational and gave both boys and girls the chance to learn together about their bodies. They all realised that what they did was very basic, and as long as a boy never risked making a girl pregnant, everything seemed to be acceptable.

Rick did not think of himself as particularly good-looking, but it was clear that he had some sort of animal magnetism, because many of the girls chose to experiment with him, which he found both fun and flattering. In Midland, he was permitted to kiss, cuddle, and touch them. Most girls wanted to play with his cock and put it in their mouths, but under no circumstances was he allowed to ejaculate. He had to warn them in advance, and they finished him off by hand.

It was all very unsubtle, but Rick loved every minute of it. he later learned that lovemaking to a woman required much more effort on his part to give a woman real pleasure. That, however, was the way it was in his teenage years, and Rick remained a selfish lover, since no one had taught him to be anything else.

One day Rick was called into the headmaster's study and informed that the railway company sponsored three students to go to the University of Western Australia, and all the tuition and expenses would be paid if he qualified. The headmaster told him that he had chosen five boys who would take the entrance exam, and he had earned the right to be involved with this through his outstanding efforts during his time at the school. Rick was delighted and asked what he had to study to get one of these scholarships. The headmaster told him that they tended to ask a simple question and expected you to write around two thousand words. They discounted one boy, interviewed the other four, and finally choose three. The University of Western Australia was highly regarded, and a degree from there would be extraordinary for a boy like Rick. H knew that his parents could not possibly afford it, and his only chance to get there was through this route.

Up until the day of the exam, he wondered what this strange question might be and how he might answer it to be awarded the scholarship, but had no idea. When Rick picked up the exam paper, a single question presented itself:

> If you were tasked with promoting Western Australia as an area of investment for foreign companies, what aspects of our state would you focus on? Please write approximately two thousand words.

Rick loved the sea, and tourism seemed an attractive option, but his many hours in the museum had instilled into him the wonderful geology and potential for mining in Western Australia, and he reasoned that with foreign investment, the returns for international investors could be substantial. In the blink of an eye, he reached 2,200 words and had to trim things back, but by the end of the exam, he had got everything that he wanted to say into 2,078 words. As Rick walked out of the exam room, he thought that he had done himself proud, but if he didn't to the next stage, it was clearly not to be.

When Rick told his parents and Gramps the question that had been asked and the way that he had answered it, they were convinced that he would get to the interview. Seven days later, a letter arrived inviting Rick to visit the university for the next stage.

Rick entered the room to see three men sitting on one side of a big table, and there was a single chair on the other. He was invited to sit down. "We really liked your essay," said one of the interviewers, "and we sensed that you wanted to write a great deal more—is that correct?" He confirmed that they were correct and informed them that geology excited him, and he wanted to become a geologist and really study the rocks and formations of Western Australia. Rick added that if foreign investors wanted to put their money to work, he liked the idea of selling that story to them.

The rest of the interview ended up with them telling him which was the best course to take and the best college to go to if he wanted to become a geologist. As Rick left, the senior man smiled and said simply, "I think that you will enjoy your studies here." Although Rick was sure that he had got the scholarship, he did not tell a soul until the letter arrived making him the offer. Rick's parents and Gramps were so happy that they shed tears, and a great deal of beer was drunk that night.

Girls don't do geology, so Rick was surrounded by boys at university, but he found out that he could have more stimulating conversations with men that with women. In the 1950s, the ladies of Western Australia were interested in marriage, family, babies, clothes, music, and suntans. The unbelievable record of Don Bradman in cricket seemed to be lost on them, and Rick's excitement about gold and copper mines and potential discoveries bored them to sobs. In Perth, there was a better class of lady than in Midland, but he was seen as very working class and much too intense. Since Rick enjoyed sex a great deal, he went out with lower-class girls who wanted sex as much as heI did and not a great deal else. This gave him a kind of satisfaction, but he knew that he was looking for something much deeper.

Rick got a first-class honours degree at the University of Western Australia and entered the best geology college in the area, with a very good reference from his university professor. Although he had to work nights in bars and restaurants to fund himself, he sailed through his exams and became a fully qualified geologist in very good time. He looked at all the mining journals for work, but it all seemed so small-scale. Most of the companies were prospectors and had little money available, and Rick sensed that getting paid might be an issue. He searched and searched, but nothing appeared, until one day he got a call from his old university professor, who told Rick that a prestigious Perth stockbroker was looking for a geologist to work in a team reviewing mining opportunities in Australia for a global audience. The candidate would have to be able to turn dreary mineral facts into sellable investment stories. "Would you like me to put your name forward?" his professor asked him. Rick told him that this was the job that he had been searching for, and really hoped that he would. The senior partner of Porter Partners knew nothing about geology, and his head of research knew little more, but they were from wealthy families, and that seemed to be enough. During the interview it was clear that Rick's working-class background bothered them, and he was deeply hurt by this. His wish was to tell them that he was really well qualified to do this job, but his social standing in a firm of this nature was going to be difficult. When the letter came, it offered Rick a job for six months at a salary that to Rick was amazing. He accepted it by return of post, and set out to show them how wrong they were.

Rick suggested to his bosses that he should visit all parts of Western Australia, review rock samples and mineral cores, and get to know the people that were good and bad. He was given a large expense account and spent two years travelling all around and building up a great knowledge base, which he believed could become valuable. Since he represented Porter Partners, the mining bosses accepted him, and learned of their prospects. But because he was the son of a lorry driver, Rick used to buy lots of beer for the local geologists and mine managers, and he gained vastly more knowledge from them, because they were willing to tell him everything, even if they had been told by management not to. Rick realised that no other Perth broker would be seen dead with these types of workers, and that gave him a real edge. Rick was pretty good at writing reports, so he submitted them regularly, and these seemed to be popular. After six months, Rick was accepted onto the full staff and got an excellent pay rise. When he told his parents what he was to be paid, they could barely believe it.

Michael Porter, the senior partner, never spoke to Rick, but in 1965 he called him into his office and said, "We have dealings with an important London stockbroker called Taylor, Dudley & Everett, and I have always dealt with a Mr Aubyn Peters. He now has an assistant called Julian Barker who is very young, very enthusiastic, and never stops asking me questions about mining. Frankly, I do not know the answers to most of his questions, and I think that you and he might get on, so please ring him and sort him out."

Rick had seen Aubyn Peters in their offices. He barely seemed to care about mining prospects in Western Australia and always disappeared with the senior partner to play golf. He was a very posh Englishman, and Rick had absolutely nothing in common with him. On the day that Rick first rang Julian Barker, he was aware that he was very posh too, and feared the worst. These fears were lessened, however, when he told Rick that he had read his report on Western Australia that had been sent through to London. He then began to ask Rick a bunch of questions, some about facts and what the implications of them were and some about interpretation. All his questions were thought-provoking, and Rick really enjoyed answering them. In the following months, the firm got lots of orders from London, and although Rick was still treated as a working-class man, he received a fantastic bonus at the end of the year.

Julian rang Rick out of the blue one day sounding very excited. He told him that his boss had retired and that he would be coming to Perth, and he wanted Rick to set up a really good trip for them both, so that he could learn first-hand why Western Australia was so exciting. Rick couldn't believe what he was saying, since this London account was treated with reverence, and for the new man to want him to organise the trip was flattering to say the very least. Rick submitted the trip agenda to the head of research, since he would have to fund a great deal of it, and after making a sarcastic comment about Rick's manners in front of an English gentleman, which upset him, he signed the document.

The trip was split into three parts:

1. The big, well-known companies
2. The companies that had made discoveries and were developing mining projects
3. Totally speculative ventures, where a good set of drilling results could lead to skyrocketing share prices

This last group Rick had put together himself by talking to the local guys and using his own knowledge of geology. As the day of Julian Barker's arrival approached, Rick was both nervous and excited, as this was his first direct contact with a client.

Julian rang from his hotel room and laughingly said, "I had no bloody idea how far Perth was from London. I seem to have been on planes for days. Are you free for a drink, because I need one?" As Rick walked into the bar of the hotel, he wondered what he would look like. He sensed that he would be tall, and he had told Rick that he was wearing a white shirt and a blue tie. He was indeed tall and stood up very straight, and although Rick knew that he was five years younger than himself, he had a sophisticated air that was a little unnerving.

He ordered the drinks, and the two of them began to talk about everything—where they had been brought up, what they enjoyed, how Rick had got into geology and Julian into stockbroking, and then up came the subject of cricket. Rick knew everything there was to know about Don Bradman, and Julian knew everything there was to know about the Ashes tours both here and in England. The love of the game was so great that it was agreed that they would link his next trip to a Test match and visit the famous Perth cricket ground, nicknamed "the Waka." They both drank beer until late into the evening and then agreed where to meet the next morning. As Rick walked home to his small apartment, he realised that Julian was the first person that he had met at work who had not treated him as anything but his equal. For Rick, that felt very special.

The trip was a huge success, and they both took lots of notes. As Julian wrote circulars for his London clients, he asked Rick to verify his facts, and they jointly agreed to the conclusions. They were together all day and every day for two weeks, and by the end of the trip, Rick believed that they had become very good friends.

The London business of Porter Partners rose and rose, and Rick got much praise from the partners, but despite all this, it remained clear to him that he was not one of them and never would be. Although his pay rose rapidly, he knew in his heart that he would never be offered a partnership, and it saddened him greatly. There were countless more trips, but visits to Test matches and fun nights out with enormous quantities of beer were always included. But of course they always worked very hard, driving many thousands of miles and producing strong investment recommendations.

In 1967, something happened that would change Rick's life forever. On the last day, they had some free time ahead of Julian's flight to Darwin. Apparently he had been asked by his boss to review a big company in the Northern Territory, and his flight was in the early evening. Rick suggested that they spend some time at his favourite beach. They sunbathed and swam and after that sat under a parasol with some beer. He do not know why I did it, but he poured out his heart to Julian about being working class, how the partners treated him, and why they would never accept him as a partner. Rick went on and on and at times had tears in my eyes. When he had finished, Julian asked in a very kind way, "Rick, do you think that any non partner in the firm earns more than you?" Rick was sure that he was the highest paid and confirmed that. Julian then continued, "If you were a partner of the firm, do you think that you would do a better job or work harder?" Clearly the answer to that was no, and Rick said so. "If that is the case, why do you feel the need to be a partner? Who do you want this for; is it you or someone else?" Although his grandfather had passed away, so he couldn't tell him, it was clear that he wanted to tell his parents that he had been made a partner so that they could be proud of him. Once Rick had told Julian this, he said, "Don't you think that your parents are ecstatic at what you have achieved? And have you ever looked at the financial risks of being a partner in a stockbroking firm? In a very bad year, it could wipe you out. My father remained a salaried partner at his firm because he didn't want the risk, and I don't blame him." He finished by asking Rick how much he knew about the partnership's funding, and he realised that he knew nothing. Julian finished by saying, "I think that you are the best, most knowledgeable researcher in Western Australia. If you go on the way you are, you will become a very rich man with no risks—is that such a bad deal?"

The feeling of relief for Rick was extraordinary, and as he dropped Julian at the airport, he knew that this young man was seriously intelligent and way more mature than his years would suggest. That night as he went to bed, he began to think of all the details of their time together, and as all these thoughts flowed through his head, he realised that he had become fully erect and was seriously sexually aroused. Rick began to think of Julian and himself together on the beach, and imagined glancing at the lump in Julian's swimming trunks. He did not know why, but he began to imagine taking Julian's off, and in his fantasy, Julian took his off as well. In this dream, they were alone on the beach, and Rick walked to him and put his arms around his neck. As they cuddled, their erect cocks rested against each other, and the arousal became intense. Rick wanted more, and they lay down on a towel in such a way that Rick's face was next to Julian's cock and his face was next to Rick's. They began to touch and stroke each other so very gently. Rick, however, needed even more and kissed him very delicately, and felt him doing the same in return. As the kissing became more arousing, he imagined the whole of his knob sliding into his mouth, and suddenly he couldn't hold himself back any longer. The climax that followed was so exquisite that Rick could barely breathe. Julian Barker had reached inside him at a level that was beyond anything that he had experienced. Rick was in love with Julian, of that there was no doubt, and he knew there and then that it would be forever.

The next morning Rick was so shocked that he physically shook. What he had done the night before was absolutely appalling. Here was a gentleman of great charisma and integrity, and all he could do was bring himself to an enormous climax thinking about Julian—it was truly terrible and disgusting. Rick decided there and then, that no one would ever know about his love for Julian, and that meant no one.

Rick questioned whether he was in fact homosexual, but the thought of sex with another man was abhorrent to him. His love was entirely tied up with this one man and not men in general. That night, he went out with his girlfriend, and after a pleasant evening, they made passionate love. The next morning she said with a warm smile, "That was the most beautiful experience I have ever had; you were so tender and gentle and warm, I cannot believe that lovemaking could ever be better." Rick agreed with her completely, but his mind had clearly been elsewhere.

CHAPTER FIFTEEN

Ambrose walked into Julian's new office and said, "Julian, my uncle left me quite a large holding of a company called the Northern Pastoral Company, and it is based near Darwin. I gather it is involved with cattle and sheep stations all over Australia. The shares, which were very sleepy for ages, have in the last few years taken off, and my holding has now become enormous. Every man and his dog seems to think that they are the best thing since sliced bread, which frankly worries me a bit. I do not want to ask an Aussie broker to dig up the drains on this one, because it might unsettle things, so I wonder if you would be prepared to extend this year's trip and visit the company." Julian was delighted to help, because this was the surest sign he could have that Ambrose trusted him, and that was important. He rang up Rick in Perth and said, "Hi, Rick, do you know who is the best land broker in Darwin? Because if you do, I would like to meet him for an informal chat." He heard Rick shouting the question across the office, and a moment later he was back on the phone. "Apparently the guy up in Darwin is Rob Dunwoody; he's a legend. By the time you get here, we will have set you up with a meeting. I gather from our team that he loves to drink. I am sure that you will be able to cope with that. See you soon." Julian thanked him and got on with his preparations for his trip.

As Julian's flight climbed out of Perth on its way to Darwin, he thought back to the events of the day. Rick had obviously been struggling with the fact that he did not feel accepted by the partners of his firm, and he distinctly remembered Michael Porter's description of Rick as he suggested that they spoke. "He is very working class but is talented and asks almost as many questions as you—I think you will get on." That, in Julian's opinion, was a truly nasty way to introduce Rick to another company—in fact, it was quite wrong. Rick was so keen to become a partner, but Julian knew that snobbery of this kind would never change, and the partners would never accept him as one of them. He sincerely hoped that the advice he had given him had helped, because he really liked Rick.

For a legend, the offices of Rob Dunwoody were very modest, and the man himself was the same. Rob sat at a desk with documents all over it and files all over the floor and cabinets, and Julian wondered how on earth that he could find anything. Rob began, "I gather from contacts at Porter Partners that you are a very bright young man and will ask me a lot of questions, but you will buy me a good lunch afterwards. I like the sound of that and consider it the fee for the information that I am about to give you, and don't worry; the lunch bill in Darwin will probably be less than a round of drinks in London. So, young man, what can I do for you?"

Julian was exceptionally nervous but began, "What I need to learn from you is the current state of the market for cattle and sheep stations in Australia, the state of the Australian agriculture sector, and whether you would be a buyer or seller of these items if you were starting today. And please, Mr Dunwoody, assume that I know absolutely nothing."

Rob, as he insisted on being called, started by saying that most of the people that came to see him thought they knew all the answers but in reality knew nothing. Hence, he was grateful to work with Julian because his opening remarks indicated honesty, and he liked that. He followed it up by stating that the market for stations was at least 25 per cent overpriced and that after a lengthy run of good times, his instincts were that bad times lay ahead. He went on to explain that a megalomaniac was buying every property that came up for sale and would not take no for an answer, and hence he always overpaid. "He says that he gets his money from long-term investors, but I know that he is mortgaged up to the hilt, and any downturn at all or any loss of confidence would expose him for the fraud that he is. If I were going to do anything, I would sell everything to this greedy bastard, but only for cash. Of course, I would never state this to anyone in our industry, because I am earning a great living selling properties and receiving my inflated commissions."

Julian decided to take a gamble and said, "You are talking about the Northern Pastoral Company, aren't you." The look on Rob's face told Julian that he was right before he had even said a word. "How on earth did you know that? All their purchases are made through agents, and no one knows who the buyer is, and Northern Pastoral never accounts for property acquisitions in a way that can be easily seen unless you are a forensic accountant. The fact is that the stock market loves Mike MacDougal. and he can do no wrong. It is my contention that he is totally out of his depth, and the financiers are leading him by the nose. Trust me, young Julian; this will end in tears." Julian lied very effectively and said that his boss was a really well-connected man, and he had heard a rumour, but it was great to get the facts from Rob to confirm his suspicions. The meeting went on until 12:30 p.m., and then the two of them went out to lunch. The restaurant that Rob had chosen was very basic, with wooden tables and chairs, but the two people that owned it were very friendly. When they arrived at the table with the menu, Rob said to them, "I want you to impress me and my young friend from London, but deliver us two large beers, which will get us started." Julian could not believe how good the food was, how much beer Rob consumed, or how little the bill was, and so he left a very large tip. As they parted company, Rob put his hand on Julian's shoulder and said, "Be very careful of what you say when you meet Mike MacDougal; he is a devious toad and a nasty piece of work. And please do not admit that you have met me; I would appreciate that. Good luck."

Julian arrived at the smart, new offices of the Northern Pastoral Company in plenty of time for his meeting, but half an hour passed, and no one came. Julian thought to himself that he had come all the way to Darwin to meet this man, and he didn't even have the courtesy to arrive at the appointed time. Just before an hour had elapsed, Mike MacDougal arrived, and far from being apologetic, he made it clear that he had an hour and that was all. Julian settled down and asked him a number of questions about how the business was financed and how much in the way of borrowings the company had. Julian asked him directly if there were any other borrowings apart from the ones shown in the report and accounts. Mike MacDougal lied without a moment's hesitation and said that all was as it appeared. Julian followed up with simple questions about agriculture to end the meeting, but he knew that he had what he needed, and now he had to act.

Julian arrived at Darwin's main post office, bought a postcard with Aborigines on it, and sent a note to Rick in Perth. It read, "Dear Rick, please thank your colleagues for the great introduction to Rob.

Our meeting was fascinating, and the lunch was superb—boy, can he drink! Achieved what I set out to. Regards, Julian."

He pushed the card into the letterbox and then went to the counter and asked the lady if he could send a telegram to Ambrose Dudley at Taylor, Dudley & Everett in London. She said that this would be no trouble, and after they had arranged the details, she asked what words should be sent. Julian thought for a moment and wrote: "Please sell as much of your large holding without damaging the price STOP All the details on my return STOP Julian STOP."

That evening he boarded the aircraft for the long haul back to England in the knowledge that he was being helpful to Ambrose, who had given him his chance in life.

Julian arrived in the office and saw a note on his desk that read, "Lunch at the Savoy today. Meet me at the office door at 12:30. All news then. Ambrose."

He spent the morning with Rebecca, who was working on his Australian notes, and Julian knew that by the end of the day, his report to the clients would be in superb English with no spelling mistakes whatever. Rebecca was a treasure, and he never tired of telling her, and she never tired of hearing it.

As they climbed into the taxi, Ambrose said, "Julian, I love your style. I send you to check out a company for me as a favour, and you come back with as strong a sell recommendation as I have heard. Stan tells me that he has sold three-quarters of my holding so far, but it is getting difficult, so he is backing off for a day or two. He reckons, however, that he will have completed the order by the end of the week. I have to admit that I am really looking forward to hearing your story, and I thought that the Riverside Room at the Savoy was a fitting venue for such a dramatic tale!"

Julian had never been to the Savoy Hotel in the Strand before. He knew that this was a place for the very rich and famous and not for the likes of him. As they walked down some carpeted steps past a piano, which was being played for guests ahead of their lunches, Julian saw ahead of him an amazing room with a vast ceiling and high windows, and beyond a few trees, there was a view of the River Thames—it was truly breathtaking to this young man.

As they sat down at the table, Ambrose asked him if he liked wine, and when this was confirmed, he ordered a bottle of white and red. Julian knew that this was to be a very exciting experience for a twenty-six-year-old. After they had given their food orders to the waiter, it was clear that the story should begin. Julian described his meeting with Rob Dunwoody and the gamble that he had taken to find out who the man was that Rob disliked. He then explained his meeting with Mike MacDougal and the downright lie that he had told him. He had independently worked out that the company would have to raise more capital in the next year or life was going to get difficult, and he agreed with Rob that the agricultural sector looked overpriced. "My conclusion is this," Julian stated, "that if Mike MacDougal can continue to hide his huge debts, the shares will drift lower, but if the cat gets out of the bag, these shares will crash."

Ambrose sipped at his wine with obvious pleasure and suggested that Julian was a really excellent presenter of a story, and he had believed every word of it. He then told Julian that no one ever died taking a profit, and even if the shares continued up, he would not mind. Later on in the lunch when a lot more wine had been drunk, Ambrose suddenly said, "Maybe we should let the cat out of the bag ourselves.

I have checked, and ten of our clients own these shares; they deserve to be warned. What I want you and Rebecca to do is write a report on this company and head it 'In the Strictest of Confidence—Sell.' Instead of sending our report out as normal, we will make individual meetings and explain what you have found out. We will then sell as much stock as we possibly can and try and get our clients the best average price possible. If you are right, and I believe that you are, this will greatly improve your status. Since this is a very sensitive document, I will want to vet every word. You may wish to describe him as a devious and rude maniac, but we have to be more subtle; I think that you know what I mean."

Over the next week, Rebecca and Julian agreed to the words of the note, and Ambrose checked everything very carefully. Julian walked down to the London Stock Exchange trading floor, sat down with Stan, and asked him, "After you sold Ambrose's shares, how quickly did the shares recover?" Stan replied, "Julian, there is still a great deal of enthusiasm for this company, and the jobbers like it, too. If you generate big orders, please ask the sellers to be patient, and I believe that I can get a great deal away. What you must stress to the clients is that any panicky actions will ruin this for everyone."

Ambrose and Julian went to visit all their holders, and Julian explained the dangers. Since the shares of the Northern Pastoral Company were nearly at their all-time high, everyone was happy to sell. All the clients obeyed the "don't panic" instructions, and six weeks later, all the clients of Taylor, Dudley & Everett were out, and the shares had only dropped 6 per cent in that time. Stan, Ambrose, and Julian went out to dinner to celebrate a really good team effort. The next day, Ambrose asked Rebecca to remove the "In the Strictest Confidence" headline and instructed her to quote the analyst of this report as Julian Barker and make sure that all the financial journalists got a copy, as well as Porter Partners in Australia.

The truth is that if you put an Alka-Seltzer into a glass, you know what is going to happen, and you are also aware that you cannot stop the fizzing until it is exhausted. Ambrose knew this, and the reaction to this sell report was extraordinary. The shares of the Northern Pastoral Company fell like a stone, tried to recover a little, and then plunged again. Julian was contacted by the Australian press, and Ambrose told him to be indirect in his answers so that the journalists would have to do the digging…and they did.

About two months later, an article came out in Australia that suggested that the banks were going to exchange their loans for shares at 80 per cent below the all-time high share price and that Mike MacDougal was to be removed as the head of the firm. Julian Barker's reputation as a research analyst was now assured.

CHAPTER SIXTEEN

Ambrose took Julian to the Savoy for lunch a second time and said that he wanted to discuss something very private away from the office.

Again after the food orders had been taken, Ambrose began, "This Labour government is going to tax us out of existence, and I have decided that I am not going to allow it. I have decided to set up an account for myself in Switzerland, and because of what you have done for me, which saved me a fortune, I am arranging things for you too. What I want you to do is to fly to Zurich and meet with a Herr Anton Gruber at the Zurich Cantonal Bank, and he will explain everything. When all the administration is done, you and I will never discuss what happens there, and you will never tell a soul about your account there—do I make myself clear? What we are doing is not illegal, but what money you make out there can never be brought back to England because that would make it fully taxable, and if you fail to declare it, then it would definitely be illegal! I have set up your meeting, and here is your return air ticket." He then gave Julian a large, brown envelope addressed to Herr Anton Gruber, which was sealed with wax, and told him to deliver it by hand. Julian was both incredibly excited and terrified at the same time. Literally in the last few weeks, he had seen a film at his local cinema called *The Thomas Crown Affair*, and in it, Steve McQueen had flown to Switzerland to arrange his highly illegal banking there—this was amazing. Julian was fascinated to know what was in the envelope, but because it was sealed, he realised that he would never find out.

The moment Julian had been dreading arrived. He had no idea what was in the envelope but sensed that if a Swiss customs officer asked him about it, he was likely to be in real trouble, and suddenly it happened. As he walked through the customs area, the uniformed officials were talking to a randomly selected group of passengers, and Julian became one of those. The customs official began by looking at Julian's passport. "Mr Barker, please can you tell me what you are intending to do whilst you are in Zurich?" Julian stood there thinking that he was about to become one of the youngest men ever to have a heart attack. Julian replied that he had a meeting at the Zurich Cantonal Bank with a Herr Anton Gruber on a business matter. The customs official went on, "And have you anything to declare to me today?" Julian knew that at this point, only the truth would do, and he opened his briefcase, put the envelope on the table, and said, "As well as my meeting, I have to hand-deliver this package to Herr Gruber." The customs official then asked Julian if he knew Herr Gruber's telephone number and if he objected to a phone call being made to confirm what he was saying. Julian took the piece of paper that Ambrose had given him with the bank's details on it and passed it over to him. Suddenly, the atmosphere changed completely, and the custom officer smiled widely. "I hope you are bringing lots of valuable business to our small country, and I hope your meeting goes very well." He placed the envelope back into the briefcase and shut it. Julian went straight to the airport gentlemen's toilet and sat there for ten minutes in a state of total and utter shock. He had never been so scared in all his life and never wanted to be again.

As one might expect, the Zurich Cantonal Bank was located in the centre of the city in a very impressive building, and only when the taxi from the airport pulled up outside did Julian start to relax a little. He was ushered into a very plush office with a large desk, behind which sat Anton Gruber. He clearly only wore his gold-rimmed glasses for reading and took them off immediately as he walked round to greet Julian. He pointed to a meeting table with six chairs around it and showed him where to sit. "Mr Barker, I was very impressed with your report on the Northern Pastoral Company, and I have read everything that you have written about Canada and Australia. Your thinking is very clear, and even us foreigners can understand the nuances of what you are trying to convey to us." Somehow Julian had never thought that his reports would be read in Switzerland or that Herr Gruber would know that he even existed, but clearly he did and was treating him as a fellow professional, which was gratifying. Julian realised that the sealed envelope was an important part of the meeting and passed it over, saying, "Ambrose Dudley asked me to deliver this to you by hand." Without hesitation the banker broke the wax seal and slid out a pile of share certificates. Julian recognised them at once. They were Royal Dutch Shell "bearer" share certificates, and one of the lessons that Julian had learned as he was trained in the back office was the difference between registered stock and bearer stock. Quite simply, if you bought the former, your name would be on the register of holders of the company, but if you owned the latter, the company promised to pay "the bearer" the value of the shares on sale, and the dated dividend coupons were attached to the share certificate itself. There was therefore no record of the investor's name, and they would remain completely anonymous.

Tom Smith at Taylor, Dudley & Everett, who knew everything there was to know about administration, had once told Julian that bearer shares were always slightly more expensive than the registered variety because they were "mobile money with complete anonymity." Without saying a word, Julian knew that Ambrose had given him a very large part of his worldly wealth, and it had left England and its Labour government without a single form being filled in. That was clearly very clever as long as Julian himself had not run off with them…because then he would have become the bearer and very rich!

Anton pressed a buzzer, and his secretary arrived. "Please check the actual bearer certificates against the enclosed list, and when you are satisfied with the accuracy of the documents, please credit Mr Dudley's account with the stock. Also, could you type out a bank receipt, which I will sign, and then we will put it in a sealed envelope, and Mr Barker here can take it back to London." Julian knew the approximate value of each of the bearer shares and guessed at how much money had been deposited in Zurich. The number that he came up with was enormous. He must never even hint to Ambrose that he knew.

Anton Gruber now turned to Julian and began, "I am guessing that you have no idea as to how we work in Zurich, so settle back, and I will explain everything to you. Your account will be unusual since it will have no money in it, but it will have something very valuable in it indeed, and that is called a 'bank guarantee.' Your guarantor, who I could never officially tell you about, but of course you know, has given me the figure of thirty thousand pounds. What this means is that as long as you obey our strict rules, you can invest in any share or shares throughout the world, and if every share goes to nothing, your guarantor will reimburse the bank from his own funds held here. We take no risk, you have no risk, and that is an extraordinary opportunity for yourself. If in years to come, you have made a great deal of money from this guarantee, you can write us a simple letter, and your guarantor will then be off the hook. I am guessing that you earn around one thousand pounds per year, so if you found exciting investments that perhaps were to rise twenty per cent, that would earn you six thousand on the full thirty thousand, which equates to six years of your current earnings. I hope that you appreciate the extraordinary generosity of your guarantor." Julian was overwhelmed by Ambrose's generosity and expressed this to Anton, mentioning the name. Anton immediately waved his finger in the air and told Julian never to mention names; he followed up by suggesting that only numbers were to be used.

"Your account will open today," Anton stated, "and you can invest immediately, but I recommend that you don't. Money is like a new toy and can be very exciting, but you do not want to break it from overuse straightaway. Think about your investments and then ring our dealers, and after they have confirmed your account, they will do all the market work here. No paperwork ever leaves this building, and they will only confirm your deals on the telephone. We always invest as 'Zurich Cantonal Bank account client,' and we settle the bargains as a bank. Should anybody ask us why a purchase or sale has taken place, we simply inform them that we act as the agent of a client, and we take client confidentiality very seriously indeed. No one will ever know what you have done—that is our commitment to you, and our reputation is built upon it. If you wish to take your family on a holiday anywhere in the world, we book your travel arrangements from Zurich, and we will send Swiss traveller's cheques to your hotel for collection on arrival. The only country that we cannot do this for is the United Kingdom, for obvious reasons. If you need to make a big purchase in the United Kingdom, like a house, we will arrange for you to get a loan from another Swiss bank in London. Your account here will guarantee that loan in London. Your mortgage deal in the United Kingdom is an entirely British transaction; only the provider of the funds in England knows of the guarantee behind it, and we never tell them who the guarantor is. The truth is that we are immensely flexible, but our fees are high—you appreciate that we have to live!" Julian saw the funny side of that and appreciated the humour.

The rest of the meeting was very detailed. Julian got his numbered account and discussed the security questions that he would be asked. Julian asked what would happen if he forgot his number. Anton said, "Don't, or you will have to fly here, and it will cause me considerable headaches. My advice is to hide numbers amongst other numbers, so in your home address and telephone book, create a fictitious person and use your account number as a telephone number, and do the same at your office. Please inform me of your next of kin's passport number, and write a personal letter to them and lodge it with your solicitor. In the letter, ask them to contact the bank, and quote your security question and answer—under no circumstances give them your account number. We will handle it from there, and the transfer and transition should be easy. You are a very young man, Julian, but death does not offer us a clear timetable, so you must be prepared. Remember also that you can update or change the letter that is lodged with your solicitor as you move through life and your circumstances change."

When Julian got back to London, he gave Ambrose the sealed envelope, and Ambrose opened it. The confirmation that all his stock was now safely lodged in Switzerland was obviously important to him, and he smiled happily. Julian told him about his brush with customs in Zurich, and he thanked Ambrose sincerely for his extraordinary generosity. Ambrose laughed and said, "It will only be generous if you make a complete ass of yourself and lose the lot, and I have seen nothing in your approach to investment that would suggest to me that you are about to mess things up. Invest as you do for our clients, and I think you will do well." Julian thought to himself that he had been offered a great chance in life, and he was not going to blow it.

CHAPTER SEVENTEEN

The year 1967 was a bad one for Great Britain and business in general. The partners walked around with a quiet demeanour, as they knew that their take-home pay that year was going to be severely restricted. Harold Wilson announced that the pound was to be devalued from $2.80 to $2.40, and then he appeared on the television and stated that the "pound in your pocket was not worth any less." Ambrose charged around the office making statements like "Is this man from another planet?" and "The man's a complete fruitcake," and when the prime minister announced that he had sold a significant amount of the United Kingdom's gold reserves, he went wild. "Everyone must now buy gold shares, since this nation has sold the only real money that it possesses." Although this statement was pronounced in a fit of temper, the firm put out a strong recommendation for gold shares, and this proved to be an outstanding call in the seven years that followed.

Julian's trip to Australia in January 1969 was a good one. Not only did they watch a bit of cricket, but they also went sailing in Rick's new boat. On the Sunday evening, they went to a cheap but excellent restaurant and started to talk on personal matters. Julian asked Rick how he was getting on with the partners, and he said that he had done a deal with them. Apparently he had come out with it bluntly and said to them, "I know that you like my work, but you think that I am too working class to be a partner of this firm, and I have finally accepted that fact. So, I want to propose a deal that will give both of us what we want. You pay me a good salary, but we split the commission that I bring in fifty-fifty. In that way, you can sell what I do, and I can become rich if my recommendations remain above average." Michael Porter thought for a moment and then replied, "I think that will work, and you are right; it is good for everyone." Rick told Julian that they shook hands, the paperwork arrived within a week, and the deal was signed. Rick thanked Julian for his great advice and told him that he was very happy with the arrangements.

Julian now told Rick about his new wife, Alice, and how happy he was. He also told him about their new house and how good he felt about his work. Rick sat quietly and listened to Julian talking. He felt very empty inside, but at the same time, he was happy for Julian. When Julian had finished, he asked Rick about his love life and specifically asked whether Rick had anyone special. Rick replied, "Yes, I am in love with someone, but it is impossible." Rick pointed at his finger and added, "Married, you know; it could never work out, but there you go." Rick went on to say that he had a very nice girlfriend, and although he had no very deep feelings for her, they had fun together. He said that he loved his work and thought of it as a hobby and not a job, and he enjoyed driving a thousand miles to see a hole in the ground and meet another mad geologist. He finished by telling Julian that he raced his boat and loved the sea, and hence he had a very full and happy life. Julian was pleased for him.

The next day they got in the Jeep and began to drive. Rick was very excited about the agenda that he had put together. He told Julian that a number of projects that he had recommended to Julian and his clients were likely to announce drill results in the next twelve months. As they travelled around, Rick suggested that a really good set of results could have a dramatic reaction in the stock market. At the end of their journey, the two men wrote up a report that itemised four companies and suggested that clients buy an equal amount of each of them, because any one of them could become a "moon shot" with the correct drill results.

When Julian got home, he wanted to publish his report, but Ambrose stopped him. He advised, "Go to the clients that you did very well for in the Northern Pastoral Company, since they think you are a star. Talk to them individually, and suggest to them that this is very private and is only being offered to a select few, and build your position slowly." Almost as Ambrose stopped speaking, Julian knew the wisdom of his words and agreed wholeheartedly. In the next few weeks, he visited eight institutions. Every one of them was happy to buy all four shares, and Rick was delighted at the amount of business that was coming from London. In the following months, the shares varied widely; some rose, and some fell, but the overall investment remained positive. Little did Julian, Rick, and the institutions realise that a day was coming very soon that would become etched in their brains forever.

CHAPTER EIGHTEEN

Alice and Julian were asleep in bed at six in the morning when, strangely, the telephone rang. Julian answered it sleepily and heard the clipped tones of the operator. "Is that Mr Julian Barker?" she asked. He answered that it was, and she went on, "Are you willing to take a person-to-person call from Perth, Australia, from a Mr Brad Donald?" Julian was now absolutely wide-awake, because Rick had once told him that if he ever heard something amazing, he would go to a Perth Hotel and ring him using a fake name. As Julian accepted the call, he loved Rick's humour. Their hero in cricket was the legendary Sir Donald Bradman, and hence Brad Donald could only be Rick.

"Julian, I made my regular call to Poseidon today, and my geologist mate there sounded a little strange. I pulled his leg and said, 'Are your cores rubbish or something?' Well, Julian, his voice dropped to a whisper so that I could barely hear him, but he told me that the drilling results were beyond belief. He told me the grades, and I almost dropped the phone—they are incredible, Julian, and he said they have been double- and triple-checked, so this is for real. According to my friend, these results are going to be announced on Monday, and it is Wednesday evening here. This information is absolute dynamite, and the directors are terrified of this leaking out before Monday. Julian, I am not going to say anything to anyone here, but I wonder if you could work out a plan so that we can all benefit in some way. I know that what I have told you is almost certainly illegal, but I am happy to leave it to you." Julian told Rick that he would give it his best shot and would ring him by Friday at the latest. The call ended. Julian sat there stunned. The fact that this information had come from a working man at the Poseidon Company and not from a director made it ten times more credible.

Julian realised that his number-one priority was to make Rick some money from this—not only had Rick found Poseidon in the first place, but this share was one of his group of four, so his clients were about to be very happy. As the train moved smoothly towards London, ideas spun through his head; by the time the passengers burst onto the platform at Waterloo Station, his whole plan was ready. He knew that what he was about to do was bad and would probably get him the sack, but technically, it was not actually illegal; Rick was wrong about that.

His first call was to Anton Gruber in Zurich, and he told him the following: "I have a very sensitive matter that I would like you to handle for me yourself; would that be all right?" Anton replied in his softly spoken voice, "It would be my pleasure, Mr Barker; what can I do for you?" Julian did not waste time. He asked him to buy Poseidon shares carefully throughout Thursday and Friday and make sure that the order would be completed before the close of trading on Friday in Australia, and the whole thirty thousand pounds was to be invested. Julian insisted that this deal was highly sensitive and confidential, but Anton Gruber made no observation and simply said, "It will be done."

Julian now got his list of the eight investors in his group of four shares and began his story to them. "My contact in Australia and I are of the belief that Poseidon will be announcing some important drilling results shortly, and we think they will be good. We do, however, have a problem, and it is this. If the results are good, Rick Jones has to tell me, and I will then ring you, and by the time we get on to buy the shares, we are going to be behind all the Australian buyers, and I think that this is silly. What I propose is this: If the results are better than I suggested in my report, I will get all of you to place orders now so that Porter Partners can be the first buyers and not the last. Of course, if the drilling results disappoint then nothing will be done."

Some clients were wary of this, but most said yes, and Julian found out that both Ambrose and Aubyn were in as well. By Friday at the close of business, Julian sent a telex to Rick. It was a firm order for three hundred thousand pounds of Poseidon shares should the grades be at an acceptable level, on any announcement from the company. Julian added that there was no limit to the price to be paid but that an average price should be reported so that all the London clients would pay the same price for their new investment.

He rang Rick and explained what he had done, not mentioning anything to do with Zurich. Rick was delighted. He now knew the results exactly, and they were wildly better than Julian's cut-off point. He said that his dealers would be ready to act before anyone else had absorbed the news. Finally, Julian asked Rick how the Poseidon share price was doing in the market. Rick said that they had moved up a reasonable amount in the last two days but nothing very dramatic. Julian put the telephone down and was relieved. He was desperately keen to ring Zurich but knew that he should stay as far away from this deal as he could.

CHAPTER NINETEEN

Rick got into his office at 8:00 a.m. on a sunny September morning in 1969 and drank two cups of coffee in a short space of time. Although he knew the results from Poseidon and they were fantastic, he realised that Julian, the man he loved, had put his complete credibility on the line for him. If something went wrong, he would be devastated. The morning dragged on, and the shares of Poseidon hardly changed. Rick got more and more nervous. But at 11:00 a.m., it came: "Poseidon NL and its Windarra Project in the Shire of Laverton, Western Australia, is pleased to announce the following Drilling Results and Grades."

The report went on, and then Rick saw what was critical: the grade was exactly what his friend had told him. Rick literally ran to the dealers and said, "Fill that order from London. Buy and keep buying until it is done. We must be the first to react, so do not be subtle. I want the whole order done by the end of the day—no excuses." The dealers heard the emotion in Rick's voice and knew that this was vital to him, and they worked throughout the day. The stock flew from A$2.50 to

A$3.50 as Rick's dealers bought everything. There was a pause, and then the dealers started again, and the stock moved to A$4.50. As the day drew to a close, some sellers emerged who were delighted with the movement on the day and happy to take a profit. Mentally exhausted, the dealers completed the London order. The back office confirmed that the average price for the whole £300,000 order was A$3.27, and the closing price was A$4.45.

Michael Porter walked into the office and stated that this order from London was the biggest single transaction that the firm had ever done in a single business day. He congratulated Rick on his outstanding research work and said that all the drinks at their local drinking establishment would be on him until the bar closed. Rick and the dealers didn't need any further prompting, and it became a wild night. Before Rick left for the party, he made sure that the trade confirmation had left for Taylor, Dudley & Everett for the attention of Julian Barker. As he walked out of the office, he already knew what the commission on the bargain was, and half of that was his. Julian had really looked after him.

Tom Smith stood at Julian's office door and said, "Bloody hell, Barker, this is fucking huge. We have split the stock up, as you requested, and the contracts will go out by the end of today. Ambrose is going to love you for this. And by the way, Stan has just told me that today Poseidon closed at A$7.50, and your buddy Rick Jones has been on the Australian TV news. I think that you should buy Stan and me a pint." Julian laughed and said, "The drinks are on me; please tell Stan and Brian, and we can make an evening of it."

He picked up the phone and got Rick, who sounded a little drunk. "I have become a TV star, and who would have guessed that? My mum and dad are so excited, but seriously, mate, the buying is just beginning. Tell your clients to hold on; we have huge orders here that we cannot fill, and the buyers will not take no for an answer. These shares are going to the moon, mate; you had better believe it. Got to go—need to buy some drinks." The line went dead. Julian was highly amused, since Rick had always called him Julian, and hearing him calling him "mate" was very funny. He was delighted for Rick, because Rick had imagination and could see things that other people could not see, and that was a very special talent. He had earned the right to get as drunk as he wanted.

Julian left for the pub and was suddenly surrounded by his own colleagues. Rebecca and Ambrose were there, and all of his clients that had been in the Poseidon deal. Rebecca had told them all that Julian was buying, and they were all invited. The party went on until the bar shut, and Julian went to pay the bill, but the barman said that it had already been taken care of by Mr Dudley. Julian staggered onto the train at Waterloo and fell sound asleep. He awoke with a start and saw the guard, who said, "You're at Guildford, Guv, and you have missed the last train." Julian meandered out to the taxi rank, agreed an exorbitant price for the thirteen miles home, and promptly fell asleep again in the taxi. The driver woke him, and he paid. Alice met him at the front door in her dressing gown—she was not amused!

As the shares of Poseidon reached A$35, which was over ten times what his clients had paid, he rang Rick and asked him a simple question: "Rick, how big could this become?" Rick thought about it and said that most of the holders would not sell, and hence the shares were likely to go higher. The nickel price was going up too because of metal demand from the Vietnam War, and everyone seemed happy to stay for the ride. What should he do for his clients? One of the things that Ambrose had taught him was that the decision to buy or sell lay with the institution and not the broker, and his role was to "advise and suggest." He then started to ring around the clients and stated that after a tenfold increase, the idea of taking some profits was not a bad concept. Julian was ignored, and the shares went on through A$100 and then through A$200 and finally peaked at A$285. Along the way, some of his clients sold some but not enough. By March of 1970, a mere seven months later, Poseidon appeared to be in financial trouble, and the shares collapsed almost faster than they had risen. Even though some of his accounts were left with worthless shares, nobody blamed Julian since he had recommended taking profits, and it was they that had ignored him.

When the shares of Poseidon had hit A$50 each, Julian rang Zurich and placed an order to sell all his holdings. This transaction raised over £500,000, and the average stockbroking salary was under £1,500 per year. Julian had to pay back the Swiss bank £30,000 plus fees and interest, but these were negligible. Julian was now a very rich man. He spoke to Anton Gruber and asked him how much money he could get to Australia without arousing suspicion. The answer was clear—this deal could not go through any bank in Australia since alarm bells would go off everywhere. Bearer shares were no good either, since they could be sold only in certain countries without too many questions. Gold worked but was too heavy to move, and so it came down to cash. Anton Gruber's advice was simple. He suggested that Julian find a project that was in financial trouble, and £20,000, which was around A$34,000, could be taken to Perth by bank courier to help fund the business. That courier would be Julian Barker. Any more than this amount would create waves, and this figure was therefore accepted.

Julian asked Rick for a company in Western Australia that was acknowledged to be struggling with its finances. Rick found a company called McNish Engineering that was clearly having problems. He rang up the *Daily Telegraph* information service and asked them if they could find a press cutting that laid out the business issues facing this company. The article arrived in the post within a few days and was perfect. It laid out all the ugly details and clearly stated that the company was in need of fresh capital. Julian set up his annual trip to Perth with Rick, but instead of his normal flight, he was to stop off in Zurich on his way.

In the bank's office, Anton Gruber gave the letter that Julian had asked him for, which released his guarantor from any liability in the future, and Julian signed it. As the secretary took the document away for filing, Julian thanked Ambrose in his mind for his kindness. He knew that his purchase of Poseidon shares was insider trading, but in 1969, although it was severely frowned upon, it was not actually a crime. Julian knew that what he had done was very wrong, and he was not going to be a hypocrite about it. He thought, you may be able to fool the world, but you cannot fool yourself. The moral dilemma for Julian was that this deal had been too good. Had he made 30, 40, or 50 per cent, he might have found a way of excusing himself, but around £450,000 profit was a lifetime's security and made him a genuinely rich man.

As Julian was having these dark thoughts, a bank official came into the room with a briefcase and opened it. Inside was Australian money, piles and piles of it, and on top of it lay a letter on bank-headed notepaper signed by Herr A. Gruber, Director. The contents of the letter were straightforward. Mr J. Barker was acting as a courier for the Zurich Cantonal Bank in providing much-needed cash to a Western Australian venture. No other details were provided. Julian now took out the press article and placed it on top of the cash and bank letter.

Anton wished him well, and a bank car took him to the airport. After a couple of changes en route, Julian landed in Perth and awaited his trip through customs. This time he felt more comfortable. Instead of waiting to be talked to, he walked straight up to a customs officer and asked to speak to him in private. The official looked a little startled but showed him into a small office. They both sat down, and Julian began. "I represent the Cantonal Bank of Zurich and some clients there. In this briefcase is a very large sum of Australian dollars, and this cash is bound for a project in Western Australia that is urgently in need of funds to continue its existence. Officially, I cannot tell you the name of the venture, but off the record, if you were to open the briefcase, I think that things might become clearer." The customs man was way out of his depth, and when he saw the piles of cash, he was awestruck. He picked up the bank letter and read it, asked to see Julian's passport, and then read the newspaper article. Once he had concluded, Julian stressed that this was extremely confidential, and he must not under any circumstances tell a soul, or it might affect the refinancing. The official thanked Julian for being so upfront about it all and wished him well.

He now had everything in place, and all that was left to do was to get to Rick's apartment. After a phone call and instructions, Julian hailed a cab and ten minutes later arrived at a block of flats that were not in the best part of town but were well located. He could see why Rick had chosen to rent here, but very soon he would be able to buy whatever he wanted. Julian rang the doorbell, and almost immediately, Rick opened the door. His outfit was the smartest that Julian had ever seen him in, and his whole appearance seemed to be very much more upmarket. Beaming, Rick said, "Welcome to my home." They settled down, and Julian placed his briefcase by his chair. He had a childish excitement building up inside him because he knew that in the next few minutes, he was going to change Rick's life forever.

Rick noticed the briefcase and pointed out that this was beer time and not work time. Julian asked him a simple question: "Where in Perth would you like to buy a property if money was not an issue?" Rick replied instantly, "They have just built some amazing apartments by the ocean, and the views are sensational, but they are around fifteen thousand dollars each, and even after the year I have had, I am still way short of that." Julian now reminded Rick that on that famous phone call from Brad Donald, he had said that he was certain that Julian would think of a plan for them both to benefit from the Poseidon news. "Well," said Julian, "I did, and it wasn't the huge order that I gave you, although on your half-commission deal, that must have worked well. No, I did something else that was far more direct. I do not want you ever to ask what it was, because I will not tell you, but the results are in the briefcase, and this briefcase is now yours. You will remember that I asked you for a Western Australian company in financial trouble. Well, I used this company to bring Australian dollars into Perth so as not to cause a stir." Almost theatrically, Julian opened the briefcase and displayed the contents, and the article regarding McNish Engineering was on top. Julian had burned the bank letter in his hotel room and flushed the ashes down the toilet, so Rick had no idea where this money had come from. Rick looked dazed but asked, "How much is in there?" Julian told Rick that it was A$34,000, and it was all his. Rick was literally speechless and said nothing for what seemed a long time. Eventually he spoke. "I suppose that putting the money into my bank account would be dumb, but I suppose cash works in this city, like most places. I will have to come up with some ideas, but I am definitely going to buy that beachfront property, since my boat is moored nearby as well."

After a great dinner in a local restaurant and lots of drinks, Rick had his plans sorted out. By the end of the trip, with the normal long drives, everything was fixed. A month or two later, Rick rang Julian and told him that he had bought two beautiful seafront apartments with sea views at A$22,500 for cash. The headline price at A$15,000 each was ignored because the builder was very over borrowed, and cash was the one thing that he didn't have. Clearly it was a deal made in heaven. Rick told Julian that he would rent out the second property long-term, and if his magic touch with mining companies ever failed, he would have a good income for life. With the other money, he was going to buy a house for his parents in Midland, and a great house there would cost under A$2,000. The remainder he called his "silly money." He told Julian that mining ventures were always running out of cash, and A$2,500 in each deal could buy him a real bang for his buck. He finished the call with a personal message. "Doing what you have done for me is so very special, and you have given me lifetime security. I love you very much." As Julian put down the phone, he thought that Rick's words were rather strange, but he put them down to an excess of gratitude and didn't think about them again.

CHAPTER TWENTY

Lord Glenconner was officially the senior partner of Taylor, Dudley & Everett but was seldom in the office. He ran his Scottish estates with a great deal of energy and was a brilliant estate manager. The city for him was a hobby, and although he was little in evidence, he knew everything that went on and had an iron-clad grip on the finances. Nothing that happened in London was missed by this man from the Scottish Highlands. He also liked to write letters, and Julian got a number. Some of these letters praised his Canadian and Australian reports, one praised his report on the Northern Pastoral Company, and the letter that he got after Poseidon described his actions as "inspired."

On his return from Perth, he was aware that Lord Glenconner was having a meeting with Ambrose and that Aubyn was there as well. Rebecca popped her head around the door and said, "Julian, they want to see you; I wonder why," and walked out giggling.

Julian shook Lord Glenconner's hand and said, "It's nice to see you, sir." The lord replied at once, "Let's forget the 'sir' business; it makes me feel old and perhaps your headmaster, neither of which I wish to be. Call me Glen; everyone else does. Please take a seat. I do not need to tell you how much we admire what you have done since you have been at the firm, and we all feel the time has come to offer you a partnership at Taylor, Dudley & Everett. Quite frankly, you have definitely earned it. Aubyn has told me his plans for his shares in the partnership and how it will affect you, but I gather he is keen to tell you himself over a game of golf. I have nothing much more to add except that if you are as good a partner of this company as you are a research analyst, the firm will be much the better for it." Julian thanked Glen for his kind words as the lord rushed out of the office to catch the *Flying Scotsman* to Edinburgh.

Before Julian could gather his thoughts, Aubyn said, "Golf at the normal time tomorrow. Come by taxi—see you then," and then he was gone as well. Ambrose opened a box of cigars and offered one to Julian, who accepted readily, and they talked and smoked together. "I don't know what you have done for Aubyn, but it must have been really special, because what you are going to learn tomorrow is amazing."

As Julian's taxi pulled up at Aubyn's golf club, he felt that this time he was ready to win, and as they went around the course, it was very close. With two holes to go, they were level, and Julian thought that today was his day. Aubyn, however, was an extraordinary competitor, and the more pressure that was put on him, the better he played. Aubyn sunk a long putt on the final green, and Julian lost again.

Aubyn ordered the wines, both white and red, and they settled into a great lunch. "Congratulations on becoming a partner of the firm, Julian; you really do deserve it. There is a part to being a partner that you do not know about, and it goes as follows: I am offered a price to sell my shares back to the business, and I get a payout that is about one-quarter of the value compared with a share in the stock market. So, in simple language, my shares are worth £100,000, but I would get £25,000 for them. One could argue that this is unfair, but my father bought into them on the same terms, and so it washes out. If you were to buy my shares, our bank would lend you the money, and in about three or four years, you should be able to pay the bank back. If markets are good, it will take less time; if markets are bad, it will take longer." Julian understood perfectly what Aubyn was saying, but he could see that there was more to come, so he nodded his approval and said nothing. Aubyn continued, "You worked hard in Australia, and through your efforts, I regained my respect in the firm. I have always felt bad about what I asked you to do, but I did always say that there would be an opportunity for me to pay you back in the future. Julian, dear boy, that time is now. Without discussing the sordid details, I am a very rich man and have invested wisely. I am bright enough to know that there are three top men in our firm who I genuinely respect, and I should invest in their best picks. I have done this with large sums of my family's money. The results have been extremely impressive. To cut a long story short, I want to let you buy my shares in the partnership for £5,000, which is one-fifth of their value but only one-twentieth of their real worth. I have already discussed this with the bank, and the papers and transfer forms will be with me in a day or two. The bank will lend you the money, and I reckon that you will be able to pay off the loan within twelve months."

Julian sat there in shock and remembered when he had thought of Aubyn as a public school idiot and a waste of space, and he felt guilty. The facts, as they had turned out, had shown him to be a legend in his own field of golf, a good judge of investment advice, and a man of honour and immense generosity as well. What could Julian say?

Julian struggled with his emotions and to his great embarrassment shed a tear or two. He thanked Aubyn for his amazing kindness. Aubyn, realising that he had a crisis on his hands, ordered the port...he knew that this would calm things down!

In the next year or two, Julian settled into the partnership. Markets were good, and his loan was paid off in next to no time. The big family event for him was the birth of his son Simon, but his birth had been terrible, and Julian had been informed that this would be his only child. To cheer Alice up, he told her that they could get a big loan from a Swiss bank in London, and therefore they could buy a lovely and expensive house. Alice had no idea why a Swiss bank in London would loan Julian a lot of money, but she simply enjoyed looking for the house of their dreams. After a short search, they found a beautiful home in a private estate called Ashley Park. It was in easy walking distance of the station to London and had a lovely garden—it was perfect.

The big event of 1971 was the collapse of the gold window. The London Gold Pool had been used to hold down the price of gold, but the buyers were now in full control. At the time of sterling's devaluation, Ambrose told everyone to buy gold shares, and this seminal moment made this a clear buying signal for gold shares and one not to be missed.

Ambrose and Julian, however, were about to learn a life lesson that is the overwhelming frustration of stockbrokers throughout the world. What is this lesson? Ambrose wrote about South African gold shares, and Julian wrote about Canadian gold shares, and *no one was listening*. More and more excited they got, and by May of 1972 when the London market finally peaked at above 540 on the FT30 share index, virtually no one had bought anything. Ambrose and Julian were frustrated beyond belief, and it was about to get worse...a lot worse.

What is it all worth?

By the end of 1972, it was clear that a major bear market had begun, and shares were falling fast. The partners at Taylor, Dudley & Everett received not a penny of bonus that year. As 1973 began, all the partners gathered together and agreed that this year had got to be better, but the nightmare had only just begun. Stockbrokers earn a small commission on the value of a trade, and if the value of the trade falls, then the commission falls too. As the markets fall, institutions trade less, and so commissions are less still. As 1973 developed, the inflation rate was rising, and so Taylor, Dudley & Everett had to do something unheard of—they had to let members of their staff go. The partners kept the costs under great control, and a few institutions were starting to buy gold shares, but breaking even was becoming difficult.

On October 6, 1973, the nightmare continued: Egypt and Syria began attacking Israel. The Yom Kippur War, as it became known, was named because the attack was made on their holiest day of the year.

On October 16, OPEC increased the posted price of oil by 70 per cent and a day or two later announced an oil embargo, because the United States was supplying Israel with arms. In the US markets, oil jumped from three dollars a barrel to twelve dollars a barrel, and the stock markets of the world collapsed. All through 1974, share prices fell and fell. Volumes dried to a trickle, and suddenly market commentators began to question whether the UK financial system could survive. Many believed that it wouldn't. Fear was in complete control, and no one could avoid it.

CHAPTER TWENTY ONE

The eight partners of Taylor, Dudley & Everett filed into the boardroom, on a cold November evening. Each of them knew that Tom Smith, who ran an outstanding back office, would have delivered accurate numbers and that they would look truly awful. Within the last month, two stockbroking companies had been "hammered," which is a financial market expression for going bust, and there was no end in sight. Was this the end of the road for their firm too?

Glen started with the facts. "If our costs continue until March of next year and our revenues do not pick up, we are bankrupt—it is as simple as that. I had a meeting with our bank this morning, and they have confirmed our overdraft limit for twelve months from today, but they cannot increase it. Our manager said that the problems in the property market swamp ours, and they are terrified to pull the plug on anyone for fear of creating a run on the banking system. Frankly, I am not sure who was more frightened at the meeting, him or me. Gentlemen—the city of London is teetering on the brink of collapse, and only the strongest will survive. The outcome of today will tell us whether we can be one of that few, or whether we will have to give up now." He paused for a moment or two to let his words sink in and then continued. "We are all going to have to invest a substantial sum of new cash into the firm to cover all the costs until March and assume no revenues at all. I asked Tom to give me the numbers. The figure is eighty-five thousand pounds, and in that period, none of you can take any salary at all. That, I am afraid, is the price of survival for now, and of course we will have to look at the numbers again in February."

Three of the partners announced that they had no liquid assets and could not put up anything. One of the three began to breathe very heavily, and Julian held his hand to steady him. He had gone white as a sheet, and there was a feeling in the room that he was very close to a heart attack. He rallied a little and then burst into tears. The atmosphere was the worst that Julian had ever witnessed, and he wondered how this meeting was going to end.

Six hours later the situation began to clear. The three partners who could not put in anything would stay at the firm, but their percentage of the partnership would fall dramatically. Three partners would put up their percentage of the new cash, and two would increase their percentage considerably. Glen could hold his position but no more, since his Scottish estates were not generating as much revenue as they had done in the past. It was Ambrose and Julian who agreed to fund the balance. Glen announced that he would stay on as senior partner until the market turned up decisively and then would retire. There and then it was agreed that Ambrose would become the new senior partner. After this injection of new cash, Julian would have the second largest position in the business.

Julian now looked at his investments in the United Kingdom and realised that all of them were gold-related. Ambrose was in the same situation. In 1971 when the gold window collapsed and the clients ignored them, they both bought gold shares themselves almost in a fit of pique. Julian had bought £7,000 worth and Ambrose over £12,000. By the end of 1974, these shares had quadrupled, and the UK market had fallen by over 70 per cent. Over a bottle of wine, Ambrose and Julian thought that it was right to sell all the gold shares and fund the partnership with these great profits. Putting new money into the firm was the same as buying UK shares after they had dropped by over two-thirds. By the time that the bargains settled and all the money was in the partnership, it was the middle of December. Nothing was getting any better, but they were still financially viable.

The phone went in Julian's office. It was Alice, and she never bothered him unless it was important. "Julian, please come home; your mother is in a state, and she says she will tell us when we are both there," she said. "I am on my way and will walk from the station and see you there," he replied.

As Alice opened the front door, he could see that she had been crying. "Your dad has got cancer, and it's bad." Julian walked into the living room and could almost cut the atmosphere with a knife. His mother was sobbing, and Jane was as well, and Alice started to cry the moment she sat down. Julian's father was the first to speak. "Julian, you know that I have been losing weight recently and have been getting dull pains in my stomach. I didn't think too much of it, but last week the pain was beginning to occur in my back as well, and I thought that I'd better visit the doctor. He took some blood and urine samples and came to the house this morning to give me the bad news. I asked him, as an ex-army chap, not to sugar coat it, as I hate waffle. He told me that it is pancreatic cancer, it is well advanced, and there is no cure. I then asked him how long I had, and he said that the body cannot function without the pancreas; it will be weeks rather than months." And then in his wonderfully clipped military way, he finished, "Going to be painful, I gather; can't be helped—bit of a bugger."

Julian knelt by his father's chair, put his arms around him, and wept buckets. He loved this wonderful man so much, and the idea of him suffering a painful death was more than he could bear. The doctor had suggested that he stay at home as long as he could and had given him some very strong painkillers. He was to take them three times a day so that the pain would be suppressed. Later in the evening, he asked Julian to walk with him. He put on his overcoat, and the two of them walked down the road. "Julian, how bad is it in your partnership? Because my old firm is hanging on by its fingernails." Julian's father had retired in 1971 and had, with the help of his firm, bought an annuity to provide him with income for life, but he still kept in touch. He went on, "One of the partners says that a big broker could go any minute now, and he has been asked to put in more than he can really afford. He admits that he is bloody terrified and says it was never as bad as this, even in the war. If you need any help, I have good savings, and I want you to have them if needed." Julian started to cry again, admiring this man who was thinking about his son on the day that he had been given a death sentence. "Dad," he sobbed, "I have got enough money to fund my part of the deal, and we are all right until the end of March. I love you so much, and you have been such an amazing role model to me." Julian's father put his arms around him and broke down into tears. "Despite all my bluster, I am not very brave. I will need you to be brave for me, and I know that you will. Support your mother and Jane; they are not strong like you—you must lead the family now." They walked slowly home, and as they got in, he said, "Will you join me in a beer, Julian? I really need one."

The onset of the cancer was terrifyingly fast, and within days, Julian's father had to go into hospital. His appetite was almost completely gone, and the only thing that he could manage was a bottle of

Guinness, which the doctor said was good for him. But the pain was dreadful, and as 1974 came to an end, so did the life of Julian's hero. On the same day, it was announced that Burmah Oil had gone bust, and the market fell further. The funeral plans were being organised by his sister Jane, who was genuinely efficient at any event planning, and she told Julian to get up to his office because they needed him. As he arrived, Tom Smith passed him with the latest numbers and said that Stan was keen to see him. The cash flow was a little better than Glen's nightmare scenario, but not much. He walked down to the stock exchange and smiled at his head dealer.

"I was sorry to hear about your father, Julian; he was much liked at his old shop."

"Thank you, Stan; I appreciate your kind thoughts. Tom says that you want to see me about something."

Stan began, "Julian, I have been on the dealing floor for a very long time, and sometimes I get a feeling. As I dig, I find that all is not as it should be. I never actually know the true facts, but I get a feeling that something is going on, and I think that it is happening right now. Let me explain how I have come to this. If I ask a jobber for a bid in these markets, his volume is small, but up until a few days ago, the jobber would joke with me and say that if I was a buyer, I could buy as much as I liked. But now they are not offering much. I keep asking all the jobbers for volume on the buying side, and it isn't there anymore. I smell a rat, but I can't prove it. I believe that there is someone with a lot of money buying shares, and the jobbers are keeping it very quiet. I am so confident of this that I have taken all my cash on deposit and invested the lot in ten major shares. My theory is simple: if the collapse goes on, the system will fail, and we will all sink together, but if I am right—someone is buying, and the market will make a bottom here. You probably think that I am bonkers, but I feel that I am onto something." As Julian left the trading floor, he saw that the FT 30 share index had hit 146, which was 72.5 per cent down from the all-time high of 542 in May 1972. No wonder they were all in the soup.

Julian rang his best unit trust customer, talked through Stan's thoughts, and asked for his opinion. "Do you know, I think we are all transfixed like a fox in the headlights of a car. If you dip the lights, the fox is gone in a second. I have never really thought about it, but what might happen if we all try to move together? Let us try something as an experiment. I will give you ten orders of £25,000 each. Only Stan must do them, and I want you to tell me how easy the deals are to do." Julian wrote down the ten names and walked them to Stan himself. The two of them walked around together and completed the orders with difficulty. When they were done, Stan said to Julian, "I once told you that if it's hard to buy, it's right to buy. These orders were tough to complete—something is definitely happening."

Julian reported the bargains back to his client and told him what Stan had said, and the client was very clear. "Please do another £50,000 for each of the ten stocks; I have got far too much cash." Stan rang Julian at the close and admitted that he had not been able to buy the stocks well; he had paid up to get the shares. He couldn't put his finger on it, but he sensed that tomorrow was going to be an exciting day.

If you light the blue touch paper on a rocket firework, it fizzles for a short time, and then, *whoosh*, it dramatically flies into the sky. So it was on the days after January 6, 1975. Prices began to strengthen as investors wondered what was happening, and then the *whoosh* came, and everyone was a buyer, but no one was a seller. For three years, investors had been selling, and now they wanted to get back into the market, but there was nothing to buy. The jobbers marked prices up again and again, and still only a few sellers emerged. The trading volumes exploded, and suddenly Taylor, Dudley & Everett was making large commissions. But it was better than that. Over the three years of the market collapse, the number of people employed at the firm had dropped from fifty to around twenty-five, and now the market had doubled in just three short months. The profitability of the firm reached levels unseen even at the all-time high, and it looked set to continue for many years to come. The money that the partners had put in to save the firm was now creating extraordinary returns.

CHAPTER TWENTY TWO

As Julian passed through the late 1970s, the firm was doing better and better and was gaining a reputation not only for natural resources but for electronic shares as well. With Ambrose as the senior partner and Julian as a well-recognised researcher, the firm attracted very bright analysts who felt that Taylor, Dudley & Everett, being a second-division firm, offered better chances for recognition than the big houses. Julian and Ambrose watched gold rise from around $200 to $850 an ounce by 1980, and the clients were delighted with the service that the company gave. More and more business came their way, and everything was good. Each year Julian had two long trips to Perth and Toronto.

Unlike Rick Jones in Perth, Phil Campbell was from an old, very well-connected family. He was in many ways like Ambrose and had great instincts for what would work and what wouldn't. He listened to experts rather than being one himself, but listening to Phil was always profitable, and he and Julian enjoyed each other's company and had a strong business relationship.

In his personal life, things could not be better. He and Alice had a wonderful marriage, and they took Simon on holidays all over the world. Swiss traveller's cheques were always at their hotel when they arrived. Julian always cashed them when Alice was shopping or doing something with Simon, so it all appeared very normal.

Simon was an extraordinary boy. He was extremely sporty and excelled at everything, and his schoolwork was magnificent. If he didn't top every class, he would be upset. Julian thought that being so good at everything might cause envy or jealousy, but his boisterous, ebullient manner seemed to make him popular too. He had a friend when he was about eleven who was struggling with his exams, and Simon told his parents that he was going to be assessed for dyslexia. Julian asked Simon to explain about this, since he had never heard of it, and when Simon explained that his friend often misunderstood questions, struggled with reading, and was a shocking speller, Julian wondered. He said nothing to Simon, but the next day he looked up the Dyslexia Association and asked to speak to an expert. Immediately, the expert said, "Is it your son or daughter that is having trouble?" Julian said that it was neither and wondered if he could take a test himself. It was agreed that he would go to their centre and would take a battery of tests.

The day came, and surrounded by eight- to twelve-year-olds, he settled down to lots and lots of questions, which he found quite testing. After the morning, he was given a verbal test, and by the end of the day, he went home full of curiosity. One of the questions he had been asked was why he needed to know, since he was clearly a very successful man. Julian's answer was heartfelt—"I spent my entire childhood feeling as though I was thick. My teachers were very reasonable, but even they lost their patience with me, and university was beyond me. It was only when I joined my current company that I was able to use a Dictaphone, and a wonderful lady called Rebecca produced my work in superb English. I have been plagued with this all my life, and just to know there was a reason for it would be a joy to me."

He had to wait a week to get the results and received a full report in the post. In it, they showed areas of high achievement and areas of general strength, but there were two items where his scores were two out of ten. In the verbal report, the link was made to all the problems he had had at school, and it was conclusively stated that he was dyslexic but not badly so.

Julian sat at the kitchen table and felt that a huge weight had been lifted from his shoulders. Throughout his career he had felt that he was an academic lightweight, even though he had moved up the management ladder at a fast pace. The sense of relief was overwhelming, and he passed the letter to Alice triumphantly. "Damn it," he said, "I knew that I wasn't thick." Alice replied gently, "Julian, my darling, nobody ever thought that you were."

He gave the report to Rebecca and Ambrose and thanked them for the millionth time for giving him the chance to join the firm after he had left school. They both echoed Alice's thoughts. He floated through that day on a cloud of happiness, because he had struggled with this for so long that nobody could truly realise what this meant to him. He remembered shaking and crying when his Common Entrance result came through, and he remembered the body blow when his great housemaster had told him kindly but firmly that university was not an option. Sometime in the past, Alice had expressed that she was surprised that he had not been to university. He still could not write good English, and his spelling was still a nightmare. But from today onward, he didn't care anymore, because he knew why…and that, for Julian, was a dream come true.

CHAPTER TWENTY THREE

When Ambrose asked Julian to join him for lunch at the Savoy, he knew that this was an important meeting. As always, they chose the lovely wines, admired the fabulous view, and ordered the food.

Ambrose began, "You remember when Glen announced in the depths of disaster in 1974 that he would wait until the market turned up, and then he would retire as the senior partner of the firm. The conversation that followed was born of desperation as all the partners clung to our potentially sinking ship. All the partners effectively told me that I should be the senior partner after Glen left, and it became a fait accompli. At the time, I knew that stability was crucial, and hence in my heart I felt that I had to do it. But I hated the idea of it, and after almost seven years, I know that I am a weak man. I love research, but I am not and will never be a leader. Julian, I do not want to retire, but I want to give up the post of senior partner. What our business needs is someone with vigour, vision, the imagination to take this team forward, and the strength to deal with the people issues that grind me down so much. The fact is, my dear fellow, that you have all these skills. You know more about how our firm works than anyone else; you have style and a natural authority, and the staff respect you enormously for what you have achieved after starting at the bottom. I want you to take over as the senior partner, and I wish to remain a partner but report to you. I suggest that I sell you a ten per cent stake at the normal terms. Then you will own thirty per cent, and I will own twenty per cent, which will be a clear sign to the other partners that I am really stepping down. I want to keep my money outside the United Kingdom, so perhaps Anton Gruber can do the transfer when we have settled on an agreed price. The others need only know what we have done and not how the financing was settled."

Julian sat there dumbstruck. Ambrose was his hero, and he had unquestioning loyalty to him and would walk through red-hot coals if he asked him to. Hence the idea of becoming senior partner above Ambrose was not in his mind—ever. He was, however, aware that in a ten-partner operation, there were many prima donnas. They gave Ambrose a hard time, and Julian was aware that he found these confrontations unpleasant. He sipped the wonderful Chablis as he prepared to respond and then said, "I would rather die than anyone think that this is a kind of palace revolution, and hence my only condition is that you present this story to the partners as you have presented it to me and that there is a proper vote. This must be democratic." Ambrose agreed with pleasure and said that he would let Julian see his presentation before it was made.

On the day of the meeting, Ambrose was in top form and seemed incredibly relaxed. A weight had clearly been lifted off his shoulders. He presented his thoughts to the assembled gathering, and it was, as it had been for Julian, a total shock. As the meeting continued, some tried to tell him to reconsider, which was rightfully flattering, but he expressed forcefully that he hated the job, and they would be kinder to let him go back to his research work where he was happy.

Julian's name was put forward, and after a lengthy discussion, he was voted in at the age of forty-one and became the youngest senior partner in the firm's history. Ambrose knew that he had done the right thing, and within weeks it was clear that all the staff felt that Julian was the right partner to take over. The fact was that the stock market continued to rise, Britain had won the Falklands War, and everyone was making plenty of money. Everything was rosy in the garden.

Julian's life went on. He watched his son, Simon, grow up through his school days and was delighted that he was extraordinary at everything. He passed every exam with flying colours and seemed to be in every sports team. Julian and Alice could not believe it when the headmaster of Simon's preparatory school suggested that he take a scholarship to the very public school that Julian had struggled to get into. On the day of the results, the letter arrived. Simon opened the envelope, and a big grin came across his face as he pronounced proudly, "I have got it; Dad, you are going to like this bit—there is to be a huge reduction in my fees because of it." Julian was so thrilled for Simon because he remembered how important these moments had been to him, and both he and Alice gave him a big hug.

Later that day he chaired a partners meeting and had an agenda point of his own. After all the normal items were concluded without any problem, he started, "Gentlemen, some years ago, I was saddened to hear that my friend Rick Jones of Porter Partners in Perth was certain that he would never be accepted into the partnership there because he was the son of a lorry driver. In fact, he is one of the best, if not the best, research geologist in Australian stockbroking, but the bigoted snobbery of that firm has stopped them from honouring this man who has given them his life's work. The point that I am trying to make is that it is not about money, since Rick is very wealthy, but it is about showing respect. Without belabouring the point, I think that Rick has been shabbily treated. In our midst are two men who have given their working lives to our firm and have never failed to deliver for us: Stan Church and Tom Smith. I know that Glen relied heavily on Tom's numbers in our crisis months in 1974, and it was Stan's instincts that helped me see the bottom in January 1975. Both these men have been here for over thirty years, and I think the time has come for us to mark our respect for them as part of our team. I know that they are both from the East End of London, and you may well think that they are not people like us, but that is our problem, not theirs. I do not want to vote on this now, but I would like your votes within three days."

Ambrose was first to speak and said something that would become the general view: "Julian, you have a wonderful way with people, and I have to admit, here and now, that I would not have thought of making Stan and Tom partners, and that embarrasses me. It is not that I do not want them here, but I simply never thought about it, and that is appalling. They have both been outstanding through the years, and they truly deserve recognition for what they have done."

Within three days, he had the votes that he needed and wondered how he would tell them. He always remembered the excitement of being told by Lord Glenconner and decided that he would tell them together at the Savoy. Julian knew that this was a little theatrical, but he guessed that neither of them had been there, so it might be an extra thrill.

Rebecca informed them both that they were to be at the office front door at 12:30 p.m. on this particular Friday, and after they left by taxi with Julian, she told their colleagues that they would not be back after lunch.

Julian began his words to them both as they sat down. "You are probably curious to know why I have asked you to lunch here today, and I hope that you will be pleased with what I am going to say. Well, it is simple: my father and my headmaster both taught me that respect should not be demanded but should be earned, and you are both here today because our partnership has come to appreciate that your combined skills have earned you the respect of everyone. We wish to invite you both to become partners of Taylor, Dudley & Everett." Julian stopped and waited. Stan Church, who was never lost for words, suddenly chirped, "Bloody hell, Julian, that is extraordinary." Tom then chipped in, "I thought that you resented me because I was shitty to you when you joined the firm." Julian replied, "Tom, I was probably a bit of a bumptious ass when I joined, but all you did was show me what was expected of me and make sure that I did it. How can I blame you for that?"

As the lunch went on, Julian told the two very happy men how the partnership worked and offered them the chance of becoming salaried partners if they didn't want to take the capital risk, but both said that they had invested well and wanted the full deal. The lunch was a very full one, and the bill was substantial, but Julian went home in a happy frame of mind. The next morning he rang Rick in Perth and told him what he had done. Rick was delighted and said, "What is so great, Julian, is that your partners offered it to them. For those working-class men, that will be worth more than anything than you can know. You're a good 'un!"

CHAPTER TWENTY FOUR

One morning in 1980, Martin Bird, a young analyst in the firm, came into Julian's office and asked if Julian would do him a favour. "I think that I have come across a really great investment story, and I hope that it is going to become brilliant. We are right at the beginning, and if I am right, this will make the firm lots of money. Mr Barker, you are great at backing very speculative exploration companies in Australia and Canada, and so I think that you are the ideal person to come and visit the company with me, and then you can decide whether it is worth doing. I am also aware that Mr Dudley would think my idea was too off the wall and strange. Will you come on my visit to the East End of London, as it isn't far?"

Julian really couldn't be bothered, but he saw genuine enthusiasm in Martin's eyes and remembered his early days, and so he agreed to go with him. "What is the name of the company?" Julian asked, but Martin told him that he should not know, as that might prejudice his attitude to the company before they even arrived.

The taxi journey to Commercial Road in the East End only took fifteen minutes. Julian realised that this was not going to take long, and he was very curious to see what had got Martin, who he considered to be very bright, so excited.

The taxi pulled up outside a building that was traditional but had clearly had a lot of renovation work done on it and now looked very impressive. The company's name on the door rang a bell somewhere in Julian's head, but he thought that they made dresses for ladies, so he doubted that this would be very exciting.

Julian and Martin were shown into a wonderful office, and all around were beautiful Mediterranean sculptures and antiques that would not look out of place in a museum. The man sitting behind the desk was clearly from the same region and had lots of black, curly hair and a very friendly smile. He noticed Julian looking at the artworks and said without prompting, "I spend so much of my time in the office that I have brought these items from my home. Don't worry; the company has not paid for any of them." Julian liked him immediately and he could see that Martin did too. As the coffee arrived, Julian said, "Mr Nadir, please assume that I know nothing about Polly Peck, which I thought made ladies' dresses, and take me through to today and tell Martin and me what your dreams are for your company. The floor is yours."

Asil Nadir, it turned out, was a Turkish Cypriot, and his family had been in the clothing industry for a long time. It was his belief, however, that there were some glaring opportunities to make large sums of money in the eastern Mediterranean without even being noticed by the major companies. He then explained that the war between Greece and Turkey over Cyprus had led to huge amounts of fruit in Turkish Cyprus rotting on the ground and going to waste.

The story he now told Julian and Martin was captivating and completely unknown at the time, and Asil Nadir explained it as follows:

"To make sense and money from this fruit situation in Turkish Cyprus, I have to be able to pack this excellent fruit, get it to mainland Turkey, and then sell it to entrepreneurial lorry drivers, who will then truck it all over Eastern Europe where the Communist regimes have not invested in agriculture and fresh fruit is really expensive.

The deal makes money for everyone. The Turkish Cypriot farmer can sell his fruit that is now rotting. I can sell it to the drivers at a healthy profit, and the drivers sell it in the markets at prices that are well below the shop prices. The end customers get great fruit at great prices, and everyone is delighted.

"It is so simple, but there is a catch. The price of imported cartons and fruit boxes are far too expensive, so for this idea to work, I need to get a local packaging company enough money to be able to provide these vital items at a sensible price, and this is where Polly Peck comes in. My family has now bought a fifty-eight per cent share stake in Polly Peck, which has a full quote on the London Stock Exchange, but I have left enough shares with other investors to retain the listing. I will now raise one-and-a-half million pounds to do the deal that will make the fruit deal work."

Julian and Martin were more and more fascinated as the story went on. Apparently, there was a brand-new machine that had been delivered to Saudi Arabia and had cost £1 million, but it had never got going because of a labour dispute. A subsidiary of Polly Peck called Uni-Pac in Turkish Cyprus had now bought the machine for just over £300,000. Asil Nadir explained that this very large machine would cost a further £300,000 to set up in the "free port" of Famagusta, but once up and running, it could halve the price of fruit cartons on the island.

At this point, Julian asked how far the Polly Peck funding had got. It appeared that Asil Nadir had many friends who wanted to buy, but he wanted a tranche of quality London buyers to come into the shares. Martin, who had remained quiet throughout the meeting, told Julian that he had a small group of institutions who would buy this story if Taylor, Dudley & Everett would write up the story.

It was agreed that Julian would get back to Asil Nadir within twenty-four hours with a yes or no.

In the taxi on the way back, Martin, who was fit to explode from excitement, asked Julian what he thought, and Julian did not let him down. "Martin, the most important thing about today is that you did not waste my time, and I am delighted to have come to meet Mr Nadir. We must now talk to Stanley Church and find out how hard it would be to buy these shares. If he tells me that it is easy, then I will smell a rat, but if he says that it is really difficult, then I will give you my blessing to write the report, and you must check every detail with Mr Nadir and me."

On their return, Julian rang Stan and asked him to look thoroughly at Polly Peck and see how easy it would be to get shares. Martin was still with Julian when Stan's phone call came back, and his message was simple. "Julian, it is bloody impossible to get shares in this one, but there are rumours of a rights issue coming. That should give me a chance, but this stock will pop if I even try to get aggressive."

"Thank you, Stan, you are a star; that is exactly what I thought would be the case. Speak to you soon," said Julian. Putting the phone down, he turned to Martin and said, "You are free to go with your report, and I will clear it with Ambrose. But tell your clients to buy carefully and slowly, because I believe that this is going to be a big story."

The funding was announced, and Taylor Dudley & Everett were very much seen as a source of knowledge on Polly Peck. The story got stronger and stronger. Fruit cartons that had been imported by multinational packaging companies at fifty-two pence a carton were being replaced by Uni-Pac cartons at twenty-six pence. Few people failed to grasp that the installation of the wonderful, brand-new packaging machine in Famagusta ensured that the Turkish Cypriot farmers were now able to sell their fruit and earn a living which had been denied to them. Unsurprisingly, Asil Nadir had trodden on toes and made enemies, not least the Greek government, who wanted the Turkish part of the island to fail. Rumours abounded that Polly Peck was stealing the fruit from the farmers, but there was no real evidence for this whatsoever.

A year or so later, Martin asked if he could update Julian on Polly Peck's latest business venture, and they sat down together. Martin began, "Julian, you know the old joke about selling coal to Newcastle. Well, I think Asil Nadir has gone one step further—he is about to sell drinking water to people who live in a desert! How good is that? He explained to me that the desalination plant drinking water that is available to the Middle Eastern countries is pretty poor quality and very expensive, because these plants are virtual monopolies. What Polly Peck has done, through a sister company, is buy some major springs off the Turkish government, which have never dried up in two thousand years. As his part of the deal, he will pay for a bottling plant and has had the mineral water tested by a third-party laboratory. Apparently, his water is in the top third of mineral waters and way above Perrier, which is interesting. He reckons that he will be able to get ninety-three million litres a year from his bottling plant. And as with the fruit to Eastern Europe, the entrepreneurial lorry drivers will buy it at the factory gate and sell it in their markets at only one pence more than the poor-quality desalination plant water. Everyone makes money, and the customer gets an excellent product. I repeat, how good is that? The man is a genius."

Julian, along with many investors, couldn't help but agree. The shares of Polly Peck were now at about eighteen pounds each, having begun life at below fifty pence. Julian did not tell Martin that after the clients of his firm had started buying Polly Peck, he had called Zurich, and Anton Gruber had invested in Polly Peck for himself. The old expression, "If it sounds too good to be true, it generally is," began to concern Julian, and at twenty-three pounds each, he rang Switzerland and sold half his holdings for a stunning profit. With no capital gains tax to pay, this was a big success, and he felt good.

The shares continued to blaze onward and upward and reached thirty-two pounds a share, and then something extraordinary happened, and everything changed literally overnight. As Julian picked up his Sunday paper, he read an article that was vicious, venomous, and vitriolic. It suggested that the whole Polly Peck story was a gross exaggeration of the facts, and shareholders should sell immediately. Julian thought long and hard about this, wondering what possible motivation the author could have had for launching such a savage attack on the company. One thing was sure, the shares would crash on Monday, and that fall would be big. The shares had closed around thirty-two pounds each on Friday evening, and Julian reckoned that they might go down to twenty pounds, such was the implied savagery of this article. On Monday at 7:00 a.m., Julian rang Switzerland and asked Anton Gruber to buy back all the shares that he had sold, starting when the shares went below twenty pounds each. As the market in London opened, the severity of the fall was terrible. The shares hit ten pounds, a fall of 68 per cent in one day. The company stated that the article was inaccurate, but investors were panicking, and Julian wondered what he had bought at what price. Julian had a strange set of emotions on that day, because he knew that the article was wrong, but seeing people in full panic unnerved him completely. It was a totally natural reaction. As the week wore on, rumours began that the journalist had been set up by the Greeks to trash Asil Nadir, whom they hated. Whatever the truth might be, that article proved the power of the press beyond all doubt.

A week later, Julian went to a payphone and rang Anton Gruber to ask about his order. "Unsurprisingly," Anton Gruber began, "you got all your stock, but fortunately, Polly Peck opened at eleven pounds each, and we completed your order at an average price of eleven pounds fifty-seven. Your sale at twenty-three pounds now looks very good." Julian thanked him and went back to the office. Polly Peck shares had now recovered to fifteen pounds each, and the crisis had passed.

About a year later, the shares of Polly Peck had reached the old high of thirty-two pounds and were clearly continuing on their upward path. Julian decided one day that taking an enormous profit was a good idea. He had made over fifty times his money, and enough was enough. Like London buses, new investment stories come around the corner every day, and Taylor, Dudley & Everett were now looking at an idea called cellular radio. According to the promoter of this story, one day everyone would be able to carry their telephone in their pocket. It all sounded a bit fanciful but certainly merited further research, and maybe Martin Bird had that type of enthusiastic brain to look at it.

CHAPTER TWENTY FIVE

Margaret Thatcher's government suggested that there were two problems with the city of London, and if they were not addressed, Britain's dominance would fall behind. The first problem was overregulation, and the second was the dominance of the old boy elitist network. The idea was to sweep it all away and lay the way for free market doctrines, unfettered competition, and pure meritocracy.

Taylor, Dudley & Everett was funded by its own partners, and if the firm overstretched itself, it would go bust. The partners took measured risks because they knew that if they got things wrong, they had had it—pure and simple.

Before Big Bang on October 27, 1986, the market was split into three major sections, which had to be separate. There were the stock jobbers, who made the markets; the stockbrokers, who found the buyers and sellers; and the merchant banks, who created the financial deals. Not one of these groups could own any of the others, and this led to power with responsibility. This was all to be swept away in an attempt to make London the pre-eminent financial centre in the world. It worked in the short term, but the partners of Taylor, Dudley & Everett saw the risks and were frightened.

Julian Barker called together a meeting of the partners well ahead of Big Bang and started the meeting in a simple way. "Nobody has any idea how this is going to work out, but after this event, nothing will ever be the same again. Please feel free to state all your views without fear of criticism, because we need to know where we fit into the new world—maybe we don't. This is a spooky thought, but if we do not address it now, we are bloody fools and have only ourselves to blame." The meeting lasted six hours, and they held a second that lasted almost as long and then a third of three hours to finally decide what the firm should do.

Julian, with Rebecca's help, wrote a full report on their deliberations, and the main points were as follows:

1. The amount of fresh capital that would flow into the city as a result of Big Bang would swamp the current partnerships. Conclusion: the partners would have to merge or sell out to a richer company, however unappealing that would be.
2. Once jobbers, stockbrokers, and banks were all owned and allowed to operate under one roof, the ethical standards would inevitably fall. Conclusion: dictum meum pactum or "my word is my bond" would be dumped from the ideals of the London Stock Exchange and be seen as a quaint saying rather than an ethical standard to be proud of.
3. Too much capital chasing too few deals would lead to lower commission rates and exploding pay. Conclusion: this would be a catastrophe for all the players in the market, and only those with unlimited cash would be able to survive.

There were many other items, but Stan Church summed it up best when he said, "I used to trade fruit and vegetables when I was sixteen in the East End of London, and if this lot goes through, I will be doing it again…this is going to be a bloody disaster." Nobody disagreed with him.

The key to this situation was to find someone with more money than sense and get out before the new owners understood what they were doing. Harsh words indeed, but not one partner in the firm did not grasp them and appreciate them. The search for a dignified exit must now begin.

Julian was well aware that his firm was highly respected, and so he mustn't appear too desperate to sell. But he also must not put off "enthusiastic amateurs" and must give them a chance to look at what they had. The time to lift their skirt a little had truly come.

PART III

CHAPTER TWENTY SIX

The phone rang at 12:50 on a Thursday, and Julian knew it would in all likelihood be a call from Canada, because no sensible UK client would dream of ringing at that time, for two very simple reasons. Firstly, he would be going to lunch, and secondly, he would know that Julian would be going to lunch too. As he answered, a Canadian voice said, "Hi, Jules, I have heard a rumour that you are about to sell out to the Yanks and the great American dollar. Knowing how insular and arrogant they are, I guess that you will be coming to New York to sign the deal." He followed this up with a glorious joke at the expense of the Americans: "You know, Jules, that most Americans think that an international investment is a purchase at Harrods—but seriously for a moment, before you sell your great firm and its wonderful London heritage, I will meet you in New York and treat you to a very special dinner at the spectacular Windows on the World restaurant on the hundred and somethingth floor in the North Tower of the World Trade Center. To encourage you to say *yes*, I will be paying and giving you the benefit of my brilliant advice…how does that sound? I know that you are about to go out to lunch and drink beautiful wines, so let's speak later."

Phil Campbell was an outstanding mining analyst and had an amazing array of contacts in the North American continent, and very little got past him. For nearly twenty years, Julian (Phil was the only person that was ever allowed to call him Jules) and Phil had shared ideas about resource stocks in Canada. Phil's stockbroking company, Beacon & Partners in Toronto, did all of Julian's Canadian business, and Phil placed all his global business outside Canada with Taylor, Dudley & Everett. It was the perfect relationship of appreciation and trust. There had never been any contracts between the entities; everything was conducted through word of mouth and a deep-rooted respect that had been built up over decades. If there were any queries, which seldom ever happened, common sense was always the arbiter and not the law, whichever party was at fault.

As Julian walked towards the restaurant, where he was to meet an important client, he wondered how on earth Phil had found out about the discussions that he, as senior partner of the firm, was having with the fast-growing New York investment banking house called Aaron Roberts. He tried to think how his three partners, who were in the meeting with him, might have leaked the story. By the time his first gin and tonic arrived, however, he realised that the leak must have come from the New York end. This worried him profoundly, and he realised that the whole cloak-and-dagger nature of takeovers and corporate finance was way outside his comfort zone, but like it or not, he was in it up to his neck. A good lunch with an important client who was also delightful company eased his worries, but the next morning he called a meeting of the whole partnership and stressed in a very forthright way that the deal had not been concluded, and there were many details to be finalised. He stressed that an aborted deal, if known about in public, could be very detrimental and damaging to them all. "The truth is," he said, "we are trying to sell our partnership for far more than it is worth, and this chance will never occur again. If we blow it, the future for us will never be the same; in fact, it could be bleak. Do I make myself clear?" As the partners absorbed his words, they were all extremely grateful that he was the senior partner of the firm. All petty squabbles, and over the years there had been plenty, were cast aside. Julian Barker had charisma in abundance, and they trusted him over anyone else to get the best price from the Americans and close the deal. This was genuinely a time to rally around their leader, and he was their man.

On that same Friday, Julian got the telephone call that he had in part been wanting but was also dreading. It was Jim Roberts, the founder and president of Aaron Roberts. "Julian," he said, "we have been through all your submissions and numbers, and I and all my board of directors want to make an offer for your firm, Taylor, Dudley & Everett." The silence that followed seemed like ages but was probably very short indeed. Julian offered the following observation: "Jim, in principle this is fine, but we have a lot of details to iron out before we can get to the signing stage—how do you want to play it?"

The telephone call continued on, and it was agreed that Julian would fly to New York on Monday and settle in, and the formal meeting would take place on Tuesday. The idea was for Julian to get his partners to give him the signing authority to commit the firm and finalise the deal. In answer to Julian's probing about the "ballpark figure" (the Americans love to have a ballpark figure!), Jim Roberts suggested thirty million. Julian, deliberately trying to be humorous, said, "Would that be sterling or dollars?" The response of "Sterling, of course" had an edge of aggression about it, and Julian realised very quickly that English throwaway humour did not work in the United States. He was flabbergasted—if the firm was sold for $30 million, he would have been delighted, since on current exchange rates that would equate to around £18.75 million. In the partnership they had come to the conclusion that any figure above £15 million would be acceptable. But £30 million was simply staggering. He had a friend at Fielding, Newson-Smith who had just been bought by the National Westminster Group for an undisclosed sum. He had told Julian over a number of bottles of champagne that they had paid a very full price and kept stating that it was now a new world, and the outlook was amazing. The executives even stated that they could take on Goldman Sachs and Morgan Stanley on a level playing field. Through their drunken haze, they laughed…that'll be the day!

It was agreed that Aaron Roberts would use their normal suite at the famous Waldorf Astoria Hotel on Park Avenue in New York, and Julian booked a room there too. The feeling was that it was an independent venue, and their three-person team and Julian could negotiate in neutral surroundings. The broad issues had been agreed, but the very important people issues had not. At Taylor, Dudley & Everett, the people were everything, and Julian was determined that no American legal wrinkle was going to be used to screw his loyal staff. It was not a family business, but the average tenure of his people was around ten years, and Julian's whole value system and everything he stood for demanded that he protect them, even if it meant shaving off something from his own payout. What made him so energised by this subject was that he had once seen an interview on television by the founder of Fidelity Investments. In it, he stated very frankly that he saw his staff as units of energy—when they ran out, he would get some more. Julian wondered whether this was some new form of American management style or, as he believed, a truly dreadful message to his workforce. He never found out the answer to his question, but he was truly ready for whatever was to come his way on Tuesday.

Flights and hotel all booked and the written note in his briefcase, signed by all the partners, allowing him complete discretion to sell

What is it all worth?

the firm and to agree to whatever terms he thought appropriate, he was ready to go. A note had arrived from the United States, stating that Julian would be negotiating with J. Roberts, R. Masters, and S. Rovick.

Before he left the office that Friday, he picked up the telephone and rang Phil Campbell. He started the call, "For whatever reason, I am going to be in New York on Monday from midafternoon and would love to take you up on your offer of dinner and your thoughts." Phil confirmed that he would book a table at Windows on the World and said to be there at 7:45 p.m. He joked that he was sure that he could find a client to see on Tuesday, and New York was an easy one-hour flight from Toronto.

That night over dinner with Alice, he said quite simply, "Next week is going to be dramatic." He was not to be disappointed.

CHAPTER TWENTY SEVEN

As his New York yellow taxicab moved easily across the bridge into Manhattan, Julian began to get a buzz of excitement. The Waldorf Astoria was a legendary hotel, and as he approached, he was filled pleasure at staying at such an august institution. Of course, it was frantically expensive, and in normal circumstances he would not dream of spending so much money on this luxury. What people tended to forget, he thought, was that in a partnership, the statement "the company will pay" meant that the partners would pay, and the larger the position one owned in the partnership, the more of that bill was effectively coming out of one's own pocket. Along with the excitement came the memory of that terrible day in late 1974, when the partners of Taylor, Dudley & Everett were told by Lord Glenconner how much they were going to have to find from their family savings to keep the firm alive. He recalled that the company's bank, who had always loaned them enough to keep things going, were in desperate trouble themselves, and the overdraft simply could not be increased. Only fresh capital would do. He remembered the tears of grown men as they realised that if they failed to come up with the money, their wonderful old business would fail; many realised too late that they had not put enough cash away for a rainy day.

Today, however, was different. As the senior partner of the company, he must be seen to swim with the big boys. They thought the company was worth £30 million, and although every fibre of his researcher's brain suggested that it was not, now was clearly not the time to point out this fact. It was Aaron Roberts investment bankers who were setting the terms, and they were buying "an historic piece of London" for the future. What they intended to do with it was very much their business.

The Waldorf Astoria did not disappoint him in any way, and Julian was treated like royalty from the moment he walked into the wonderful hotel lobby. The staff member who took him up to his room on a high floor ushered him over to the windows to see spectacular views of the New York skyline. For some reason, as he marvelled at what he saw, he remembered arriving on his first trip to Australia, utterly exhausted after twenty-eight hours on aeroplanes, and the extremely modest hotel he had stayed in as a very junior research analyst.

Time zones play tricks on you, and the five hours between London and New York leave one in a bizarre situation. Julian had got up at 6:00 a.m. at home, and getting everything together plus getting to London Heathrow in the rush hour was not relaxing. Then, he spent two hours in the terminal, seven and a half hours on the plane, and finally the better part of one and a half hours to get from John F. Kennedy Airport to the hotel. In UK terms, it was 8:00 p.m., but in New York, it was a sunny afternoon at 3:00 p.m.

Julian telephoned Alice to say that he had arrived safely and then set his alarm for 5:00 p.m., just in case he fell into a deep sleep, which of course he did. As he turned off the alarm, he felt disoriented. Where was he? Then slowly he focused and had a further look around his magnificent room. The bathroom was enormous and very tastefully furnished, but being over six foot, he found that the bath was a bit cramped. Truth be known, Americans do showers and not baths, but his surroundings for his evening out were prestigious.

As Julian looked up at the twin towers of the World Trade Center, he felt very small. These beautiful buildings certainly symbolised the awesome financial power of the United States. As he entered the elevator, as they like to call it, the button showed "106–108 Windows on the World Restaurant," and this made him think about just how far he himself had risen.

Phil Campbell was already sitting at the restaurant table and admiring the view. After greeting Julian warmly, he said, "Do you realise that we can look down on the Empire State Building from here; how amazing is that?" Phil went on, "I love this place; the food is great, the wine list is terrific, and I always feel that I have achieved something in being able to afford to come here. Tonight we are going to drink a very special red wine called Firestone."

"What?" said Julian. "That is a tyre, not a wine!"

"Aha, my dear Jules, you don't know as much as you think. The great Harvey Firestone began his industrial business, and of course the Firestone tyre is a famous brand, but his son Leonard saw the potential of winemaking in California and planted a vineyard there in 1972. So proud of his family heritage was he that Leonard called his wines 'Firestone' to continue their great tradition. Trust me, Jules, when you taste their best wine, you will not be thinking of tyres; it is very special, and by the way, the price is too!"

Julian acknowledged that the wine was probably the best he had ever tasted, and a second bottle arrived as Phil began to impart his advice. "The problem with the vast majority of Americans is they think that they are the best at everything. In reality, however, it is their awesome financial power that really makes the difference. The great American dollar is well received everywhere in the world, and to be a little bitchy, they buy their success. Take your business as an example—for the last century, your people have used a very limited amount of capital to create a global network of contacts, like my firm and many others. If a client comes to you and asks you about Japanese electronics companies, you might not know the answer, but you will have a trusted friend somewhere in the Far East that will give you the answer willingly as a favour. And that same person can ask you about European chemicals, and you will pass on the information without any question of a payment. The word is respect and all that comes with it. Jules, I would no more lie to you than fly in the air, because I know that you would never lie to me. This bond is beyond price, and the Americans simply don't get it. What they do not understand, and they never will, is that if you and your colleagues left the firm, I would not need to deal with your company. Under US ownership, you are just another outfit touting for my business. And finally, to end my rant, they really think that buying you for lots of money guarantees that you will appreciate and respect them. Someone famous once said that they know the cost of everything but the value of nothing." Julian sensed that Phil had had some bad experiences with Americans, but he said nothing and let him go on. "Jules, promise me one thing above all else: do not let them pay you in Aaron Roberts shares. You must organise it so that you get cash, and please negotiate the shortest possible lock-in arrangements—absolutely not more than two years, and less if possible—and get good contracts for your staff drawn up under English law." Phil now lifted his glass and told Julian that the lecture was over, and they could now enjoy the evening. Julian realised that most of the items Phil had mentioned had already been discussed in London, but having Phil explain it so fervently in New York made him realise how important his observations were. As they left the restaurant and entered the elevator, it dawned on Julian how long it took to get to the ground floor. It seemed a long way.

CHAPTER TWENTY EIGHT

Julian found the business suite and walked into it at one minute to 9:00 a.m. In the room was the Aaron Roberts team of three: Jim Roberts, whom he had met in London; a short and very overweight man; and quite simply the most beautiful woman that Julian had ever seen. He was stunned. Sam was the short man, and Robyn was the Hollywood star. As he stood there, he was trying to think of a film actress that was the equal of this vision, and he couldn't.

The price of £30 million for Taylor, Dudley & Everett was pretty much agreed in five minutes, but what caused the problem was Julian's insistence that the partners be paid in cash. Sam, who proved to be the most aggressive and sweated a great deal, was unwilling to give up on the idea of paying for the transaction in Aaron Roberts shares. But Julian, with Phil's voice pounding in his head, would not back down. He stated as politely as he could that he was selling his business and was not buying a share stake in theirs. Jim and Robyn grasped this, but Sam kept saying, "Don't you trust us or something?"

Jim rang his company's brokers and asked them if the shares being issued could be placed with US institutions. The broker asked how many shares were being talked about, and Jim stated 833,250 at their current price of fifty-five dollars. On the speakerphone, they all heard the sucking in of breath, but suddenly he came back and said, "Mr Barker, if you will let me place them at fifty dollars, it's a done deal." Julian replied that at fifty-one dollars, it was his. The broker sounded excited and said, "When shall I do it, today or tomorrow?" They all agreed that the legal papers would be done by the next morning, and Julian would contact the broker when the final documents had been signed.

The conversation about lock-in arrangements and staff contracts went on, and Sam was very prickly about everything. Quickly Julian realised that Robyn was not only the most beautiful woman that he had ever seen, but she was also amazingly clever. Jim valued her judgement and deferred to her a number of times over the day. Julian was finding it awkward, because in a normal business meeting, it never occurred to him what person he was looking at. He assumed that he looked at men intently as he made important points, and he guessed that he looked at their eyes and face, but with Robyn he didn't know what to do. She was wearing a very well-cut, white blouse and a black skirt. She wore a most attractive silver bracelet, and in the opening of her blouse, she wore a delightful silver charm held on a silver chain. Her taste was impeccable, and Julian could not take his eyes off her as they conversed. Her eyes were a soft blue, her hair was blond, and her breasts were in perfect proportion to the rest of her body, and he struggled not to look at them. By the end of the afternoon, he knew that on that matter, he had failed, but in the business matters, everything had been concluded. As he walked out of the suite, he remembered something Glen had told him years before: "The best deals are the ones where both parties come away thinking that they could have done better." Julian mentally thanked Glen for his advice and knew that he had got as much as he might reasonably have expected. He and Jim had rung both sets of lawyers, and the final deal would be ready for signing at 10:00 a.m. the next morning. They all agreed to take an hour break and reconvene in the Waldorf bar for drinks.

Julian rang Alice and excitedly told her that they were nearly there, and he spoke to Simon, who at sixteen thought that this whole deal was really cool. He rang the lawyers and mentioned a few points, but nothing that caused concern, and then he rang Rebecca. He told her the main points of the day and asked her to pass on the news. Julian then had a shower and got ready for drinks. He could not stop thinking about Robyn.

Julian was first in the bar and told the waiter that he would order his drink when the others arrived. He took a few green olives that were on the table and enjoyed them. Jim and Robyn walked into the bar at almost the same time, and Sam was a minute or two behind. Both Jim and Sam were wearing dinner suits and informed him that they had to go to a big Jewish charity do. Jim laughed and said, "We are expected to be there!" Robyn was wearing a beautiful dress that accentuated every part of her glamorous body, and the silver jewellery had been swapped for gold. The totally discreet neckline of the day had moved to a subtle but delightful presentation of her breasts. Julian kissed her on each cheek and delighted in the aroma of her body and perfume.

Drinks lasted for about an hour, and then Jim and Sam excused themselves as their driver came into the bar, and off they went. Julian said to Robyn that he thought that she would be joining them, but she told him that she was not Jewish and was not invited to such things. Julian asked her if she had plans, and she replied that she didn't. They agreed that they would eat dinner together in the hotel.

The next two or three hours were some of the most wonderful that he had ever spent. As they told each other about their lives and upbringing, it was evident that they were becoming very attracted to each other. He learned that she was not married and found relationships difficult. Her fast rise in the world of business and her dramatically rising income were undoubtedly negatives to men of her age, and she also found that here friends, both male and female, were quite jealous of her success. She even admitted to Julian that she was often lonely. She asked about his young days, and he told her about his difficult schooling, his wonderful family, and how his travelling around the world had been so fulfilling.

They had reached the coffee stage of the meal when it happened—Julian looked into her soft, blue eyes and saw in them something that captivated him, and her look back was something that he had never seen before. His erection under the table was throbbing, and he could clearly see her nipples through the material of her dress. Julian's mind went off on the most wonderful fantasy. He imagined his lips kissing those beautiful nipples and the glorious exploration that would follow. In his dream, he was kissing her clitoris as she asked him to enter her so that they could have an exquisite mutual climax. He could actually imagine himself entering her vagina, and then suddenly he returned to reality as he heard Robyn's voice. "Julian, I know that you are married and I am not, but I am incredibly attracted to you, and I would really like us to make love together. Are you shocked?"

Julian suddenly saw Alice in his mind and thought how unfair it was for a wife of over twenty years to have to compete with the most beautiful girl in the world. Then he thought of Simon and his brilliant exuberance, and finally he thought of the unquestioning bond that he and Alice had. He loved her more than he ever could have imagined possible, and to lose her would be impossible for him to bear.

He spoke softly, "Robyn, you are the most beautiful woman that I have ever met, and the idea of you and I making love fills me with desire. I want you now with every fibre of my body, and I sense that there is a magic between us, but I am afraid that I must be strong and say no. There is an unseen bond between a happily married couple, and it is an unbreakable trust that there is no betrayal in either one. I would probably never be caught, but I hope you understand what I mean." Robyn looked a little embarrassed and appeared to be lost for words but eventually said, "You are the most honourable man that I have ever met, and that makes you more desirable to me than you could possibly know, I understand what you are telling me, but it is a shame as I think we would have been wonderful together. Please tell the waiter to put the dinner onto our suite. Good night, Julian." As he saw her walk out of the room, he was still fully erect, but sadness overwhelmed him. He realised that he had upset Robyn badly. For her to offer herself to him and be rejected was harsh, and although he knew that he had done the right thing, he didn't feel good about it and went to bed feeling very low.

Julian arrived in the business suite, and Jim, Sam, and Robyn were there with another man who was obviously their lawyer. Gary informed Julian that the two law firms in London and New York had worked through the night; everything was agreed, and the contracts were ready for signature. About an hour earlier, Julian had spoken to his legal firm in London and confirmed that all the little wrinkles had been ironed out, and they felt that Julian could sign off the deal without apprehension.

Jim signed for Aaron Roberts, and Sam witnessed his signature; Julian signed for Taylor, Dudley & Everett, and Gary witnessed his signature. The deal was done, and a further little piece of British history was now owned by the United States. Julian hoped that they would care for it. Whilst the signing was going on, Robyn rang the company's broker and then passed the handset to Julian. The deal to place all the partners' new shares in Aaron Roberts Investment Bank was now in progress and would be completed before the day was out. So excited were American investors about the "Big Bang in London" that after the placing was complete at fifty-one dollars, the shares closed the day at fifty-six. Julian was thrilled, Jim was delighted, and a New York broker had earned a great commission. The only losers from this deal would be the investors who bought the shares, and their loss would be slow, painful, and substantial.

CHAPTER TWENTY NINE

Julian arrived home to a hero's welcome, which was unsurprising since all the partners were now worth a great deal, and it was all in cash. No more risks—and although the contracts demanded that they work for two more years, that was hardly a sacrifice because the payments for these two years were enormous. The twelve years up until Big Bang had made everyone a great deal of money, and now this huge sum of cash was a bonus on top. Stan and Tom were ecstatic because they had only been partners for a few years, and now they had lifetime security. They thanked Julian for all that he had done for them with genuine sincerity.

Julian got calls from Glen, Aubyn, Rick, and Phil congratulating him. All of them were amazed at the price that Aaron Roberts Investment Bank had paid for the London brand name of Taylor, Dudley & Everett. Phil Campbell was extremely complimentary of the way that Julian had got the partnership's new shares placed and got them all cash, which he had strongly advised.

When the celebrations were over, Julian spoke to the partnership in a serious way. "One of the reasons that our partnership has been bought for such a high price is because we do our jobs well, we have excellent client relationships, and we are seen as honourable, and that is not going to change. I have been told that Sam Rovick will be coming to London every month and will work with us on strategic planning. Aaron Roberts are very interested in derivatives, and they want to feature them in the years ahead. I am certain that after our lock-in period, many of you will stay, and some will go. But the name of Taylor, Dudley & Everett will always stand for something special, and that is integrity."

When he had heard a few days before that Sam Rovick was to be the connection between New York and London, he was both pleased and disappointed. Sam was not his type of individual, and he knew that they would clash endlessly. But he also knew that if he saw Robyn Shelley every month, his ability to keep his hands off her glorious body might not survive. Undoubtedly it was better for everyone that he should not see her.

The city of London became an entirely new place to work. The huge wave of new capital bid up the salaries of the best people, and bonuses became extremely large. Commissions, which had averaged 0.65 per cent before Big Bang, were now a maximum of 0.3 per cent, and with the highly inflated cost structures, big losses began to emerge. Within eighteen months of Big Bang, one large bank announced a trading loss of over £100 million! But the markets went up and up, fuelled by the excitement of "the new, deregulated city." The Wall Street market joined in, prices flew, and there seemed to be no end to the enthusiasm.

Julian felt confused because all his warning instincts were flashing red. He wondered whether he was being old-fashioned, and so he rang Phil Campbell and asked how he was feeling about things. Phil was animated. "In my opinion, the US economy is like a one-hundred-truck railroad train that takes two miles to stop and is currently one mile from a landslide across the rail lines, and the driver is saying—so far so good." He continued, "I do not know when this is going to hit, but it is an accident waiting to happen!"

Julian told his clients to take some profits, but as in 1971, they were not listening, and so the market rose. When the change came, it was sudden and brutal. A deal failed to complete in New York, and that spooked the traders. And then a huge storm hit the south of England, and one million trees were lost in one night. Markets went into meltdown, and Julian could do nothing. Within six weeks, New York had lost 40 per cent of its value and London 32 per cent. It was at this point that Julian began to question his worth to the city as a broker. This new world was much more volatile, and the idea of researching a share and putting it away for three to five years was beginning to look out of touch with current thinking. This feeling was only made worse during his monthly meetings with Sam Rovick, whom he was beginning to dislike.

Aaron Roberts told Julian that twenty experts in derivatives would be coming to London and asked if he could find them space. The answer to this was no—there was no space. "Get new offices, and I mean now," shouted Sam. Julian replied that office space was becoming expensive; had they done the numbers to justify the investment? "There are wider issues at stake here, and you just don't get it, do you, Julian? You don't own this firm anymore, and you will do as I say," Sam thundered. Julian decided there and then that when his lock-in was over, he would leave, and up until then, he would smile and do whatever Sam asked, however stupid it may be.

The new offices were palatial. At the same time, it was agreed that the name of the firm would be changed to Aaron Roberts Stockbrokers, and Taylor, Dudley & Everett would disappear. Julian hosted a wake for all the staff who had been at the firm for ten years and found that only fourteen people qualified. It was a great function, but it showed Julian one very sad truth: loyalty to a firm or of a firm to its staff was a thing of the past. The traders were "guns for hire," and they didn't care where they sat as long as the pay was great and the bonuses enormous. Every dread that his partnership had feared had come to pass, but it was worse than they ever could have imagined.

The losses at Aaron Roberts Investment Bank were massive, and the shares of the business had fallen to below twenty dollars by the time of Julian's retirement dinner.

CHAPTER THIRTY

Julian answered his phone, and an American voice spoke to him in a respectful tone. "Mr Barker, I have been given your name by Robyn Masters of Aaron Roberts in New York. She asked me to contact you about the new technological service that we offer to your group. I gather that you run Taylor, Dudley & Everett in London; is that correct?" Julian answered that it was and suggested that he continue. "My name is Nick Waters, and I work for a subsidiary of General Electric called GEISCO, which is General Electric Information Systems Company. What we do is create for customers an electronic information arrangement that allows you to pass notes to anywhere in your group at the press of a button. This, I must suggest to you, is state-of-the-art technology, and Aaron Roberts have signed up for the GEISCO system. All I need from you is the names of your key staff that would be likely to communicate with New York from London. If you could kindly let me have the names of your people, I will set them up on our system myself and will send the entire electronic address book to you by tomorrow morning." Julian was then given a code that he should log into on his computer, and the phone call ended. As he sat there, he thought to himself what a waste of time and money is was to send notes around the offices of Aaron Roberts, and he went back to what he was doing.

The following day he turned on his computer and saw a red, flashing signal that spelled "GEISCO message." He typed in the code he had been given, and a note from Nick Waters was there waiting for him. With a polite introduction, it showed him every name in Aaron Roberts Group, with all his key staff on the list. Apparently, all he had to do was click on a name and type in a note to the recipient. Julian sat there slightly awestruck by all this and very nervously clicked on the name Nick Waters. Instantly, a blank page appeared, and he typed into it, "Thank you for the list; is it really as easy as this? Julian Barker." Within three hours, Nick Waters replied saying, "You forgot that I was asleep in bed when your message arrived, but GEISCO runs twenty-four hours a day every day, and *yes*, it is as easy as this. Thank you for responding so quickly. Regards, Nick."

Julian sat there in utter amazement and was bright enough to realise that what he had just seen was remarkable. He then went to each name on the London list and found out that they all had a note on their computers, and he gave them the code to sign in and access it. When they opened their GEISCO page, the note from Julian to Nick was shown with Nick's reply to Julian, and it finished with a sentence: "Welcome to the world of GEISCO." Everyone wondered what they would do with it, but they were all staggered at the technology. Before Julian went home, he sent a note to the three key players in New York saying, "London loaded on GEISCO and ready to roll. Very best wishes, Julian." As he caught his train home, he knew that this message to three individuals was entirely unnecessary, but in a childish way, he had really enjoyed sending it—the idea of his note crossing the Atlantic Ocean in seconds excited him.

What is it all worth?

When he got home and poured himself a drink, he wandered into the kitchen and, putting the glass down, wrapped his arms around Alice from behind her. Both he and she loved this little ritual, and for fun, she always told him that supper might have to be delayed if he continued cuddle her. They laughed, and he began to tell her about his extraordinary day and the world of GEISCO. As they sat down for dinner, Alice, who was very bright, started to talk more and more about this new invention. "Julian, do you remember when you played cricket and the captain had to send out the team to all the selected players by postcard? Can you imagine if he could tell everyone electronically? I fix tennis games with the ladies, and it is a fag. This system would be great, but I suppose it will always be too expensive for us ordinary people." Excitedly, they thought of all the wonderful things that could be done. It never occurred to them that the world of the Internet was fast approaching and would change the way things were done forever.

CHAPTER THIRTY ONE

In the days before finally leaving stockbroking for good, Julian spent a pleasant evening with a friend where too much drink was consumed, but everyone had a great evening. Julian left the restaurant with the intention of getting a taxi to Waterloo Station to catch the late train back to his home. He was aware that he was a little the worse for wear. As he walked down the dark street, he sensed something but was not sure what it was. The night was wet, and he quietly cursed that no cabs were available. He turned into a quiet street. Too late, he heard something behind him, and the assault began. His hooded assailant punched him repeatedly and kicked him as he lay on the ground, but mercifully, the event did not last long. As his attacker turned away, Julian was sure that he heard him say, "This is just the beginning." As he lay on the wet pavement, he sensed that the accent was American, but he wasn't sure. He staggered to the nearest place that was open, which happened to be a hotel, and asked them to contact the police and an ambulance.

The pain was excruciating as he waited, but eventually he was taken to hospital, where he was joined by the police. He found out that he had two broken ribs, but although very painful, the rest of his injuries were thankfully just very bad bruising. He looked terrible, but Alice and Simon told him that he had been very lucky. His admission of being slightly drunk guaranteed that the police's first reaction was not a very positive one, and they suggested that it must have been an opportunist mugging. Julian was indignant and showed them that his wallet was still in his jacket pocket. He added through his painkiller-induced sleepiness that his attacker had spoken, and once he informed them of what was said, they suddenly changed their tune and took the event much more seriously. Sleep overwhelmed him, and the police told Alice and Simon that they would return in the morning.

Alice and Simon were joined by Ambrose in the morning, along with other members of the firm, and everyone was completely shocked but equally perplexed at what had happened. The police asked everyone whether Julian had made enemies. The general sense was that any American investor who had bought shares for the purchase of Taylor, Dudley & Everett, who had now lost around 60 per cent of their money, might be disgruntled, and over the years Julian had written a number of damning reports. So in truth, the list of suspects was large.

Broken ribs, as anyone who has had them knows, are really painful, and laughing is terrible. Somehow we laugh more times in a day than we realise, and Julian was no different. But he was surrounded by his friends and family, and for the moment he felt safe.

After two days, Julian, Alice, and Simon got into the car and very gingerly drove the twenty-odd miles to Walton-on-Thames. As they entered their driveway, it was obvious that a break-in had taken place. As Simon went in first to investigate, he came out and said that the contents of the house had been trashed in a violent way. The police were round in lightning-quick time, since there was a note on the broken living room glass table. It read, "Not nice, is it, you insufferably arrogant bastard—your next meeting with me will end it."

The police immediately gave the note to a handwriting expert, and within a minute he declared that the man that wrote this was extremely mentally unbalanced and was quite capable of violence. If Julian's attacker had simply wanted to terrify him and his family, he had certainly been successful. The story made the television news programmes, but no one had any idea as to who might be behind this.

Everything went quiet, interest in the matter died away, and the police, with no leads whatever, began to drift back to their everyday work. Julian had now fully recovered, but his nerves were bad, and he lay awake a great deal and had bad dreams. He knew in his heart that this maniac would return, but when might that be?

About four months later, Julian received a telephone call. They collected him and drove him to his golf club, and the scene there was unreal. Police and their technical experts were there, and the clubhouse had been closed. Apparently, at 6:30 a.m., a brick had been hurled through a window, and attached to it was the message, "They think I have gone, but they are wrong." The note did not name Julian, but everyone knew who this act of destruction was aimed at, and they were really panicked.

There is an old expression that states that every black cloud has a silver lining, and so this third attack was to offer the forensic team its breakthrough. The team took the two notes and checked them under the microscope, and it was agreed that the paper was identical. The scientists then analysed this paper in minute detail and proved beyond doubt that this paper was made and sold in Australia and nowhere else.

Even though it had been nearly twenty-five years ago, Julian immediately made the connection. His "sell" note on the Northern

Pastoral Company had been dramatic, and Mike MacDougal had lost much of his money, but what would have upset this arrogant man was that he got sacked and was treated by the Australian press as a fool. If the handwriting expert suggested that this man was unbalanced, Julian had little doubt that he was very dangerous.

The flight records from Qantas showed nothing, as did British Airways. But his name appeared on a flight to Singapore, and a Singapore Airlines flight had brought him to London Heathrow. Once the police knew who they were looking for, they set about their task brilliantly. He had arrived in England and had stated that he was here on holiday. His first hotel was in London's West End, and his initial attack had been three days later. He checked out of London, and after a lengthy search, he emerged in a large hotel near to London Heathrow.

The police informed Julian that he was booked on a Swissair flight to Zurich in two days' time, and very subtly Julian was shadowed. The attempted murder occurred in the car park of a local supermarket. The police, who had pictures, saw Mike MacDougal before Julian did and intercepted him with an aggressive rugby tackle well before he could pose a danger, and he was taken away to be charged. On his person they found a large carving knife.

The investigation uncovered the event that triggered the attacks: an article in the *Financial Times* that announced the pending retirement of Julian Barker from stockbroking. This article stated that Mr Barker was a much-respected figure who had made his name in exposing an Australian entrepreneur for serious wrongdoing.

Apparently, Mike MacDougal had been in and out of mental institutions over the last twenty-five years but was not considered to be dangerous. He ended up being returned to Australia on the condition that he be held in an institution for the criminally insane.

CHAPTER THIRTY TWO

Julian was angry with the way things were going, but one morning on December 12, 1988, an event occurred that put his frustrations into true perspective, and it frightened him.

He got his normal train from Walton-on-Thames station, arrived at around 8:00 a.m. at Waterloo, travelled on to the city, and was at his office desk by 8:20 a.m. Within half an hour, someone stood at his door and said, "Thank goodness you are all right. There has been a major train crash at Clapham Junction, and initial reports suggest that many are dead." Julian turned on the television in his office. Apparently, the crash had happened at 8:10 a.m., about fifteen minutes after his own train had passed through Clapham Junction. He walked around the office—everyone was accounted for except one, but he was on the list as going to the dentist that morning. Everyone prayed that he was having a filling or was stuck in a train behind the crash. Later in the day, he rang in and said that he had been on the train behind the accident for four hours. It was a small price to pay when he heard the news in the evening.

Julian knew that one of his merchant banking clients called Graham Livingstone commuted from Farnborough, and he rang his office immediately. It was clear at once that all his colleagues feared the worst. One told Julian that he caught the same train each morning and got in at around 8:35 a.m. Julian asked if they could let him know when they heard any news.

The news showed the severity of the crash. One train had stopped at the signal on a bend just outside Clapham, and the fast train careered into the back of the stationary train. To make matters worse, an empty train travelling the other way hit the debris, and the carnage was terrible. By that evening, the suggestion was that thirty-five were dead and five hundred were injured, and no one had heard from Graham. Julian had never experienced anything like this in his charmed life, and it shook him.

The good news came the next morning. Graham had been taken to St George's Hospital in Tooting and had been unconscious for some hours; he had broken his arm and three ribs and had head injuries. Many in the dining car of the train had perished instantly. After a day or two, it was suggested that Julian could visit him. When he saw him, he wondered how he had survived—he was swathed in plaster and bandages, and his face had obviously been savaged by flying glass. When Julian reached the bedside, Graham smiled and said, "This is not the best way of getting a week or two off work!" Julian spent about twenty minutes with him but realised that he was too weak to talk for long. One thing he did say, which struck Julian as extraordinary, was that the last thing he remembered was seeing his coffee leaving its cup as a block, and then he realised that he was flying through the air too, and then it all went blank.

As he left the hospital, he realised how precious life was and determined not to let the petty tyrannies of the new owners worry him.

Graham had been saved, but many families had to face the reality of losing a loved one simply going to work. He shuddered to think that had he caught a later train, he could have been killed as well.

The day of Julian's retirement came, and Jim Roberts, Sam Rovick, and Robyn Masters arrived in London to attend the farewell dinner that had been arranged. Alice had been invited to join them; the function would begin at 7:00 p.m. A little before he left the building to connect up with Alice, Robyn Masters walked in, shut the door of his office, and sat down. She looked as beautiful as ever. "You, Julian Barker, have a lot to answer for," she began. "After you rejected me, I confided in my best girlfriend. She told me that I needed to buy myself a vibrator, and then I could imagine making love to whomsoever I wished—and I did, so I have made love to you many times!" They laughed, and he couldn't help wanting her badly. Before she left, she said, "I am looking forward to meeting the woman that you threw me away for—she must be very special," and the door shut.

His retirement function was wonderful. Everyone was there, including Glen and Aubyn; they all told stories, and the champagne flowed. Julian was still just below fifty, but he had decided that stockbroking was no longer for him. As they settled into the car that was to take them home, Alice, who had drunk plenty of champagne, said, "That Robyn is unbelievably attractive, and the way that you looked at her was very charming. I am delighted that she is going back to New York; I am nowhere near in her league." As Julian was trying to think of something to say, she rested her head on his arm and fell fast asleep. Alice never mentioned Robyn's name again.

Julian loved doing research into companies and finding special ideas. He liked dealing with Phil Campbell in Toronto and Rick

Jones in Perth for the natural resource sector, but what he really hated was coming up with a great idea and having his idea rejected, as had often happened in his working life. He therefore decided to become an investment manager of his own money, and he had plenty of that. What with his payout from Taylor, Dudley & Everett, which was over £5 million after tax, and his "special fund" in Switzerland, he decided that this was the future for him, and he loved it. He made and lost money, but by 1993 he came across a deal that excited him.

Phil Campbell told him that there was a project in Busang, Indonesia, that was on the Ring of Fire. This geological structure, named after its many volcanoes and earthquakes, is also famous for some outstanding gold mines. These tectonic plates run up from New Zealand; through Papua New Guinea, Indonesia, and Japan; over to Canada and the West Coast of the United States; and down to Chile. The California Gold Rush was on it, Japan's most valuable gold mine was on it, and the famous Bougainville mine was on it, so Julian hoped that Busang in Indonesia might prove to be rewarding.

Julian did his research and found out from Phil in Canada where this company, called BreX, was quoted. In Phil's opinion, the people behind it were "stock promoters" and potentially questionable. He talked to Rick in Perth about the geology in the area; his view was that a few good drill results might prove to be spectacular. He said, "It is a bit like Poseidon; the geology looks good, and you should be able to make some money before they ever have to build a mine, which is where all of these ventures come unglued. I'll tell you what I will do. I will buy some, and then at my own expense, I will go up there and tell you how long you should hold the shares." Phil Campbell was delighted to have someone of Rick's talent on board, and they all bought BreX stock at C$3.25 in a private placement to finance a drilling programme.

Rick's report was great. "This project is shit-or-bust time. The geology is fascinating, and if the first results are good, the shares will fly. Once this sort of share gets on a roll, there is no knowing where it might go. But make no mistake, this deal is very high risk, and we must make sure that our chairs are near to the exit!"

The three hardy investors waited, and the shares climbed from under C$5 to C$20 to C$50. The results became more and more remarkable. What occurred now was accidental, and no one could see it coming, because this had never happened before. The shares of BreX went into an index, and the investors that tracked that index *had* to buy the shares, whatever their price, to fulfil their duties. As the stock rose to C$100, the index trackers had to buy more and more. Rick rang up Julian and Phil and stated quite categorically, "This deal has gone crazy, and I no longer understand it. I have made nearly thirty times my money, and I am selling, and I think you both should too."

Julian and Phil needed no further encouragement and sold out for a mammoth profit. The story of BreX was to get stranger. The shares now had gone up so much that they were admitted in the main Toronto index, at which point those investors that "tracked" that index *had* to buy, and the share went on up to C$286. Then came the devastating news: the drill results were incorrect. Were they false? Many thought so. The shares collapsed, and BreX became the biggest bankruptcy in Canadian corporate history. Investors lost nearly C$6,000,000,000, and rumours began to circulate. It was said that a company director fell out of his helicopter in Indonesia, and his body was never found. Phil, with his wonderful humour, suggested that this director had to be the first man to fall out of a helicopter in Indonesia and land in the tax haven of Bermuda!" The three investors who had made a fortune all agreed that fact is stranger than fiction, and one simply could not make a story like this up.

What is it all worth?

By now, Julian's son, Simon, had started work at a headhunting firm called JMG Recruitment and seemed to be doing very well. Simon always did well at everything, and Julian enjoyed watching his success.

CHAPTER THIRTY THREE

Something occurred in the last part of the 1990s that was truly strange, and it threw everything that Julian had learned into the dustbin. When he reviewed a business, he looked at the numbers, the management, and the story, and based on that, he decided whether a share was a buy or a sell. The fact was that Julian had been doing this for just short of forty years, and his track record was very good.

As the end of the twentieth century loomed, events began to unfold that made no sense to him, and he happily admitted to anyone that he was bemused and even decided that he must be a dinosaur. The stock market was ablaze; there was no other way to describe it. Shares with no profits burst into the top 100 companies in the index. Vodafone became valued at five times what Julian thought the shares merited and was now one of the largest companies in the world. Telecommunications was the thing, but a new sector emerged, and it became known as the "dot-com boom." If a company had any connection with the Internet, the shares would rocket. Companies floated on the stock exchange, and with the slimmest of research in their documents, the shares soared to ever greater heights.

Julian was invited to a lunch in the city and travelled up on the train, looking forward to learning why he was so out of touch. The lunch proved to be highly amusing, and Julian learned a great deal, but it was not what he expected at all. He met his old friend who was now in charge of the entire operation. Julian ordered a gin and tonic but noticed that all the young fund managers were on sparkling water. Julian asked one of them why he was willing to buy Vodafone shares at about five times their realistic value, and his answer was both illuminating and insulting. "Mr Barker, we are in a new paradigm, and this is something that you older chaps cannot understand. The world is different now, and your old rules do not apply any more. These shares are all going up a lot more. I am afraid that you will all miss this great opportunity because you will not adapt and change."

Julian resisted the temptation to wring this arrogant idiot's neck but offered to bet one hundred pounds that Vodafone's shares would halve in the next three years if the fund manager would offer him ten-to-one odds. With ever increasing pomp, the manager said, "Vodafone shares cannot halve; that would be impossible. So why don't I offer you one hundred to one?" Julian agreed and asked his friend to confirm the terms of the bet. As he left, he rang up his own pension manager and asked him to sell every share that he owned and hold it in cash. His manager was rather startled. "Mr Barker, why would someone of your knowledge and experience sell out of everything right now?" Julian thought about it for a moment and then replied, "I have just met the biggest buffoon of my lifetime, and if he is an example of who is running pension and investment funds today, the world has completely lost it. I may be wrong, but I very much doubt it, and I would rather have good, old-fashioned cash than crazy shares. This new breed of managers might be sober, unlike in my day, but it doesn't stop them being certifiably stupid."

Within three months, the lunacy ended, and the telecoms and dot-com bubbles burst. Julian was wrong, because Vodafone shares did not drop by 50 per cent—they dropped 80 per cent. Markets, as Julian always told people at dinner parties, are governed by greed and fear. The greed was truly amazing, and it is unlikely that those stupid valuations will return again for generations to come.

Julian had a very good friend called Chris Cartwright who ran a business in medical sciences, and although they never had much in the way of business dealings, he respected his opinions greatly. They often met to discuss things over a pint or two of beer at a local pub and the Plat de Jour. On this particular day in the late summer of 2001, they were enjoying a relaxed lunch, when suddenly the barman suggested that they move into the other bar, because something bad was happening in New York. Julian and Chris picked up their pint glasses and walked into the other bar. The TV screen was showing one of the twin towers of the World Trade Center burning; it had apparently been hit by a commercial aircraft. Chris said," I have often flown into La Guardia Airport, and you come in directly over the city of New York. I suppose this was probably an inevitable accident waiting to happen." The three of them chatted about this, and then suddenly in front of their eyes, a second plane flew directly into the other tower. "Oh, shit," they all said at once, "that is no accident." At once they realised that this was the greatest act of terrorism in the history of the Western world. For the next hour, they were glued to the television, along with almost everyone else. The pictures were ruthless and terrifying.

The moment that he got home, there was only one person that he wanted to discuss this with: Phil Campbell, who in 1987 had taken him to dinner at the Windows on the World in the World

Trade Center, introduced him to Firestone wines, and offered him outstanding advice. He sat at his desk and dialled the number that he knew by heart. After two rings, Phil's secretary, Joyce, answered the phone. With his high-quality English voice, Joyce knew at once who it was and said, "Oh, Mr Barker, we are in a complete state here, because we know that Phil is in New York, and there is no cell service at the moment, and we cannot get him, and we do not know what to do." Julian, although very shocked, tried to be a calming influence.

"Joyce, who was he meeting with, did he tell you? Because I know that he can be a little casual about these things."

"He said that he had a meeting with a hedge fund manager called Joe, and I do have his office number, but I don't know his surname."

"Joyce, ring the number on a landline, find out how many Joes they have, and find out which of them knows Phil and when are they meeting. When you have the information, please can you ring me and tell me what you have found out? Thanks."

Julian put down the phone, and Alice was standing beside him. She had realised the gravity of the situation and asked Julian to explain. "Phil, you know, loves the Windows on the World restaurant and took me there many years ago. He has often said that it is favourite place in New York, and he generally invites his clients there for breakfast meetings. The views of New York in the mornings are spectacular; he reckons that he sells more of his research work because of the setting than he ever would in the office, and I know that he is right. Joyce says that he is meeting a hedge fund manager called Joe today, which means that he is selling an idea. I know Phil's habits, and I am fearing the worst. Look at the TV—the Windows on the World restaurant is above the flames, and if he is in there, I do not think that he has a chance." He put his arms around Alice and burst into tears, and the words came out—"If he is there, he will die."

Thirty minutes later Joyce rang him and said that there was only one Joe in the office of the hedge fund, and he had not arrived yet. In his diary was a note that said "Diamonds PC." Julian's heart sank, since Phil had been talking to him about a big diamond pipe being discovered in Canada that he reckoned could be worth C$1 billion, and the company that owned it was valued at C$75 million. Julian had accepted Phil's story and was himself a shareholder. As he continued to speak to Joyce, he found himself shaking. Joyce was crying, since she now feared the worst and was looking to Julian for support. He tried to pull himself together and asked for details as to his family and what they knew of his travel plans. Joyce had all the information. Phil had got the late flight from Toronto to New York the night before and had stayed in a hotel near Wall Street, where he always went. There was nothing in his diary except "NY."

Phil's wife was getting frantic. She told Joyce that he was a very good husband and would have found a landline and rung home to put everyone's mind at rest. Julian and Alice sat in front of the television and watched each tower collapse one after the other. They held each other by the hand and wept. They now sensed the worst was approaching.

The next day came and went. Joe and Phil were still out of contact. Julian spoke to Phil's wife and tried to be as supportive as he could, and he did the same for Joyce, but he knew the reality long before the final facts were confirmed. The news actually was given to Phil's wife by an executive of Phil's cellular phone provider—they apparently were logging Phil's phone, and it finally went dead at the exact time that the Windows on the World collapsed with the Twin Towers. No phone signal was ever recorded after that. Phil's and Joe's bodies were never recovered and had obviously been cremated in the savage temperatures of that terrible moment.

Julian and Alice were devastated, since Phil had been a part of their lives for nearly thirty-five years. Alice really liked Phil and he was often in London and had come to dinner parties at their home. Phil's wife spoke to Alice and asked what she could suggest to do about the funeral, since there was no body to bury or cremate. Alice came up with the old London tradition of a memorial service, where people could pay their respects and celebrate a great life.

Everything was agreed, and Julian and Alice boarded the plane for Toronto to say good-bye to a very good friend. The memorial service was held just north of Toronto, and everyone came. All the partners and their wives and a huge array of clients and friends from Canada, America, France, Germany, Switzerland, and the United Kingdom were there. Phil's best friend, who had known him since childhood, gave the eulogy, and everyone struggled to deal with the enormity of the September 2001 event in general and Phil's loss in particular. As they drank during the wake at Phil's golf club, where Julian had played many times, Julian struggled to get to grips with the whole event. Phil was a lovely man who thought of everyone and wouldn't hurt a fly. How could it be that his wonderful spirit had been snuffed out by a group of terrorists who wanted to teach America a lesson? He wasn't even American; he was Canadian.

As he and Alice went to bed that night, he suffered from indigestion and slept fitfully. The next day, they flew home. During the flight he was pleased to think about something else. One of the partners of the firm that his son Simon worked for wanted to retire, and Simon had suggested to his father that he should buy his shares in the company. Julian knew that he could easily afford it, but he mustn't make it too easy for his son. Simon must be made to show him why he should own it. As he constructed his plans, sleep overwhelmed him, and he nodded off.

CHAPTER THIRTY FOUR

Simon Barker was now aged thirty and had started work at JMG Recruitment at twenty-three. He had a first at Oxford in history and had been in the university blues golf team for three years. He always wanted to work with people and thought that getting candidates good jobs was a great career to follow. Success chased him around, since this man could do no wrong. He was a star, and his bosses knew it.

Martin Graham Johnson had founded the firm and decided that JMG (Johnson, Martin Graham, as his school list referred to him) Recruitment worked as a name. He put everything he had into starting it and found another businessman in the field, Michael Edwards, to put up some money and join him. The early days around 1988 were a little haphazard, but as the years progressed, they saw the city of London and financial recruitment as the place to be. Despite some ups and downs, the two founders did well, the business grew, and their own numbers increased.

In 1994 when they interviewed Simon Barker, who seemed to be top of everything, they knew that they had a thoroughbred in their midst. Simon had a way with people and placed candidates in companies with ease, and candidates came to him if they wanted to change jobs. By 2001 it was clear to everyone in the firm that Simon Barker was the number-one business getter at JMG and was challenging many of the bigger names in the industry for placements. It was at this time, however, that Michael Edwards was diagnosed with a terminal disease and would have to bow out of the company. Everything he had was tied up in JMG Recruitment except his house, so he had to find a buyer for his stake in the business. Simon, ever the entrepreneur, told Martin Johnson that his father had been a top stockbroker and would be the right person to help sell the shares.

Simon talked to his father at a million miles an hour, and Julian learned nothing. "Simon," he said, "write me a quality presentation in the following way, and I will discuss it with you. You must start by telling me what you are going to tell me, then tell me, and then tell me what you told me. If you achieve that—and believe me, it is not easy—then I will see what I can do."

Simon thought for a long time…what was he trying to tell his father? The final document that he gave to his father was long, but the main gist was as follows:

JMG Recruitment was a business in the financial headhunting arena. It operated in London and had shown very fast growth over the last decade. One of the original shareholders now wished to sell his 50-per cent stake because of ill health, and an opportunity existed for an investor or investors to buy now. The outlook was very exciting. (Simon felt that this should tell his father what he was going to tell him.)

Mr Stephen James Bamford

The next section—tell him—went through the growth of the business, how JMG got its clients, how they worked with the employers, and finally, how the costings of the business worked. Simon explained that basic remuneration was reasonable but could be outstanding if a member of staff placed a number of good candidates in good jobs. This was motivational for the individual at JMG but also kept the overheads low during bad times. Simon also explained that the assets of the business were the people, and hence the company did not have to pay out large sums of capital for factories, plants, and machinery, but they kept a good team together.

The last section—tell him what you told him—was more difficult since Simon didn't want to simply repeat the first section, so it came out like this:

"The financial markets in London are increasingly seen as the most dominant in the world. Whilst New York and Tokyo are very large, it is London where everyone is basing themselves. London can speak to the Far East in the morning and the Americas in the afternoon, and although Frankfurt is trying to compete, their language remains an obstacle. The outlook for JMG Recruitment is therefore extremely good, and this sale of shares, which is only happening because of personal tragedy, can only happen once. Hence, there will not be another opportunity to buy into this exciting business again."

After his father had read the document, he offered the following comments to Simon. "This presentation is good, because I now know what you are selling and why you are selling it. I also know that you have a robust financial structure and a good outlook, but there are a lot of questions that you have not answered, and you will need to. For instance, you do not say what the cost of this stake will be. You do not mention how you stop your staff going off and beginning their own firms. And how does my potential client get out in the future, or are you telling me that he is stuck in this investment forever? Simon," his father concluded, "do not get me wrong; your report has got me interested, and that is important. What we now have to do is to meet with your bosses and answer all the outstanding questions, and then we can get this show on the road."

Simon was deflated but happy as well. He had at least interested his father, but he had also learned how little he knew of the "real world." Over the next few weeks, they had a number of meetings with the two founders, and they went well. Julian explained the dangers of buying a "people business" and told them of the failure of the acquisition of his own firm. He was blunt: "Most of my partners were queuing up at the exit door once their lock-ins were over, and that cannot be good." He explained a rolling bonus plan that was extra to the normal annual package and related to JMG's success. What this plan does is reward loyalty after three years and then every year thereafter. If people go elsewhere, they forfeit this plan and leave a lot of money behind. Finally, he explained how they had bought and sold shares at Taylor, Dudley & Everett over the decades and suggested a similar pricing model.

A figure of £2 million was worked out. Julian suggested that this was a logical and explainable price, albeit not generous. Michael Edwards understood his options and the needs of his family after his death, and he agreed to these terms. Two weeks later Julian returned and said that he had received an offer of £1.5 million from what he rudely referred to as a "vulture fund" and a second offer of £1.75 million from a fund who insisted that the company go public on the stock market within two years.

Martin Johnson and Michael Edwards sat there in silence. Simon was thinking to himself, "What bastards these people are to take advantage of a dying man." Julian now spoke with great authority and charisma. "My recommendation is that you politely reject these offers and walk away. In my world, I always try and have a plan B. I do not always succeed, but in this case I have one, and it is simple. I said to you, Michael, that two million pounds was not generous, but it was both logical and explainable. You did me the courtesy of accepting this figure with good grace, and I admire you for that. My suggestion for you and Martin is this: I would like to buy your shares myself for two million pounds and join your board as a non–executive director. I have no intention of interfering with the day-to-day running of JMG, but with Michael gone, I feel that I can add strategic thinking and work with Martin to help him through the difficult months ahead."

Michael was becoming a little emotional, and tears were welling up in his eyes. Martin came to the rescue and spoke. "Julian, during our recent discussions, I have come to value the way that you go about things, and even if you were not buying Michael's shares, I would be delighted to have you join our board. I am certain that Michael will agree with me in saying how pleased we all are at this outcome, and we welcome you as our equal largest shareholder." Julian smiled and produced a stock transfer form from his briefcase and his cheque for £2 million. "If you sign the form now, you can take this cheque home with you today, and our deal is done. I will complete the paperwork in the next day or two." Michael shook Julian by the hand and said, "You are a true gentleman, sir; you didn't have to do this." Simon was so proud of his father, because he knew that what Michael had said was true. Two months later, Michael died.

In the six months that followed, Martin and Julian worked on a strategic plan that would move JMG Recruitment towards a London Stock Exchange listing. This, as Julian described it, was not urgent, but it was an excellent idea for financing the next stage of growth. Simon's stellar advance continued, and the happy and successful team around him grew.

Julian was plagued with indigestion, and it irritated him. He took milk of magnesia tablets like dolly mixtures. One day he was sitting in his living room with a cup of coffee, and he could hear Alice humming happily as she did the ironing in the adjoining room. He thought to himself how lucky he had been to have such a loving and wonderful wife. Despite his dyslexia, he had gotten a great job—Ambrose was a star, and Aubyn had turned out be a gentleman, but he still had never beaten him at golf. Then there was the tragedy of Phil's death; Rick, his long-time Australian friend; and of course, his magnificent son, Simon. As these thoughts meandered through his head, he felt pins and needles in his arm, and the pain in his chest got really bad. These were the last memories of Julian Barker.

Alice finished the ironing and put it away and then joined Julian in the living room. He looked to be asleep in his chair, but some alarm bell deep inside her told her that this was bad. When she touched Julian's hand, it was cold. She did not scream or become hysterical but sat down slowly, rang the local health centre, and simply said, "I think my husband is dead; please, can someone come round now?"

She then rang Simon and Jane and asked whether they could come too.

PART IV

THE FULL CONFESSION OF SIR SIMON ANTHONY BARKER

CHAPTER THIRTY FIVE

Some years ago, I met a wise man who gave me a piece of advice and told me that if I followed it, I would avoid many unpleasant incidents in my life. His advice was this: If someone or something makes you very angry or distressed, the natural reaction is to lose your temper or to lash out. This, he told me, is a very bad idea, because things once spoken or written cannot be taken back, and after calm reflection, it becomes obvious that you should have waited before reacting. At this stage, an apology is way too late. His proposal was simple: write a letter to yourself, with all your anger exposed, telling the offender of the fucking error of his ways and suggesting to him exactly what you think. Once complete, this note should be put in a drawer and not looked at for a month. After four weeks, reread your letter and realise how silly it sounds, and then tear it up and get on with your life. As I am sitting here in front of my computer, I know that I must write this letter to myself, because it is me, Simon Barker, that I am so angry with.

The facts are these. I have just been knighted in the 2013 Honours List, I am loved by my staff, I am loved by my shareholders, I am loved by my wife and children, and I am a multimillionaire—so what, you may ask, is my problem?

Well, if you believe in the politics of Niccolo Machiavelli, who suggested forcefully in the fifteenth century that the end justifies the means, then I am in the clear. But my wonderful dad always told me when he was alive that "You can fool the world, but you cannot fool yourself," and this is what I am struggling with right now.

The fact is that I have lied, cheated on my wife, had bizarre sexual experiences, and bent every rule to get what I want and win. This is my life; I always win, and defeat is not an option for me—it is not in my dictionary. The horrible truth is that if this confession fell into police hands, I would certainly go to jail. I think, therefore, that I must put my whole life into context and see if I can explain my actions.

I was born in 1971 of wealthy parents. My mother's family made their money in engineering, and my father's family were stockbrokers, and we lived in a private estate in Surrey. My birth was a bit of a nightmare; Alice, my mother, had complications, and this left her incapable of having other children. As an only child, I wanted for nothing. We travelled on exotic holidays, and I guess that I must have been spoiled. I did, however, have something very special, and my parents loved it—I was brilliant at everything and won everything. It didn't seem to matter what it was; I always seemed to end up victorious. One thing is odd to me—with this amount of success, you would have thought that I would be disliked by the boys at school, but strange as it is to report, I was always good with people and hence had lots of friends.

On my first day at school in a nearby town called Cobham, I distinctly remember the headmaster telling us that we were all going to take some tests to see whether we would be in the upper set or the lower set. This was "red rag to a bull" for me. Even at eight years old, I had to be top, and nothing else would do. Although we were not told the exact results, it was clear from the headmaster's reaction to me that I had done very well and was in the top set for all subjects. The same thing happened in sports, and my reaction was exactly the same; I had to be the best, and I was. Lord knows where this came from since neither of my parents was really very competitive. My dad, Julian, loved cricket and golf and was not bad at tennis. My mother was very keen on tennis and was always trying to improve her game, and she still plays today in her sixties. By the time I reached the under eleven stage, I was being made captain of teams, and I loved every minute of it. By twelve, I was put down to take a scholarship to my father's old school. I had little doubt that I would get it, but the school was famous for its sports teams—I wanted to get into them as well, and I knew that I would. As I write this, I know that I sound incredibly arrogant, but actually I am not. If you are really good at things, you do not show off, because it comes so naturally.

An incident occurred when I was eleven that I can remember like yesterday because of the effect that it had on my parents. A friend of mine asked me what I knew about sex, and I said that I had heard a few things, but I didn't know much. He then suggested something that happened between a man and a woman that I thought was very interesting, but I wasn't sure that it was right. Well, if ever I wanted to know anything, I always asked my parents, so shortly afterwards on a Sunday morning, I went into their bedroom and asked my mother the question. "Mummy, do you kiss Daddy's willy?" She looked totally shocked and replied, "Simon, you can't ask me a question like that," and then she fell silent. "So that means yes, then, I assume," I chirped and ran out of the room. I am sure that I heard laughter as I went downstairs, and now that I am older, I can certainly understand why—oh, the innocence of youth!

At our school, we were expected to board for the last year as preparation for going to public school, where most students boarded. I knew that I would like this since I had friends in the year above me, and they seemed to get into fun scrapes and have a wow of a time. I couldn't wait. Before I went, my father decided to give me my official sex education presentation. I say presentation because he had laid it out like one of his research documents at work. Mum had typed it, because he wasn't good at that. He went through the whole thing, and I was fascinated if a little embarrassed—how many people like to think of their parents making love? He told me about making a woman happy before myself, and he explained about masturbation and that it was natural for a boy and not a sin, as some might say, and he told me about condoms and AIDS and…well, it was thorough. "Keep this presentation," he suggested, "and reread it when you get older and it becomes more relevant." I always remember the last sentence of his note, which read, "The aim of every man should be to become a thoughtful and good lover." *Good* did not work for me; I aimed to become a magnificent lover.

I took my scholarship to public school and felt that I should succeed in getting one, but it was only when the letter arrived that reality struck me. In the letter from the school, I was told that I had got a scholarship and that the fees would be much reduced for my parents. This was a real eye-opener for a thirteen-year-old, since I took school for granted and never really thought of the cost and sacrifices that parents had to go through to give their children a good start in life. This was a big day for me because for the first time, my actions had given someone else a benefit, and this felt really good.

By this time, I was playing junior competitions at both my golf and tennis clubs in St George's Hill, where my parents were members of both clubs. Interestingly, they are having their centenary celebrations as I write this story. I enjoyed all sports, but I knew that golf would be my passion, and I set about becoming really good.

School and exams were fun for me, and I achieved top grades throughout my time there. I learned an awful lot of things that would be of absolutely no relevance to me in my future life, but it had to be done to "tick the box." One thing about me is that I was never a rebel; if it had to be done, all I cared about was being the best at it.

Pornographic magazines were all around the school, and many of our pupils who came from overseas brought in the very explicit ones. I was no different than anyone else—I read them all! One day, however, I saw a long, wordy article in one of the magazines entitled "Are You Willing to Become a Great Lover?" The moment I read the title, I knew that this was manna from heaven for me, since I always had to be the best, and this instruction manual was going to help me achieve it.

The article was actually very medical and not dirty at all, but it was clear in its message: no athlete will win medals unless he or she trains over a long period of time, and to become a really good lover requires a great deal of training.

Without going through the whole article, which would be boring, the items that stood out for me were as follows:

1. You cannot be a really good lover unless your PC muscle is very strong. As I read the article, I learned what a PC muscle was, having had no idea before.
2. The article explained about Kegel exercises and how by doing them every day, a man could develop a very strong PC muscle.

3. Male multiple orgasms exist. I had heard of women having multiple orgasms, but not men. The article explained that a male climax occurs before ejaculation, and if a man practices hard enough, he can have climaxes without ejaculation and hence can keep going for a very long time. This I found fascinating.

My character, being what it is, demanded that I become outstanding at all these things, and for the next period of my life, every masturbation became a challenge to me to have more climaxes without ejaculation and to last for ages. The article finished by stating that just because you can do all this, it doesn't mean that you have to. The main aim of lovemaking is to give your lady partner the greatest pleasure possible, and that was important.

By the late 1980s, a good-looking man did not have too great a difficulty in getting girls into bed, and I was certainly "up for that," so to speak. I chose my first girl carefully, since I wanted at least one of us to know what we were doing. Through all the magazines, I was very familiar with the mechanics of what I had to do, but there is something about that first time that is terrifying, and I was no different. As the evening came to an end, we went into some nearby woods and started stroking each other. We had drunk a lot, but we very alert, considering. No one had ever touched my cock before, and my arousal became very intense. I spent a long time stroking and caressing her breasts, which were small but very responsive, and she clearly wanted me to go on as she moved one breast and then the other towards my mouth. She stroked me so well that I had a climax but just held off the ejaculation. I moved to stop her stimulating me and began to kiss her clitoris, and she came very quickly. I was fiddling around with the condom, and I just managed to get it on and entered her. My mind said, "Make this last and be a superstar," but my body was having none of it, and my ejaculation exploded very quickly! It was a great first experience, but I knew that I had to get a lot better, and I very soon did.

All public schools rate themselves based on how many of their students get to Oxford or Cambridge, and so it was inevitable that I would be pushed in that direction by my academic tutors. Cambridge was a long drive, and Oxford was a short drive, so the latter was chosen. I had heard odd stories about the interviews at these famous universities. The one that appealed to me most was when the interviewer gave the candidate a brick and asked him to throw it through the window. The candidate was a little surprised but did so and broke the glass. The interviewer said, "Excellent, but the successful student would have opened the window first!" I was therefore ready for any weird question that they might throw at me. What happened instead was that the interviewer asked me to confirm that my golf handicap had reached scratch. I confirmed that this was the case, and he started talking about Oxford and Cambridge matches in all sports and how important it was to play for the university team. I reasoned that if I appeared very positive about this, it would help my cause, so I did. He started talking about my history course, and that was that.

There was something very special about Oxford, and representing the university at golf for all my three years there against Cambridge was incredible. I attended Brasenose College, which was founded in 1509, and the whole university gives the history course that I was taking real meaning. The parking situation in Oxford is a nightmare, but the city is truly remarkable. There were ladies at my college and a relatively recent arts festival, so the social side of the student life there was a truly wonderful experience. I had many liaisons with fellow students from both inside and outside my college and learned about "intense relationships." Some girls in my experience got incredibly serious about me, and I simply couldn't cope with it. I had never fallen in love; all I wanted was to be with like-minded girls who were having a wow of a time. Many from day schools were experiencing their first freedoms from parental control and loving it. I was always very respectful about the use of condoms and was never irresponsible. We were having far too good a time to muck it up with unwanted pregnancies and sexually transmitted diseases.

My tutor at university suggested that I should go for a PhD postuniversity after it was clear that I had got a first-class honours degree. It was all very flattering, but I felt that the real world awaited me, and I wanted to get started. I did, however, have a problem, and it was a simple one—I hadn't the faintest notion what I was going to do. At school all the sixth formers were put through something called the Morrisby Test. I found it useful since it created a profile of one's personality traits and assessed skills and suitability. I came out as someone who should work with people, and on the skill set side, I could do most things.

My father was very amusing, since he had just left his company and said, "Anything apart from stockbroking!" We spent many a long hour talking about the matter and came up with a short list. Advertising, media, and personnel management were the main ones. Dad put me off retailing since he said that they work on Saturdays, and he laughed and said that it was my golf day.

I got an interview at the BBC, which went well. The main person there suggested that I should get into the world of programme making, but after I heard how long it took to make thirty minutes of TV, I reckoned that I might get bored. I didn't write it off, however. My second interview was at a global advertising agency in London. I could see myself running ad campaigns but soon realised that the job that I would be getting was many rungs lower on the ladder than that. Public relations appealed, and as with advertising, there was a high female component to these companies, which I liked. With my training from the porn magazine and three years at Oxford, I was now a sexual athlete of quality and needed to find plenty of beautiful young ladies. If you asked me whether I was promiscuous, I would probably say yes, but I had not fallen in love yet—for me, I was more bothered about getting really good at lovemaking and having a great time with girls who enjoyed it too. Love could wait.

One day my father brought in the *Financial Times* and prodded an advertisement for a young associate at a headhunting firm called JMG Recruitment. He suggested that in this line of work, one would always be dealing with people and finding candidates a new job, which might be very rewarding emotionally as well as financially. We talked it through, and the next day I replied to the advertisement. The lady asked me what I had done during university in the way of work. Fortunately, I had an answer and told her that I had been working for a fast-growing interior design company in all my holidays, since I was sixteen. She liked my answer and told me that she would send me the date and time of my interview.

CHAPTER THIRTY SIX

I need to back up a little here to explain my last statement, because it actually has the merit of being true.

My father has a marvellous sister called Jane, and we have always got on really well. She is very bright and always joked with Dad about how much cleverer she was than him at school. They have always been very close, and that became obvious around the time of my grandfather's terrible death from pancreatic cancer. My mother always tells me that Jane was a saint at that time and took on everything, however horrible it was.

So, Jane in our house was seen as a superstar. She did well at school, but in 1957 at age eighteen, middle-class girls were on the lookout for men to marry and have children. Jane was definitely happy with that idea, but she was brilliant at art and design and asked my grandfather if she could go to a really exclusive college in London. Everyone in the family tells me that Grandpa was very military and strong, but he was putty in Jane's hands. He was the doting father of his pretty daughter. He agreed at once, and off she went. Postwar, money in England was tight, and many of the big, old family homes were being sold to pay death duties or be split into maisonettes and flats. Jane, however, told me that although there was not that much work around, it was a brilliant time to learn the trade, and she did learn it well. The college was in a smart part of London, and one day, Jane tells me, a very good-looking man came in and said that he needed someone, not too expensive, to help him remodel his recently deceased father's home. Jane admitted to me that she moved the fastest of anyone and went off with him there and then. Whether it was the job or the good looks, she never divulged, but I have my suspicions.

It turned out that this man's father had been a lord, and now this man, in his late twenties, was a lord as well, since the death of his father. The house was in Eaton Square, looked architecturally fabulous, but was badly in need of a coat of paint. As they walked in, it was obvious that the old lord was not house-proud in any way. In Jane's opinion, it had massive potential, but you needed to have a good eye for these things to see it. It was clear to Jane that Lord Michael Peel didn't! Jane told me that she began to fall in love with him when she asked him how he liked to be addressed. She loved his answer: "I would like you to call me Michael, and I will sack you immediately if you call me Mike, but I will respond to Sir at a push!" What appealed to her so much was that he didn't mean a word of it, but he obviously had a great sense of humour.

As with many of the landed gentry, they were long of assets and relatively short of cash, but Jane saw something that was to help Michael a great deal and was undoubtedly the reason that he married her. The assets were all property and land, and Jane and Michael went through the entire estate and worked out what must be kept and what could be sold. In the 1960s, we had the Beatles, but America just loved anything English and would pay well over the odds for the right property that was beautifully furnished. Within three years, what Jane and Michael did was remarkable. Jane would identify the design of a specific building and make it perfect at a sensible cost. Then Lord Michael Peel would personally take American buyers around, and in front of His Lordship, they would pay an excellent price. There were twenty serious properties in the estate and the main stately home in Wiltshire, plus of course Michael's London home in Eaton Square, which was now quite beautiful. I went there many times as a boy, and it was breathtaking. Jane and Michael married in 1963, and she of course became Lady Jane Peel. For tax reasons, Michael suggested that a company be set up and called Lady Jane Interiors. At the time Jane felt that Michael was being a little over the top, but the future proved that Michael was right and Jane was wrong.

The early days of their marriage were idyllic, and they enjoyed improving the Peel Estate together. As they sold more properties at high prices, they built up a war chest of cash and started buying run-down houses in London and making them look beautiful. The properties were always well located, and they kept some to rent out and sold some to keep their borrowing levels in check. Jane and Michael had William in 1967 and Mary in 1969, and I got on with my cousins really well. Some of my favourite childhood memories were of visiting William and Mary at their stately home in Wiltshire. I do not remember how much land there was there, but if I said it was over a thousand acres, I would not be far off. For young children it was heavenly—we climbed trees in the forest, built camps, rolled down hills, and swam in a lake that was perfect on a hot summer's day. We only returned to the house when we were exhausted or hungry.

Jane also built up her business in our home area. For those of you not familiar with our part of Surrey, there are some important private estates where very rich people live, and these were Jane's clients.

Many of you will know the Wentworth Estate near Virginia Water, where the famous golf tournaments are played. In Weybridge and Walton-on-Thames, there are three: St George's Hill, which is the best known probably because John Lennon and Ringo Starr owned homes there; Burwood Park and Ashley Park, where I was brought up; and over near Esher and Oxshott, there are Blackhills and the Crown Estate.

Jane was very bright, as I have mentioned before, and she focused solely on these key areas. What she realised early on is that money looks for a safe place. The early buyers came from Iran when the shah there was replaced by religious leaders who were less friendly. Then it was South Africans who feared for their future, and then Iraqis who were disliked by Saddam Hussein and decided to leave their country in a hurry, and now it is the Russians. The list is endless, but they all share a common view—Surrey is a safe place to invest millions in bricks and mortar, and these properties, whether new or renovated, have to be presented in the most immaculate way. At this point Jane gained a huge advantage over the competition, and it was simple—she was Lady Jane Peel and was part of the English nobility. The fact that her work was brilliant was not important to many, but because they had lived with fear and corruption in their own countries, they simply wanted to deal with someone that they could trust. Her business took off from day one, and she is still doing extremely well today. As I write this, Jane is seventy-five, and she still loves her work.

Marriage, however, did not work out that well for Jane, although she is still married to Michael. He suffered from a problem that afflicts many men, and that has been created by three things in his case. He has always been good-looking and funny, he is a lord, and he has money. With no disrespect to the ladies of London, this is an unstoppable combination. He was irresistible to them, and sadly, I must report that he did not resist at all! The expression "serial philander" comes to mind, and although he was always kind to Jane, William, and Mary, he could not stop himself and caused havoc. Jane and Alice, my mother, had endless discussions about what to do and eventually decided that Jane should come and live near to us in Surrey and her work and let Michael get on with it. Initially, Jane was very bitter and angry, but in the end she accepted her strong position in the family and came to understand that Michael loved her very much. This took decades to resolve, but as they say in Yorkshire, "There's nowt so queer as folk!"

CHAPTER THIRTY SEVEN

This brings me back to my interview with JMG Recruitment. I arrived and gave a sealed envelope to Mr Martin Johnson's PA, which had been given to me by Jane. She said it was a reference. The PA opened the letter, read it, and then disappeared to deliver it. I waited for about ten minutes, and then I was called in. There were two men in attendance; it turned out that they were the founders of the business. On the table in front of them was the letter that Jane had written—I knew this because I had seen her headed notepaper many times before.

One of the two started the meeting with a question: "Have you read this letter?" I told them that I hadn't, and then he continued, "I think that you should hear the contents."

He began to read the letter, and this is broadly what it said, since I have never read it or seen it again:

"To whom it may concern,

"For the record, I must immediately declare that Simon Barker is my nephew.

"He first came to work for my interior design company aged sixteen as a holiday job, and he has always asked me if he could come back holiday after holiday ever since. He is working for me now, until he begins his full-time career. I pay him pretty basic wages, and he accepts them without complaint.

"What has always impressed me about Simon is his ability to deal with people from all walks of life. From day one on-site, Simon was introduced to plasterers, painters, electricians, plumbers, carpenters, and cabinetmakers, and he treats them exactly the same as his uncle, who is a lord, and is very popular with them all.

"During his seven years with my firm, he has visited houses with all kinds of owners. Frankly, the only thing that my clients have in common is wealth. Many have good taste, some have taste that does not work in this country, some wish to receive help, and some have a stubborn streak and are beyond help. What I have tried to instil into Simon is a respect for others, whilst encouraging him to 'advise and suggest.' I have also taught him that he must learn when a client is bad and develop the ability to walk away from a deal, however financially rewarding that contract may be. He is a very quick learner, as his academic record attests, and I feel that in the world of recruitment, which is not so very different to mine, Simon will add value after the appropriate training.

"Yours faithfully,

"Lady Jane Peel"

I sat there both proud and happy and thought, Jane, you are very special. The interview continued: they asked me lots of questions, and I think that I did well. I asked them a lot of questions about what the company did and finally gave them a straightforward and direct one. "What, in your opinion, is the best and the worst thing about your business in recruitment?" They looked at each other, smiled, and agreed their answer. "The best thing about our business is when you place a candidate in a company and it works well for everyone. Maybe ten years later, the candidate wants to change direction and comes to us again because he had a good experience the first time. Simon, that is as good as it gets, and maybe he might come to us later for that big job. The worst thing about our world is that an event outside our control leads to panic amongst our clients, and they start a recruitment freeze. Generally, we have a difficult six months, and then the freeze ends and life gets back to normal. How does that sound to you?"

I am not quite sure what came over me, but I told them that I completely understood those two differing situations, and if they were to offer me a job, I would definitely take it. I was never quite sure whether that was rude or enthusiastic. But they offered me the job nonetheless.

CHAPTER THIRTY EIGHT

From the first day that I started at JMG Recruiting, I knew that I had made the right decision. The team around me were fun and talented, and we were a firm to be reckoned with. We came across the majors in the industry, and some job placements we could not get, but if we got to present to the client, we often got the project. I lapped up the training and worked incredibly hard, since it was natural for me to want to be the best. Without doubt, my numbers were rising very fast, and my bonuses reflected my success.

Tragically, Michael Edwards was diagnosed with a terminal illness, and I suggested that the two founders talk to my father. He made me deliver a presentation to him as to why he should get involved. To cut a long story short, he found some buyers for Michael Edward's shares, but they tried to screw him. My father, who was a remarkable man, priced the shares fairly and bought them himself, and he became a nonexecutive director of the company. Michael sadly passed away, and Dad helped a great deal in the twelve months that followed.

I was working on a placement one day when my mother called, which was rare. She spoke to me very softly and said, "Simon, please can you come home? Something terrible has happened—your father has had a heart attack and is dead." Having told Mum that I would be with her in as short a time as possible, I sat at my desk, and tears rolled uncontrollably down my face. We worked in an open plan situation, and very soon everyone was aware of my emotional state. Eventually, one of our more outgoing associates asked what was wrong. I told him that my father had had a heart attack and had passed away, and he was only just over sixty years old. I also asked him to tell Martin Johnson, because I could not speak the words to him, and I would be going home.

As I got on the train, Martin rang me and said how sorry he was and told me to take off as much time as I needed. People in the carriage kept looking at me, since I cried all the way from Waterloo to Walton-on-Thames. When I arrived at my parents' house, Jane was already there, and the ambulance had already taken my father's body away. We all hugged each other as the enormity of what had just happened began to sink in. I asked what I should do, and my mother and Jane suggested that I inform everyone of the news. This, I thought, was a nightmare of a role, but I also realised that it had to be done.

As I walked into my father's study, I saw a note that was written in Dad's italic style, and it said, "Ring Rick re Iron Ore." As I read it, I realised that the time difference meant that he could not do it until Rick got up. I looked at Dad's phone and saw on the stored numbers "Rick Home" and "Rick Off." Rick Jones from Porter Partners was a legend in Dad's eyes and he always told stories of their trips around Western Australia and the work that they did together. All my young life, Dad went off to Australia in January for two to three weeks and visited Rick, and although he now went slightly less, the two of them continued to work closely together by phone. Clearly, iron ore was to be the current topic. I rang Rick at his home at about 7:30 a.m. Australian time and told him that Julian Barker, who was my father, had had a heart attack and died suddenly. I remember distinctly that there was a lengthy silence, and then he said in a voice that was beginning to break up with emotion, "Thank you, Simon, for ringing me. I really appreciate it, and please can you let me know when the funeral is to be held? I wish to be there to pay my respects." I told him that no one expected him to travel all the way from Australia for a short service and a few drinks—everyone would understand. "Simon, you must understand," he said, "that my dealings with your father go back over thirty-five years, and I simply have to be there. Please can you e-mail me the details as soon as you have them?" I realised there and then that this man had made up his mind, and it was silly to argue. Jane organised the service, which was to be held at a very tasteful crematorium in nearby Leatherhead; the buffet lunch and drinks would take place at a hotel close by. I e-mailed all the details to Australia and a number to people throughout the world that I found on my father's e-mail address list.

Letters flowed in to my mother, and they all had the same theme of how much Julian had been respected and appreciated. The letter from Phil Campbell's widow was very poignant; she stated that Julian had been a tower of strength to her in the aftermath of Phil's tragic death. One letter stood out for me too. It was from a Robyn Masters from Aaron Roberts Investment Bank of New York, and although short, it was powerful and said, "Julian was the most honourable man that I have had the pleasure to meet in my life and epitomised everything that is great in Great Britain." The sentiments were truly wonderful, but Dad never had a good word to say about the firm that had taken over Taylor, Dudley & Everett. In fact, his words were more flowery than that; he actually said, "This lot should be a case study on how to fuck up a one-hundred-year-old business in less than five years!"—and this from a man who hardly ever swore.

The day of the funeral service came, and the organisation of Jane and my mother worked like clockwork. There was a huge congregation in attendance—many people had to stand, and the doors remained open to accommodate more. My mother, who had remained strong up to this moment, finally fell apart as the first few bars of my father's favourite song were played and the coffin came slowly into the chapel. Seeing this was too much for Jane, William, Mary, and I, and we sobbed uncontrollably. Ambrose Dudley read the eulogy, with plenty of funny stories gathered from me, his friends, and the golf club. My overriding memory of the service was that it had been beautifully done. I did notice, however, that one man was crying apart from me, and it was Rick Jones. He appeared very distraught. I thought of the massive effort that he had made to get to the service from Australia, and my heart went out to him.

The wake was held at a very pleasant hotel about a mile away. People from everywhere came to me and told me what a wonderful man my father was. Stan Church, the head dealer, and Tom Smith, the head of the back office at my father's old firm, told me that he had believed in them and given them the chance to be partners of the company. Their sentiments were identical—Julian Barker had respected them for their talents and was not the remotest bit interested in the way they spoke or the fact that they were both from the East End of London. Lord Glenconner was there, and Aubyn spoke eloquently about the way that Dad had always handled himself. Rebecca and her husband were there, and she told me about my father's problems with writing but then said that making his reports into perfect English was one of the most exciting jobs that she could have had. She also told me that Dad had negotiated a special bonus for her from the Americans, and as a result they had been able to buy a beautiful house without a mortgage. I knew that everyone was being "super nice" because my father was dead, but I have to say that these outpourings of emotions appeared very genuine.

As the afternoon wound down, Jane took Mum home with Michael and her children and asked me to sort out the bill. I had not at that point spoken to Rick, since he had rallied and was enjoying plenty of drinks. You could hear his strong Australian accent over the general hubbub in the room. Having sorted out the admin, I return to the garden-facing suite and joined the final three that were there—Ambrose and his wife and Rick Jones. I thanked Ambrose sincerely for doing the eulogy so well, and they left.

Rick had chosen to stay at the hotel where the wake was being held and hence did not have to leave for anywhere. I filled up two glasses of red wine, and we sat down together. I told him how much I had loved the stories of the outback of Australia and my father's trips to see him and the characters that they had both met. We talked for some time, and then I pried a little more and told him that I had seen him crying, and he appeared very distraught. It was as though a floodgate had opened, and he began, "Simon, I feel that I know you really well, because when you drive in a four-by-four for two weeks every year for thirty years, there is virtually nothing that doesn't get discussed. I know about every success that you have had at work, your first at Oxford, the fact that you played golf against Cambridge, and your rapid rise through JMG Recruitment. Because of this, I am going to tell you something today that I have never told to a soul, and that includes your father. It was my only secret from him. Please let me tell you everything before you speak, because it is very important to me that you know it all. The fact is that I loved your father more than any human being on this planet and have done so since the late 1960s. Please do not think of this as a homosexual admission, since I have no sexual feelings for men in the slightest. What I realised early on is that Julian understood me in a deeper way than anyone has ever done. My love for him has never been expressed, and if he were here today, he would be as shocked as you. The truth is that he thought of me as a close and real friend, and I knew that. He told me of his very deep love for your mother and that he had very nearly been unfaithful to her once but somehow had stayed strong. He always told me that he really was happy that he had not slipped. Simon, as I said, he thought of me as a great friend, but for me, he has been the love of my life. Perhaps you will now appreciate that I simply had to be here today to say my good-bye."

I realised at that point that tears were rolling down my face, not because of my father but for this poor man who had never ever been able to express his love for my father until this moment. This was way beyond anything that I had learned about at school or university, but it was as real as anything that I had ever been taught. We stood up, hugged, and wept.

CHAPTER THIRTY NINE

Two weeks after the funeral, a letter was hand-delivered to the house by my father's solicitors. I found this a little strange, since the will of Julian Barker had been read, and there were no real surprises contained in it. Dad had left legacies to William and Mary rather than Jane, which had been agreed in the past. I was left the 50 per cent shareholding in JMG Recruitment, which Dad had paid £2 million pounds for, and my mother got the house and about £2.5 million. Julian Barker's early life had been blighted by dyslexia, but he certainly had been a success by anyone's standards.

I opened the envelope. It contained a covering letter and another envelope that had "Simon" written on it in my father's distinctive handwriting, and it was sealed with wax. I read the letter from the solicitors, and it told me that my father had given instructions that the sealed letter should be given to me two weeks after the funeral. I broke the seal and took out the letter, which I have in front of me now in 2013 as I write this story. It said:

"My dearest Simon,

"The fact that you are reading this letter means that I am now dead. Even in your time of distress, please could you and Mum try to think of the good times and not allow your grief to run riot?

"What I am going to tell you now will surprise you and possibly shock you, but that's the way of the world. I have tried to live a good life and show respect for others, and of course, I have loved you and your mother very deeply. Some years ago, I was seriously tempted to make love to a very beautiful woman, and I only just managed to resist the temptation. I told myself that if I had done it, I could fool the world, but I could not fool myself. I would have broken a bond of trust with your mother, and that would have tortured me terribly, even if she had never found out. Simon, when you marry, please understand this: in today's cynical world, not getting caught is seen as very clever, but truly it isn't. If you truly respect and love someone, why would you cheat on them? It makes no sense at all.

"Back in the 1960s, I must admit to you that I did something that was not against the law, but to use one of your favourite expressions, it was very dodgy! I might have been able to forgive myself if the damn deal had not worked so well and made me so much money. I could be a hypocrite and say that it was one mistake in a lifetime of good deeds, but that would be a total fabrication. What I did was wrong, wrong, wrong, but it gave me a lifetime of financial security! Your father, I am afraid, is not a paragon of virtue after all.

"I want you to contact a Herr Friederick Weiss at the Zurich Cantonal Bank and go to see him with an original of my death certificate. When you get there, he will tell you everything. His contact details are attached. Simon, you have been a wonderful son to me, and I could not be more proud of you if I tried. I am so pleased that you will now be an equal partner with Martin Johnson at JMG Recruitment. Keep learning from him, and the future looks excellent.

"Lots of love, Dad"

I sat there puzzled. I had understood from Rick Jones that Dad had had a brush with infidelity, but what was this dodgy deal? I had got eight original death certificates from the registrar of deaths, so it was no problem to take one with me to Zurich. The taxi drive into Zurich was quick, and within no time, I was in the office of Friederick Weiss. He told me that Herr Anton Gruber, who had handled my father's affairs, had now retired, and he had been appointed to take over.

Friederick Weiss began, "Your father has invested very well since this account was opened in the middle of the 1960s. Today the account simply owns gold and Swiss francs. The last time that I saw Mr Barker, he was highly amusing. He told me that when Mr Harold Wilson sold a part of Britain's gold reserves, the price rose from forty dollars to two hundred dollars, and now Mr Gordon Brown has sold more gold in the low two hundreds. This, your father said to me, was the best buy signal that he could have, because Britain's prime ministers had a one-hundred-per-cent record of getting it wrong! The value of your father's account is ten million one hundred sixty-eight thousand one hundred twenty-three pounds, and he told me to tell you to keep it for a rainy day. I am going to give you a credit card in the fictitious name of Mr Brad Johnson. I want you to sign this form three times in your normal writing and then sign the back of the card. With this card, you can draw out as much money as you want, anywhere in the world, and each month we will clear any drawings automatically. Never draw any money in England ever, do I make myself clear? And do not draw money from UK banks abroad. We can protect you, and if you are sensible, we will never be forced to tell a soul about your account here, and you should not tell a soul either."

My father's papers were verified and returned to me, my security questions were settled upon, and I left for home. Ten million quid—wow, what a figure! Something for a rainy day...I laughed out loud.

On my return, events settled back to normal. JMG Recruitment powered ahead, and the suggestion of the company going public on the London Stock Exchange appeared on the horizon. We appointed a team to prepare us for this event. I have never seen so much meaningless paperwork in all my life. Everyone appeared to be protecting their own arse, and I guessed that if the business failed, the only people to lose money would be the poor old shareholders!

The costs of this exercise were outrageous, and Martin and I had to be diluted to 15 per cent each to raise £20 million of fresh capital. Martin sold a further 5 per cent to other younger members of the team, which left me as the largest shareholder. Martin became the chairman, I was appointed the chief executive officer, and the shares were launched at one pound each in 2005.

It was in that year that I met a lady who was about five years my junior, called Annabel Ferguson. She was not classically beautiful but exuded sex appeal, and she organised business conferences, which was why I met her. JMG Recruitment had a stand at the conference, and she came to talk to me as the CEO. I still find it odd that from the first time that I met this girl, I knew that she was different from anyone else that I had been out with. I normally ran a successful chat-up line, and within a date or two, I had them in bed—and of course there I impressed them. With Annabel it was different. She seemed happy to see me but not that bothered, but she captivated me with her charm.

It was weeks before she agreed to a date, since she was always busy and could never make it. I was beginning to think that I was losing my touch—she always kept me interested but always at arm's length. We finally had a date, and it went well. I felt very relaxed in her company, and there was something between us that seemed to me to be different. I wanted to have sex with Annabel but sensed that she would not react well to my normal, forthright approach. As the evening ended, I kissed her gently on each cheek and said that I hoped that we could see each other again, and I left as she walked through her front door.

Within weeks, I was in love, but she still appeared to be nervous about sex, and I didn't understand why. So one day over dinner, I asked her straight out why she appeared not to want to have sex with me. I dreaded her answer, but when it came, it was nothing like what I had feared. She said to me simply, "I have just ended a long relationship, and as we parted, he told me that I was a terrible lay, and I do not want to lose you because I am so crap in bed." I could see the tears in her eyes, and for the first time in my life, my heart melted. All I wanted to do was to cuddle and kiss her and make things right. That night we got into bed together and kissed and touched and aroused each other very slowly. I did nothing at all that might make her nervous, and when we made love, it was so gentle and sensual that our emotions were completely aligned. For the first time ever, I was not trying to be a gold-medal-winning sexual athlete; I wanted to be certain that everything was perfect for Annabel. The reward for me was that that night, I discovered that true lovemaking was completely different from rampant sex. Let's not be silly about this, since both have their place, but our lovemaking that night took our relationship to a wholly different level. We married in 2006, I at thirty-five and Annabel at thirty-one. Both our careers were going very well, and we deferred the idea of children until later.

CHAPTER FORTY

At the time of the stock exchange flotation of JMG Recruitment, two statements had been made, one by Martin Johnson and the other by me. His comment was that he intended to retire in 2007, when he reached his sixty-fifth birthday. Being a recruitment agency, we were ideally placed to find ourselves a new chairman. Our final choice was a John Barrett, who had been in the merchant banking sector for most of his life and had concentrated on human resources in recent years. He understood how the city worked, he understood staff requirements, and he was a respected figure in the Square Mile. He was ideal as our new chairman. Martin was delighted to go gracefully and told me at his leaving party that I would always have his support.

My comment at the time of listing was that a large amount of the new money should be used to build up our brand in the new financial centres as they emerged. By 2006, I knew that Hong Kong was obvious—it was already established as a financial centre, and it was also the window into China. We had to be there. Singapore was also obvious. Under their revered leader Lee Kuan Yew, this tiny outpost of the old British Empire had become a powerhouse of the Far East. His leadership style, as he once described it in a television interview, was that of benign dictator. He made sure that the rule of law was adhered to and that business was welcomed. I knew that Singapore was the right place for us. The last centre was Dubai. This was slightly more of a gamble, but the financial plans for the region were large, and of course the Arabic world had the money in the Middle East to deliver it. My strategy was easy to explain. JMG Recruitment was doing very well in London, and now we would spend £20 to £25 million to set ourselves up in the emerging world. Within five years we would have a global footprint outside the United States and Japan, and although that might not make us unique, we would be very rare indeed.

I set about putting this all together and travelled a great deal. I recruited key executives to head up the operations, discussed locations, found offices, and worked out how long it would take to get this huge undertaking to become profitable. My conclusion was that by mid-2009, we would be seeing the first green shoots from our newly planted fields. The stock market loved our plans, and our share price rose to £1.75 or 75 per cent up from our issue price, which was exciting for everyone.

During a trip to Hong Kong, I had finished dinner with my colleagues; they went to their homes, and I was left alone in the bar. For some reason, I was not tired, and I noticed two very attractive young ladies sitting at a table together. Until I had visited the Far East, I had never realised how beautiful the young ladies there could be—the vibrant colours of their clothes, their wonderfully slender bodies, and how gorgeous they looked. I walked over to their table and introduced myself, and we all began to talk. I found out that one was called Li, and the other was named Anna. I was particularly struck by the beauty of Li, and fortunately, Anna had to go. We talked, and I became sexually aroused. Li sensed what I wanted and agreed to come to my room.

I was captivated by the fragrance that she was wearing, and I breathed her in. We kissed, and our clothes fell to the floor. As I took her bra off, I feasted my eyes on her small but perfectly formed breasts. She pulled my pants down and started to stroke my excited cock. As I pulled down her panties, I got the shock of my life—in front of me was a fully erect, circumcised cock. I had heard of ladyboys before, but this was extraordinary. My thoughts were a jumble. This woman was absolutely delicious, she looked beautiful—no, she was beautiful—she smelt amazing, and her breasts were perfect. A friend of mine once said, "A risen cock has no conscience," and this was about to be proven. Despite my shock, my erection was still at 100 per cent, and Li was touching it as though nothing had happened. I never like to be defeated, and this was no different, so I brazened it out. Although this was a totally bizarre experience, I felt that I was with a gorgeous woman, and as I played with her breasts, my arousal became greater. I suddenly wanted to play with her penis and did so. I stroked it very gently, and then, to my eternal shame I kissed her knob and put it in my mouth. She did the same to me, and we hurtled towards climax. Before the end, I removed my mouth from her, gently stroked her through to her climax, and watched her ejaculation. Although I am utterly shocked at what I did that night, I will not lie—it was nothing like anything that I had ever experienced before, but I found it incredibly exciting.

In Singapore, I found proper ladies' company, which I paid for as with Li, but in Dubai, I never strayed. Why? If you are caught stealing in the Middle East, under religious law, you can have your hand cut off. So, I was certainly not going use my cock to commit a crime... goodness knows what might happen! As I write this confession, I saw no harm in what I was doing; I was just paying to have company and sexual fun. I saw it no differently than paying a green fee and playing a round of golf—in fact, I did that as well. This had no bearing on my relationship with Annabel at all. As the years have passed, I now feel absolutely terrible about my disgraceful behaviour, and I know how dreadful it is because I would not divulge this to anyone in this world—that is the measure of my sins, and I regret them most terribly.

CHAPTER FORTY ONE

In the interview for my job at JMG Recruitment, I asked the question, "What are the best and the worst things about this sector?" When mentioning the worst thing, the founders informed me that an external event that led to a recruitment freeze was bad news. Well, in 2008, the roof caved in!

It all started in New York, when people began to realise that the financial world had gone mad, but it was way worse than this. The institutions were getting more and more overstretched, until one day in 2008, the bubble burst. I am not going to go through this nightmare in excessive detail, but some facts about this lunacy are illuminating even five years after the event. A well-run, conservative bank will raise capital and then lend up to eight times that sum to a range of customers. It will keep just under 30 per cent of the bank's balance sheet in cash or near cash to deal with any traumas along the way. This is how it has been done for centuries. Banks do go bust, but this model is sound in all but the very worst of circumstances.

But it now became clear that banks all around the world had become completely irresponsible. Using unintelligible derivative contracts, the major US investment banks had reached not eight but forty times their capital. To this day, I am aghast at the absolute folly of this situation, and no one has ever explained to me how it was allowed to happen. The crisis started with Bear Stearns, then Merrill Lynch had to be bought out to save it, and then the famous Warren Buffett bought a stake in Goldman Sachs to make sure that they didn't topple, and then Lehman Brothers went bust. Our banks in the United Kingdom were in a mess; the Bank of Scotland was going down; RBS, which owns NatWest Bank, was going down; and Northern Rock and others had to be rescued. The phrase "too big to fail" emerged, and the poor taxpayers of the world were obliged to bail them out. There is no other way to describe this—it was a total and utter shambles, born of greed and ineptitude. My father would turn in his grave if he could see this mess that the world of bankers had got us into.

Well, of course, poor old JMG Recruitment was right there in the firing line. What was our sector speciality? It was the financial sector. The stock market dropped by 50 per cent, but if you had exposure to the financials, your share price was obliterated. The shares of JMG dropped from a high of £1.75 to a low of 60p, which was 40 per cent below our original listing price. The press were all over me like a rash. "How bad is it? Will you close your international offices? Can you survive?" To suggest that our world became a nightmare would not be overstating things. Recruitment freezes were the norm, and we limped through the remaining months of 2008.

The central banks of the world started a new thing called quantitative easing, which Grandpa would have called "borrowing to save up." On and on it went, and they are still at it today as I write my confession. The long-term price we will eventually have to pay for this funny money is not yet known, but I am certain that it will end in tears.

In 2009, we were limping along, and the one-off costs of setting up our international operations were still badly affecting our profits. Their business plans were not going to meet target, but only a fool would blame the people there. This was an external event of monumental proportions; it was no one's fault at JMG. I tried to be mature about all this, but I was scared as well—it was hard not to be.

In March of 2009, an event occurred that was to change my life completely. My phone rang, and it was an official from the London Stock Exchange. He was clear in his wording: "We have just had a notification from an American company called All State Manpower, Inc., who are making an all-share offer for JMG Recruitment valuing your shares at one pound twenty-five. Your shares closed last night at seventy-five pence. Please send me a holding statement before four in the afternoon, and I will have it published." My first thought was eff off, but I doubted that the stock exchange would approve that!

By the end of the day, I had created a statement that was more measured. It broadly stated that All State Manpower was a totally US business and brought nothing to JMG's operations or its shareholders and that it was very opportunistic and undervalued the substantial investment that the company had made in recent years. This statement went out at 4:00 p.m., and I called a meeting of the board immediately.

John Barrett, as our chairman, was top-class. I knew about headhunting, but what I knew about corporate takeovers was negligible. By the end of the meeting, we had decided that we needed a top investment bank, a public relations firm, and our lawyers. I had stated that I did not want an American firm, because of potential conflicts of interest, and there were no UK banks left except NM Rothschild. The name that appealed to me most was Deutsche Investment Bank. John knew someone there, and after a phone call, we were informed that a top executive would meet us at our offices at 9:00 a.m.

What is it all worth?

Although lots of English people work for Deutsche Bank, it was a Reinhardt Schultz who arrived. He was tall and slender and had black hair. He spoke perfect English but had a strong German accent, and after a few minutes of talking, I knew that this was a man that I could trust and work with. He started by asking me to imagine that I was the chief executive of All State Manpower and explain to him why this was such a great acquisition. I realised, at once, how clever this approach was. What Reinhardt was asking me was to explain the merits of JMG from a US viewpoint so that he could understand the Americans' motivation.

I knew exactly why All State Manpower wanted us—it was obvious—and I began to explain it. "All State has a very powerful position in New York within the Wall Street community, but they are also very strong in Madison Avenue in advertising and PR. They are a good outfit, but they are entirely inward-looking. They have never ventured out of their home base, and if you asked them to point out Dubai on a map, they would be struggling. My guess is that they think that the Gulf War is the Gulf of Mexico. The fact is that they know we have been hammered by the financial crisis at a time when we have invested a great deal of money in making ourselves a brilliant global brand outside the United States and Japan, and they also know that from 2010 onward, the one-off costs of setting up in Hong Kong, Singapore, and Dubai will be fully absorbed, and after that the payoff begins. Their CEO must be salivating at my final point. I know already that our figures to December 2009 will be the worst we have ever produced. They will show the end of the set-up costs and the worst trading period in our history. Clearly, I do not know the actual figures, but they are going to look horrific. All this means that he can fight me when I have one hand tied behind my back. Frankly, I am very impressed with their timing; it could not be better—if they win, they get a ready-made global brand, and within two years, their management team will look heroic. They will be a truly worldwide business, and their shareholders will dwarf ours. This, sadly, will massively dilute the benefits of recovery to my people after they have taken all the strain. Quite simply, it isn't fair." Reinhardt looked across the table and said softly, "But who said life was fair?"

By this time my blood was up, and I almost started saying, "We will fight them on the beaches." Reinhardt was impressed with what I had told him and loved how passionate I was about my strategy. He suggested that he contact a lady called Clare Sherman, whom he had worked with before. She was a public relations expert, and she was very good at handling the press. Reinhardt said that he would be honoured to work for us and would do everything in his power to win, but he warned me there and then, "A contested bid like this will get nasty. Cruel and untrue things will be said, and All State Manpower will do everything they can to discredit you. They know that you are the largest shareholder, and the way that you have spoken today, they will fear you, and they will try any dirty trick to bring you down. Simon, if this bid goes through, you will be a rich man from the sale of your shares, and they will have to pay you off in millions of pounds. What's it all worth to you to fight this ugly fight when there is a fair chance that you will lose anyway? Think long and hard before you undertake this battle, because the financial markets take no prisoners. You are apples and oranges to them; they just want the best price." Blimey, he thought that I was passionate! This man laid it on the line and made me think, but my character is very black-and-white, and as I have said before, defeat is not in my dictionary…as far as I was concerned, let the battle commence.

Within twenty-four hours, the paperwork appointing Deutsche Investment Bank was submitted. I signed it along with John Barrett, and the fight of my life began.

CHAPTER FORTY TWO

Clare Sherman walked into my office with Reinhardt, and it was clear that they got on well. She was a very elegant lady of around the same age as me. I asked her to tell me, as the new boy to these corporate battles, what she did. She told me that there were two parts to her role; one was proactive and the other reactive. In the first area, she had to work with me to make sure that my message to the market was precisely what I wanted it to be. Once we had our ducks in a line, she would go and find the right journalist and media outlet and work with them to get the best column inches in the press. If we wished to play any dirty tricks ourselves, she knew some dubious characters who could find out most things about our opposition. She then discussed her reactive role and explained that sometimes, articles came out that were bad news from our point of view, and we had to react to them. She finished by saying, with a glance towards Reinhardt, that getting the press right for your shareholders was as important as the defence document. I asked her how she had ended up in this work. She told me that in her early days as a journalist, she was fed up with senior people at the newspaper trying to get her into bed, but now she was giving good stories to their papers, they treated her with much more respect.

Now that the team was in place, we began to work on the defence circular which was to be sent to our shareholders. All State Manpower would send out an offer document telling our shareholders why they should accept the offer for their shares and then why our combined group would be so much better than JMG remaining on its own in an uncertain world. Our defence circular would be a rebuttal of their document and would explain that our shareholders had taken all the financial strain, and to accept an offer now would dilute their recovery. The documents were a little pantomime-like, and we traded blows like Punch and Judy at the seaside. As we worked on our messages, I have to admit that I enjoyed getting close to Clare, because she always smelt so good. I have no idea what her perfume was, but it was very alluring.

Reinhardt now explained that we had to start visiting the institutional shareholders to see how the land was lying. He got up, went to the whiteboard, and drew a line down the middle with a black marker. On the left side he headed it "For," and on the right he headed it "Against." He then wrote "Simon 15 per cent" in the "For" column, then "Martin 10 per cent," and then "JMG staff 5 per cent." At the bottom of the page, he wrote "Private holders 10 per cent" and "Institutions 60 per cent." He told me quite firmly that this board would be a constant reminder in simple terms as to where we needed to get our votes. He suggested that we leave this board in our meeting room until the closing day, and it could be amended as events unfolded. He then said that my performance in front of the various institutions would have to be impressive. He did offer me a little encouragement and informed me that most of his clients didn't start with 30 per cent in the "For" column.

The next weeks were exhausting. We had lots and lots of 1 and 2 per cent holders, and every meeting was as important as the last. I tried to stay really passionate, and I had success—the "For" column grew to 38 per cent—but the "Against" column rose to 7 per cent. I then had the meeting that Reinhardt had feared. The client was a unit trust group, and they had shares in a whole range of funds run by many managers. Their total holdings came to 10 per cent, so this was important. It started badly and got worse. The main man was called John Thomas, and I struggled to keep a straight face. He was late. Reinhardt suggested that we start without him, but the others politely said no, and we waited. Thirty minutes later, which seems a very long time when you are waiting, he arrived, and he looked like he was about to explode. I knew at once that the cause of his lateness was not tardiness but straightforward bad news. He sat down and gestured to me. "Get on with it, then; we haven't got all day." I normally quite like Welsh accents—Jonathan Davies, who commentates on rugby for the BBC, sounds fantastic—but this voice I did not like, and I resented the way that he spoke to me. After I had told them my story and believed that I had done it pretty well, he started on me. "It strikes me, Simon, old son, that you have tried to run before you can walk. You have overdone it, and now you have had your arse bitten. I can see little here that makes me want to support you; in fact, I am a little pissed off that your shares have been such a bloody awful investment. What's more, if All State Manpower hadn't come along, it would have been a bloody sight worse." I answered questions for fifteen minutes more, but that creep kept interrupting anything that was positive and smacking me down. At the end of the meeting, he informed me that he made the final decision. That bloody man's voice still rings in my ears. As we walked out of the building, Reinhardt told me to calm down, since one always had a bad meeting during a road show. I updated the board with 10 per cent more in the "Against" column.

I met with a large life company, and their attitude was totally different. The chief investment officer there informed me that they had done a lot of work trying to understand our plans and liked the overall strategy. He stated that the financial crash had given them cause for further research, but they had concluded that JMG Recruitment was a share that they wanted in their long-term portfolios. He then gave me copies of the signed forms rejecting the offer. As we returned to the office, we stopped at a wine bar and shared a bottle of wine. We now had 48 per cent in the "For" column, and Reinhardt felt that the private holders would split 5 per cent "For" and 5 per cent "Against," which would suggest that we were home and dry. We enjoyed our evening, but a series of shocks awaited us that would destroy our joy completely.

On Sunday morning, I glanced at the front of the business section of the newspaper and saw a picture of myself. The headline said "Time to Sell JMG to the United States." As I began to read the article, Clare rang my mobile. She sounded very edgy. "Have you read the article yet, and have you seen what John Thomas has said about you? Please meet Reinhardt and me in the office as soon as practical." I apologised to Annabel for having to duck out of the lunch we were going to, but she understood that this was a crisis and had to be dealt with. As I entered the room, I tried a little humour to help, saying, "This John Thomas is something of a cock, isn't he!" Reinhardt, being German, didn't get the joke at all, and Clare was so stressed that she ignored my comment completely.

She started at once. "This is the nightmare scenario for us, Simon. In this article he rubbishes you completely. He calls you an egomaniac who is trying to live up to his father's memory, and he rubbishes your shareholding by saying that you got given it by you rich father. He says that All State Manpower is a first-class outfit, and he would rather have a smaller return and be a part of a decently run company, not one run by a relative youngster who has an overinflated opinion of himself. Simon, the whole basis of our defence document is that you are a first-class manager with flair and vision, and if this article blows that image, we are in deep shit." Reinhardt tried to calm Clare down but struggled because she was in full panic mode. He said, "All we have to do is keep telling our story, and I think we will just get over the line."

As the next few days went by, I kept rereading the article, and it hurt. Dad had given me the shares, and with the benefit of hindsight, I had opened all three offices overseas in eighteen months, but how could I have seen the financial crisis coming? No one else had. I was feeling very bruised, when Reinhardt told me that Martin Johnson wanted to see us on Thursday.

Martin had only been retired for a year, but he looked quite old. As he picked up his coffee cup, I noticed that his hand was shaking a little. I wondered if he was going to tell us that he was ill, but what he told us was gut-wrenching. He spoke with a little wavering in his voice and looked straight at me. "Simon, all I have is a house without a mortgage and JMG shares, and if this company goes bad, I am done for. I have thought long and hard about this, and I have concluded that I do not want to sell to the Americans, and I do not want all my eggs in one basket with you either. Please can you or your friends buy my share stake at a discount to the offer price and let me take the cash?" Reinhardt interjected immediately and told Martin firmly, "Martin, if we buy any shares, we have to offer the same terms to every other shareholder, and we do not have enough money to do that. If we get another person to buy your shares, that is against the rules, and if we get someone to buy your shares and fail to tell anyone, we will all go to jail. This law was set up some years ago because financial gangsters would quietly buy up to fifty per cent of the target company in different accounts and only announce their bid after they had already won. You remember that Ernest Saunders and Gerald Ronson went to prison for this exact crime in the Guinness/Distillers battle. I beg you to reconsider." Martin was now in quite a state and said, "I will begin selling tomorrow. I know that gives you problems, but that article over the weekend has really spooked me. I am really sorry." He got up and turned to the door, apologised again, and was gone. As he left the room, I couldn't help but say in a loud voice, "Martin, you are an absolute bloody shit."

The next twenty minutes were brutal. We moved 10 per cent from "For" to "Against," and things looked grim. Reinhardt informed me that anyone who traded in shares and owned over 3 per cent must declare their trade within forty-eight hours. "Oh, Christ," exclaimed Clare, "the press will have a field day. I can see the headline now—'Founder of JMG Recruitment sells his shares and cannot support Simon Barker.' This is worse than anything that I could have feared. I am at a loss as to what to suggest." Reinhardt sat glumly in his seat, and I felt physically sick. At last Reinhardt spoke. "Simon, you are not responsible for any of this—not the financial crisis, the clever timing of All State Manpower's bid, or the vindictiveness of John Thomas—but I think that you must prepare yourself for the worst next Friday."

I thanked Reinhardt and Clare for all they had done and suggested that we meet again on Monday and work out how we could bow out with honour. I asked to be excused and left the office to get some fresh air.

CHAPTER FORTY THREE

The two pieces of news came out on the same day. Martin Johnson had sold his entire 10 per cent shareholding at a price of £1.16, which was a discount of 7.2 per cent to the offer terms. Everyone in the office was distressed. It was made worse when, an hour later, it was announced that a Bermudan investment fund had bought the stake. Reinhardt explained what arbitrage was, since I had never heard of it. "The buyers take the stock today at one pound sixteen, and they then accept the offer at one pound twenty-five. After the bid, they have got out at the bid price, and they have made over seven per cent in about a week. Their only risk is if the deal fails, and I am now certain that it will go through."

I went home to Annabel, told her the whole sorry tale, and explained that we were now certain to lose. I also told her that because I had fought so hard against All State Manpower, I was certain to be fired, and although I would get a big payoff, I would be out of work for a spell. We cuddled on the settee and discussed whether we should start a family. Annabel said that she had done all that she wanted to do at her company and was ready to concentrate on the really important things in life, and those were me and our potential children. I didn't sleep that night as I went over every permutation, and I decided to make an important speech to my staff the next day. I arranged to speak to the entire team, and all our international offices were patched in on speakerphones so that they could hear. I spoke from the heart.

"I have to tell you all honestly that by the end of tomorrow, we will be owned by All State Manpower. I have fought with everything that I have to win this battle, but I am afraid that it is not to be. In recent years, I have been proud to lead you all and help in the founding of our future strength in Hong Kong, Singapore, and Dubai, and if I had my time again, I would do exactly the same again. We are brilliant in London, and now the JMG footprint is spreading across the world and will become ever stronger.

"Please, I beg of you, work with our new owners and show them what you have shown me—that you are an amazing group of individuals but an even better team. Every word that I have said in this takeover battle is true, and as 2010 begins and the set-up costs of our international division drop away, our real value will show through.

"In the nature of these things, I will be removed as CEO, but you must not worry about that. I am rich in money, and I will leave here rich in happy memories. Good luck to you all."

I have to say that the cheering went on for some considerable time, and I felt really uplifted.

The next morning, I told Annabel that if we lost, which was now certain, I and a number of my colleagues would get very drunk, and so I would stay in London and spare her that. She kissed me and said

What is it all worth?

that I could get as drunk as I liked, but could I ring her with the result before the drinking began? I agreed.

Reinhardt had told us that our deal closed at noon, and when all the forms were counted by the registrars, the result would be rung through to the boardroom no later than 12:30 p.m. The registrar confirmed that most of the forms had been logged, but there were a few stragglers left. In the boardroom were Reinhardt and Clare, our corporate lawyer, John Barrett, and of course, me. We waited, and the air of expectation rose. Suddenly, the phone rang. John Barrett answered it, and he pressed the speakerphone button so that we could all hear. The voice of the registrar came through very clearly—those in favour of the bid by All State Manpower, 47 per cent; those rejecting the bid, 53 per cent. Reinhardt spoke first and said, "How can that be?" The registrar went through all the numbers, and they made poor reading. Only 3 per cent of the 10 per cent of private holders supported me, and 20 per cent out of 60 per cent of the institutions supported me. But the Bermudan Investment Fund had rejected the offer, and that had helped us cross the finishing line.

There was mayhem in the office. I kissed Clare a great deal, shook hands with everyone else, and went into the open office, where I was greeted by cheering. It was amazing, and I rang Annabel at once—"We won, we won, and it's bloody brilliant, and I am now going to get drunk, but for different reasons. See you tomorrow." It occurred to me that whenever anything exciting happened in my dad's life, he always ended up at the Savoy. My secretary booked us a table for five, and off we went. As we travelled there by taxi, I told them that this was on me, and we were going to drink James Bond champagne. Dom Pérignon it had to be. Reinhardt was ecstatic, and Clare was in sparkling form. John Barrett kept laughing, because he had already spoken to a headhunter about a new job, since he was bound to be replaced. Our lawyer was unusually boisterous and enjoyed every drop of wine that came his way—and there was plenty—and of course, the meal was delicious.

Even on the most wonderful of occasions, there comes a moment when people leave. Our lawyer, who was completely gone, went to the gents and never returned. We guessed that he had staggered home and hoped that he would be all right. Reinhardt said that he was going to an opera in the evening and was certain that it would be Wagner, which he hated but his wife loved, and he was bound to go to sleep. He told us that she didn't mind as long as he didn't snore, which he only did when he had drunk too much, and then she kicked him. "Tomorrow I will be black and blue!" John Barrett played with his second cognac and said, "Simon, today has been the best day of my career, and I hope you want me to stay on, because I wish to see all that you have predicted. And screw that cock, John Thomas, from here to eternity." This time everyone laughed.

John went, and Clare and I sat there. Nothing had to be said—we were going to have sex; of that there was no doubt. I don't know what it is about winning, but the adrenaline rush is extraordinary. We found our room upstairs, and as we got through the door, the passion that had been building since John had left exploded. We stripped each other's clothes off, and Clare spoke with obvious arousal: "I want you inside me now; take me from behind, and thrust me as hard as you want." She literally fell onto the bed face down and spread her legs open, and I was inside her instantly. I drove inside her as hard as I could, and we climaxed together. It felt amazing, but we both knew that that was nowhere near enough. We lay arm in arm, touching and arousing each other, waiting for that moment when our sex could recommence. It wasn't long. Clare sat on top of me, guiding me inside her and sitting astride me, and she started to play with her breasts. Her eyes closed, and I wondered what fantasy was going through her head. We climaxed again and again. At nearly 10:00 p.m., she got up and showered. When she returned to the bedroom, she said, "Don't worry about pregnancy; I have been on the pill for years. You know that this can never happen again, and this is a completely one-off deal." Then she said something that quite shocked me. "I don't love you or anything like that, but I just wanted to fuck you, and today was absolutely the right day. See you soon, and I am really looking forward to my fee for the work I have done. It should be huge, like you. *Ha ha.*" And she was gone. The fact that I had just been appallingly unfaithful to my wife didn't seem to register in my brain, and all I could think of was that she had sort of used me—how absurd is that?

CHAPTER FORTY FOUR

They say that the darkest part of night is just before the dawn, and so it was for JMG Recruitment. From that blackest of black moments when Martin Johnson bailed out on us and we believed that we had lost, everything started to turn around. Clients flooded to us, because they could see how passionate I had been in fighting off the US invader. Even more important, clients in Hong Kong, Singapore, and Dubai had been impressed that the company had never pulled back from its international plan, whilst other firms had cut back savagely during the financial crash. As a result, clients wanted to deal with us and not them. The terrible figures that I had predicted through 2009 proved to be nothing like as bad as I had told the market, and when they came out, our shares, which had fallen straight down to £1.00 after our victory, were now trading back at the £1.50 mark. I knew that the comparison from these numbers to the next year's numbers would be brilliant, because all the set-up costs for our international division were now behind us, and these new emerging market offices were becoming the powerhouse of the group. All State Manpower continued to grow, but it was pedestrian compared to JMG Recruitment.

Clare was now in charge of our press relations and was doing a great job—our image in the media was getting better and better. She was true to her word, and nothing sexual ever existed between us again after our victory night performance. Actually, I was glad. Annabel and I had started to try and have a baby from the first night that I returned from London. Our lovemaking was so intimate that in a Hollywood movie, she would have come to me a month or so later and told me that she was pregnant. It didn't quite happen like that, but our baby was on its way very soon.

Henry Arthur Barker was born in September 2010, and both Annabel and I were thrilled to bits. My mother, Alice, was besotted by the little chap and came out with the most wonderful nonsense. She said things like, "I think that he has got the Barker nose." I reckoned that it was utter twaddle, but it was so nice to see Mum happy again. She missed my father terribly, and although she was a good-looking woman, I do not think that any man will ever match up to the love of her life, which my father certainly was. There were times when I wanted to tell her that Dad had never strayed in all their marriage, but I knew that it was irrelevant, because she had a respect for him that never needed to be confirmed. That love, that trust, tortures me terribly when I know how despicable my own behaviour has been.

During 2011, JMG shares reached £2.32, and an announcement came to me from the registrars. It simply said that the 10 per cent shareholding held by the Bermudan investment company had been sold to a variety of institutions at that price, and they had no further stock. At our board meeting, I said to the other directors that I wished we could thank them. One of my more verbal directors said, "You did—they doubled their money in just two years, and that can't be bad." I suppose that I had to agree.

Recently, Annabel has given birth to a beautiful baby girl, and we have called her Olivia Mary Barker. We now have the perfect family of a boy and a girl, and I could not be more delighted. The shares of JMG Recruitment have just touched £3.00. This was caused by a stockbroker's research note that said that we were the best-run company in the sector and had great staff retention, and this was due to the charismatic leadership of Simon Barker. It appears that I have come a long way from the days of being an egomaniac who was trying to run before he could walk!

The rumours started shortly afterwards, and there was a whisper that I might be given something in the 2013 New Year Honours List. My letter came. It politely asked me if I would accept an honour, if I was to be offered it. Well, of course, I wrote back and said "*Yes.*" I thought that I might get an MBE or an OBE, but a knighthood was way better than I had hoped for. I kept the news completely confidential and only told my mother and Annabel the day before. My mother was so happy and proclaimed that we had two "ladies" in the family. Annabel laughed and said that Lady Jane Peel was way further up the list than she would be. Those days were such fun for everyone around us. And then, the demons began for me, and I began to wake up at night in a sweat. I was not a happy man.

CHAPTER FORTY FIVE

As I write my confession in 2013, I am struck by a story that has been in the press a great deal recently, and that is the return of Asil Nadir of Polly Peck fame, who has returned voluntarily to stand trial for the many things that he has been accused of. I am fascinated by this story because in my teenage years, my father's stockbroking firm wrote reports on the business of Polly Peck, and Dad had wonderful stories that excited me. He told me of selling fresh fruit from Turkish Cyprus to the Eastern Bloc before the Berlin Wall came down, selling drinking water to people who lived in a desert, creating a TV and consumer electronics business in Turkey, and building a luxury hotel in Antalya, Turkey, as an emerging holiday centre within Europe. It all sounded so great, but sadly, it ended in tears. What fascinates me is that Turkey is now a booming economy and one of the fastest-growing in Europe, and Turkey has become a hugely popular holiday destination. Polly Peck did most of the right things but clearly wrong things as well, and that is sad, because the vision of the company was extraordinary. I heard through an old friend of my father that Mr Nadir was told by a high-ranked individual in the Security Service that there was a "contract out on his life," and if he didn't disappear immediately, he would be dead in a week. What a story! As a reader, you may well wonder why I mention this in my confession. The fact is that here is a man who could live in the lap of luxury in Cyprus for the rest of his life, but he so believes in his innocence that he is willing to come back to the United Kingdom and have his leg "tagged" and face trial at the Old Bailey. Contrast this with me. I know that I am guilty, and I would not dare to face a jury, as I would certainly end up in prison. My story is one of deceit and treachery, and it can never be known. I have read recently that Mr Nadir has been found guilty and sent to jail. Whatever people think of the man, he came to face the music and believed in his innocence. I certainly respect him for that.

If I were to let anyone read my confession, by now they would think that my sexual antics and bizarre activities were unkind to my lovely wife, Annabel, but why have I got such inner demons torturing me and causing me such excruciating pain? The truth is that it is all about a little word called "respect." It is a small word, one that anyone could so easily pass over or indeed ignore completely, but one shouldn't. Respect for me has taken on enormous meaning, because I am respected by everyone, but I am a total and utter fraud. I am a devious and malicious liar, and people should hate me—if they knew the whole story, they really would. What is so awful is that I am surrounded by people whom I admire enormously, my father has told me of people in his life that earned his respect, and here I am living a totally phoney life. I want to honour those people right now, because I am so depressed at what I have done.

My father spoke so highly of Tom Smith, who worked his whole life in the back office of Taylor, Dudley & Everett, never bitching about his role, which must have been tedious in the extreme. He never let his standards drop.

To Stanley Church, who headed the dealing team at my father's firm. He knew that he had reached the top of a short ladder, but he worked tirelessly and professionally to do the best that he could for a firm that he never expected to become a part owner of.

To Aubyn St John Peters, whom my father came to respect enormously. He knew that he was a truly great golfer but could also see that he was a dreadful stockbroker, and after he had made his arrangement with my father, he never forgot his debt of gratitude. He found the right moment to pay back Dad in the only way that he was able.

To Ambrose Dudley, who was a legend in the world of stockbroking research but was willing to acknowledge that being a senior partner was way beyond his talents. He recognised that he should step aside and let the right man take the helm.

To Rick Jones, who fell in love with my father but respected him so much that he knew that he could never tell him of that love. I have come to respect him so much, because he has to be the most unselfish man that I have ever had the pleasure to meet.

To my grandfather, whom I never knew but my father and Jane worshipped. He knew his limitations, yet he lived a fulfilling and quality life. His end was devastating, but he showed extraordinary bravery, although he wept in my father's arms as he told him how frightened he was. His fortitude to the very end earned everyone's love and respect.

To Jane, who has committed her life to her family and philandering husband. She truly made the best of a bad job. She never ran away and never looked to divorce to justify her own position. She simply knuckled down and built a life for herself, William and Mary.

To my wonderful mother, Alice, who married my father and loved him deeply until his untimely death. What a mother she has been to me, offering discipline where it was needed but love and support to me throughout my life. I could not have wished for better.

And now, to my father. Even beyond the grave, he admitted to wrongdoing. He needn't have done so, but he didn't sweep it under the carpet; he took responsibility. At his funeral, everyone but everyone used the word "respect" about this man, and the American lady wrote that he was the most honourable man that she had ever met. How can I even dream of living up to his standards? It would be impossible.

And finally, to Annabel, who is so kind and loving to me and trusts me implicitly. If she were to ever know what a truly awful person I have become, it would destroy her. I respect her so much that I have decided that I will never stray again. She is far too wonderful a lady to be put through such pain, and I never want to inflict this upon her.

And against these extraordinary people, who never demanded respect but received it wholeheartedly because of the way that they conducted themselves, I must look at myself, and the comparison is stark. I have written about my sexual antics, but it gets a great deal worse.

I go back to that awful day during the takeover battle with All State Manpower, when Martin Johnson came to the office and told us that he was going to leave us high and dry, and Reinhardt told us that there was nothing we could legally do to acquire his 10 per cent stake. I was utterly poleaxed. It had never occurred to me for a second that the founder of the business would simply want to walk away. Of all the variables that we had reviewed, this was never one of them—it was beyond comprehension. When Clare then told us that the press would have a field day when they got hold of the story, I knew that she was right. Now the seeds of an idea came into my head, and it grew very quickly. It was based on a lovely old expression: if you want a job done, do it yourself.

I excused myself from the meeting, because I was feeling sick and needed some air. I walked out of the office and wandered about until I finally knew what my plan was. I now went into the Carphone Warehouse, bought a "pay as you go" mobile phone, and paid for it in cash. As I got out of the shop, I threw the receipt in the rubbish bin and walked to a park bench. I looked up a telephone number on my normal phone and then dialled the number on my new one. The phone rang, and it was answered by Friederick Weiss. I told him who I was; he knew me straightaway and asked what he could do for me. I told him that my father had always told me that the money in my account was for a rainy day. Well, I told him straight that I was in the middle of a torrential thunderstorm, and he laughed.

I now gave him my instructions: "A large amount of JMG Recruitment shares are about to come onto the market tomorrow morning, and I want you to buy them all. Every penny in my account can be used, but your dealers must get them all. This deal is totally illegal, and I will definitely go to prison if this gets out, so you must do it in a way that is utterly untraceable. You are never to contact me on this subject. When you have got all the shares, you must vote against the current bid for the company by All State Manpower that closes next Friday." He read back my instructions very methodically, and he had got the whole story right. He then confirmed that it would be done. I hung up and threw the phone in a different rubbish bin. I reckoned that once the refuse collectors had done their job, there would be no record that my call had ever taken place.

When the news came through that a Bermudan investment company had bought Martin Johnson's shares, I was as surprised as everyone else. When Reinhardt described the process of arbitrage, I had to try very hard to keep a straight face, but I feigned interest effectively. I now rang the registrar and asked him how many rejection forms had been received. He confirmed that 43 per cent were in at that moment. I knew that with Bermuda, it took us to 53 per cent, and I had already won. The next week was such fun as I lied and lied and took everyone in. My speech to Annabel was truly despicable, but I felt that I had to do it, and my speech to the staff was utterly disgraceful. I spoke with such sincerity about how we were going to lose, how they should work hard for their new bosses, what an honour it had been to lead them, and, of course, how I was about to be fired. It was the most appalling piece of deception that one could possibly have undertaken. It was a tissue of lies from start to finish, and as I am writing this, I am shaking at the thought of it. The depths of my depravity are truly dreadful, but it has been done, and it cannot be undone. As I have written before, "defeat" is a word that is not in my dictionary, but to what levels of behaviour have I stooped to gain victory? I ask myself again and again, "What's it all worth?" In my quest for defeating my enemy, I have sacrificed every value and standard that my wonderful parents ever taught me, and I must live with this.

On the day of victory, I sunk to new levels of depravity. Very early on, I planned to sleep with Clare if I could. I told my dear, sweet Annabel that I was going to get drunk and drown my sorrows, and she felt sorry for me, but truthfully, I was preparing the way for a potentially great sexual encounter. I might not have pulled it off, but I had to prepare the ground in advance. Our lunch was really good fun, but I kept admiring Clare's body, and I wanted her. Of course, I do not know, but I think that she became aroused by me fairly early in the lunch. Our eyes kept meeting; she caught me looking at her breasts, and she was enjoying the attention. Once everyone had gone, there was never any doubt as to what was going to happen next, and it was wild. We were both so utterly aroused and full of adrenaline that it would take many hours of passion to satisfy us both. When I think of the complete betrayal of my lovely Annabel, it haunts me, and yet I planned it all. There are no redeeming features for my actions—none whatever.

The trouble with lying and deceit is that once you have done it, you cannot change it; you have to go on with it. I received a letter from the CEO of All State Manpower, and in it he congratulated me for the passion that I had defended my company with. He said that they had no idea how dogged I would be and admired me even in their moment of defeat. If they could guess at what I had done, they would be appalled.

The staff of JMG Recruitment love me, since I am their passionate leader who will go to the ends of the earth for them, and hardly anyone leaves the firm because of me. If they had any conception as to what an awful man I am, surely they would leave in droves.

At £3.00 per share, my holding is now worth £45,000,000, and that makes me an extraordinarily rich man. Maybe this is acceptable, because I have built the company up, but even here I have a dark secret that I have to admit to. When the shares of JMG had doubled in value, I rang Friederick in Zurich and asked him to discreetly sell all my holdings. He did this, and there is now £22,000,000 in my "rainy-day account" that no one knows about. On the announcement of the disposal of shares by the Bermudan investment company, when I told everyone that it would be great to thank them…it was pure theatre and no less bad for that.

And now they have knighted me, and this is why I am writing my confession, because when the queen touched my shoulder with her sword, the true enormity of my sins hit me like a train. My crimes have taken in everyone from the lowest to the highest in our nation, and the truth will never be known. The facts will fade into the mists of time, and Sir Simon Barker will be remembered as a legend of his generation. When I have completed my confession, I will smash my laptop to pieces with a hammer and drop it at the tip so that there will be no electronic trace of these words to be found.

In four weeks' time, I will reread my confession and decide whether, as Niccolo Machiavelli would suggest to me, "the end justifies the means" and I should be proud of what I have pulled off, or alternatively accept that "you can fool the world, but you cannot fool yourself." If that is the case, then I will have to learn to live with it in the certain knowledge that I am a terrible human being and do not deserve respect from a living soul. Either way, these pages will be burned to ashes and put down the waste disposal unit, and my story will be lost forever.

Truly, this is a dilemma, isn't it?

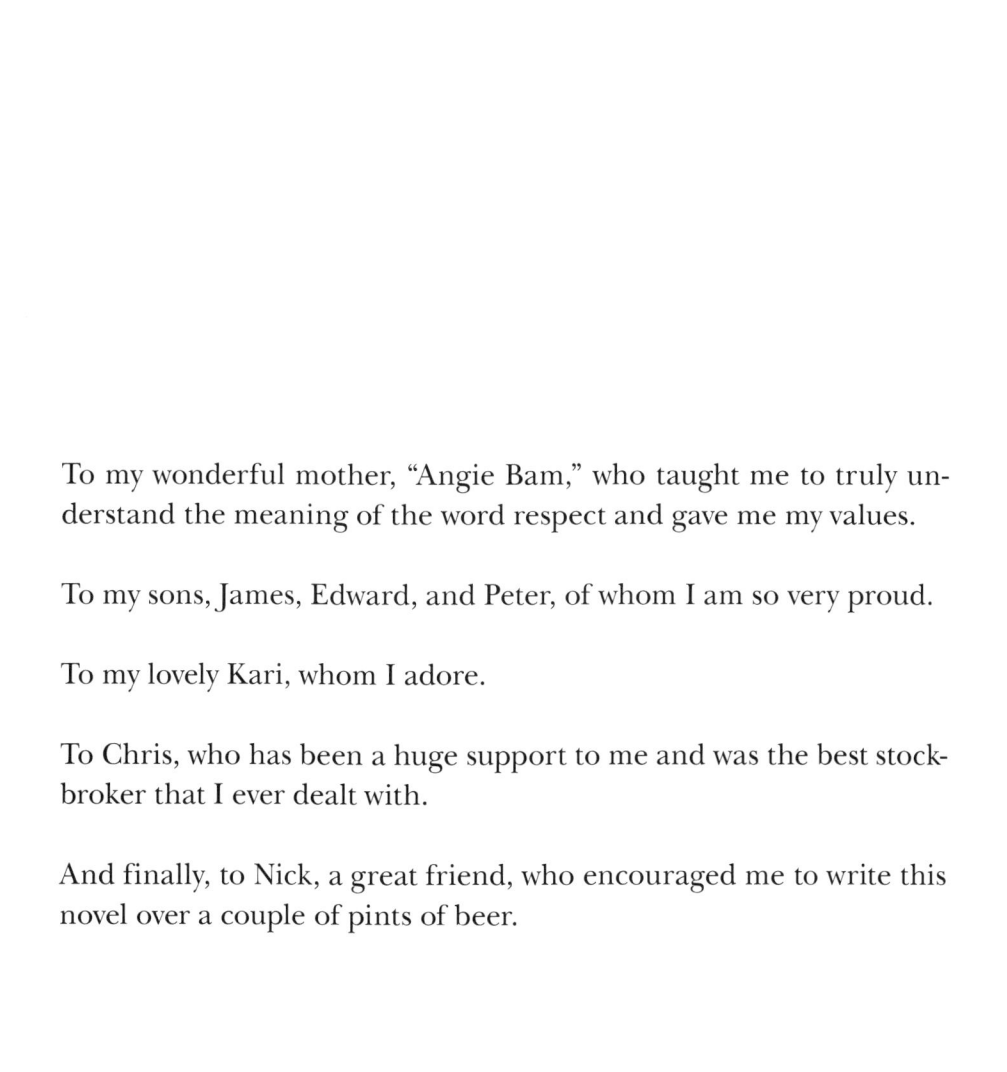

To my wonderful mother, "Angie Bam," who taught me to truly understand the meaning of the word respect and gave me my values.

To my sons, James, Edward, and Peter, of whom I am so very proud.

To my lovely Kari, whom I adore.

To Chris, who has been a huge support to me and was the best stockbroker that I ever dealt with.

And finally, to Nick, a great friend, who encouraged me to write this novel over a couple of pints of beer.

ABOUT THE AUTHOR

Stephen Bamford was born in May 1950 and went to Worth Abbey School. He did not go to university and began his career in the back office of the Kleinwort Benson Merchant Bank. He became the investment director of the NatWest Unit Trusts and later founded the international investing arm of MetLife of America. He won three Public Investment Awards during his twenty-six-year career. He has never been a stockbroker. He is a fellow of the Chartered Institution for Securities & Investment. After his investment career, he became a nonexecutive director of Fitness First plc and is currently the chairman of Ximax Environmental Solutions plc, a specialist water treatment business and is a director of Sulnox Fuel Fusions plc. He is divorced and has three sons. His hobbies include golf and wine, and he has been a member of a book club for fourteen years.

© CRS Registration No. 2801330750

Printed in Great Britain
by Amazon.co.uk, Ltd.,
Marston Gate.